Roping the Wind

He smiled and her stomach did that peculiar flip. She stiffened as he reached out and touched her full lower lip with his callused thumb.

'Who shoved the stick up your ass that makes you think you're so damned perfect?'

She tried to laugh. 'I'm not perfect. You've never liked me because I didn't immediately lie down and worship you.'

He repeated the subtle caress. 'Hell, I wouldn't want you lying down yet. On your knees would be good enough to start with.'

Helen glared at him, waiting for the anger simmering inside her to explode. He was her patient. He'd just received devastating news and this was obviously his way of dealing with it. She had to remember that.

'You should go.'

'Why? Am I scaring you? Are most of the guys you date too intimidated to cross you?' He leant in and brushed her mouth with his own. 'I've had a lot of leisure time recently and I've been dreaming about doing this.'

Before she could do more than take a quick indignant breath, he nipped at her lower lip and thrust his tongue into her mouth. She half-expected anger but he kissed with a slow thoroughness that weakened her resistance. Within a few seconds, her hand was buried in his thick hair, holding him close.

When he drew back, she was panting. His big body held her pinned against the door. She could feel the heat of his erection against her stomach. Nancy laughed in the hall just outside the door. All she had to do was scream and someone would hear her.

By the same author:

Where Have All the Cowboys Gone?

Roping the Wind

Kate Pearce

In real life, always practise safe sex.

First published in 2007 by
Cheek
Thames Wharf Studios
Rainville Road
London W6 9HA

A catalogue record for this book is available from the British Library.

www.cheek-books.com

Typeset by SetSystems Ltd, Saffron Walden, Essex

Printed and bound in Great Britain by CPI Bookmarque,
Croydon, CR0 4TD

The paper used in this book is a natural, recyclable product made from
wood grown in sustainable forests. The manufacturing process conforms
to the regulations of the country of origin.

ISBN 978 0 352 34158 7

Distributed in the USA by Holtzbrinck Publishers, LLC, 175 Fifth Avenue,
New York, NY 10010, USA

Prologue

Jay Turner wrapped the bull rope securely around his gloved right palm and closed his fingers over it. Beyond the delivery chutes, the thumping sound of AC/DC's 'Hells Bells' blared over the packed crowd at the Sacramento Arco Arena. He hardly noticed the noise and the smell of bull shit anymore. His whole attention was fixed on the two thousand pounds of bull that shifted uneasily between his thighs.

He had to qualify tonight or he'd be going home without a dime again. Five weeks without reaching the final fifteen made a man look like a has-been. It would leave him too close to the cut and ruin his chance of making the finals for the third year in a row. Rampage, the bull he was attempting to ride for eight seconds, was getting more restless. Jay rammed his Stetson down hard on his head and nodded to the gate man.

The bull erupted from the chute with an explosion of power and strength. Jay kept his free hand high over his head and his balance over the center of the bull despite its best efforts to throw him off. A wild sense of exhilaration filled him as the crowd roared in approval. There was nothing like this feeling apart from sex, and hey, if he did OK tonight, he'd make damned sure he got some of that as well.

He spurred the bull to earn those vital extra style

points and tried to make it look like he didn't have a care in the world. The buzzer blared in his ear. He untied his rope and jumped clear, managing to keep to his feet as the shock of landing tore through his knees. One of the bullfighters slapped him hard on the back and handed him his hat.

'Great ride, Jay,' he yelled. 'That should get you in the final round.'

Jay looked out at the crowd and waved his Stetson. His grinning face appeared on the huge screens at either end of the arena. A lot of the female fans told him he looked like a young Robert Redford. He couldn't see it himself, but it was OK by him if it got the girls screaming his name. He punched his fist in the air as his score came up. Eighty-nine points would keep him up there and into the last fifteen.

As he exited the arena and headed for the locker rooms, Jay's confident grin faded. Christ, his right knee hurt like hell. He'd been avoiding the sports medicine team all weekend because he already knew what they were going to say. He needed surgery on his knee. Surgery that would put him out for the rest of the season.

After enduring another round of back slapping from his fellow competitors, he made for the privacy of the locker room and sank down on a bench. Bull riding was a young man's game. Only an eighteen year old with a gut full of bravado and no brains could get on a bull and not worry about the consequences. Jay wasn't a kid anymore. His confidence had eroded like a sand dune in a desert over the past twelve years. He grimaced as he dropped an ice pack on his knee.

Trouble was, after the last set of injuries, he'd started to worry about getting hurt. And as soon as a rider did that, he became less able to sit on a bull, less capable of shutting out the fear. Jay sighed as he leant his head back against the metal locker behind him and closed his eyes. One more round and he'd be able to go back to the hotel and soak in a long hot bath. Hopefully with a couple of Buckle Bunnies to scrub his back and any other part of his anatomy they fancied.

Jay frowned as he studied the list of the top fifteen riders. He'd come in sixth overall and had drawn one of the worst bulls in the final round. A monster called Destroyer who seemed determined to live up to his name and had a growing reputation for dumping the elite of the bull-riding world on their butts.

For a second, despair washed over him. He'd given up on his dream to become an all-round rodeo world champion after his first set of knee injuries three years ago. His half-brother Grayson had paid for his surgery that time. Jay had no intention of asking for his help again.

He coiled his bull rope into his hand. Despite his doctor's warnings, he'd switched to bull riding, figuring it would be easier to focus on one thing. Of course, he'd immediately damaged the other knee as well.

Jay stared out at the crowd, allowing his eyes to adjust to the bright lights and the constant ripple of movement. Silently, he struck a bargain with God. If he could just make it through this year, he'd have the surgery. He'd find the money somehow.

The rock music rose in volume and the ground vibrated beneath his boots. He made his way to his assigned bucking chute. Time to cowboy up and get the job done.

Destroyer looked calm enough, his brown flanks heavy with muscle, his tail hardly twitching. But there was a stillness about him Jay didn't like, a watchfulness in his eyes that spoke of barely leashed wildness. Jay touched his mother's wedding ring, which he wore on a chain around his neck. He always imagined her looking down at him from heaven, protecting his ass.

As soon as he nodded his head and the bull jerked under him, Jay knew he had a problem. The sudden force of the bull's vertical jumps and belly rolls almost pulled his arm out of its socket. He slid to the right, tried to correct, but it was too late; the big bull was on to him.

He was flung off but his hand was still trapped in the tight binding of his rope. He fought to unwrap his hand as the bull fought just as fiercely to get away from him. Jay could only hang on and try not to panic as he worked at the knotted rope. Again, his shoulder was almost wrenched from its socket and a searing pain shot down his arm. The bullfighters yelled at him to stay on his feet but it was impossible. He tried to avoid a kick and slipped to his knees. Over his head, Destroyer reared up and came down on his right leg.

A thin scream pierced the air. Jay only realized it was him when it stopped and he crashed into unconsciousness.

When he opened his eyes, he was still in the arena. Beyond the solid barrier of bullfighters and the sports medicine team who circled him, he sensed the big crowd holding its collective breath. This wasn't the way he planned to end his career, face down in the dirt.

'I think his neck is OK. Can we get him on the back board, boys?'

'Oh shit, not *you*,' Jay whispered.

He shut his eyes again but it was no use. The quiet female voice was all too familiar. Why was *she* here?

4

Where was Dr T? Of all the people he would least like to see at this moment, Dr Helen Kinsale was probably first in line. He knew he was in for a lecture.

He clutched the side of the board as four guys hefted him up and turned toward the exit. The crowd clapped and whistled as he managed to wave his hat at them. Dr Kinsale walked alongside him, her cool slim fingers wrapped around his wrist as she continued to monitor his pulse.

The guys parked him on the gurney and left. For once, the treatment room was empty apart from the nurse. His flashy blue chaps were unbuckled and laid neatly over the back of a chair along with his Stetson. Jay inhaled the scent of antiseptic along with his own sweat and fear. Dr Kinsale washed up and pulled on a clean pair of surgical gloves. He gritted his teeth as waves of agony washed through his right knee. He wasn't stupid. This was bad.

'Hey, doc, can you give me something for the pain?'

Shit, he hated to ask her for anything but he was going to start rocking and moaning like a baby if the torture didn't stop soon.

She came toward him, her pale-blue eyes calm, her blonde hair held back from her face in a neat ponytail. She wore jeans and a black shirt bearing the PBR logo. There was no sympathy on her face, only a businesslike sense of purpose that unnerved him. At least she hadn't said I told you so.

'I'm sorry, Mr Turner, but I have to check the extent of the injury first. I can't give you pain relief in case we need to anesthetize you later. I'll be as quick as I can.' She touched the leg of his jeans. 'Could you take these off or shall I cut them?'

He tried a smile. 'Hell, doc, I didn't realize you wanted me so bad. But then, these are my lucky Wranglers.'

She didn't smile back. If anything her expression became more glacial. How a stuck-up woman like Dr Kinsale had ever got involved with the rough world of rodeo was beyond him.

'What are you doing here tonight? Where's Dr T?'

She turned away and took something off the tray of instruments beside her. 'He's operating on another rider. I offered to stand in for him.' She revealed the scalpel in her hand. 'And I like to see how my old patients are getting along.'

He stared at the scalpel, his mouth dry as she gestured at his jeans. He tried to think of a joke, any joke. 'I don't think I can take them off fast enough to satisfy you.'

'I'll cut them then.' With a quick precise slash of her scalpel she sliced away the fabric from ankle to thigh to reveal his right leg. Jay almost threw up. His kneecap was a bloody swollen mess. He tried not to howl as she gently examined him. With a sigh, she turned to her assistant.

'Can you notify the local hospital? We'll need to take him in for X-rays and possible surgery.'

Jay grabbed her elbow. 'Can't you do something here? Patch me up, let me go back to my hotel and do the big stuff at the end of the season.'

She removed his hand from her arm and held his gaze. He hated the sympathy he saw in her eyes even more than her previous disdain.

'I'm sorry, Mr Turner. This is too serious. If you don't get this fixed now, you might never regain full use of your leg.'

Chapter One

Six months later

'Shit.'

Jay muttered another obscenity as he sliced his finger with the lethal blade of his penknife. He tensed as his half-brother came up behind him.

'Do you need a hand with that?' Grayson studied the mangled remains of the bagel Jay was attempting to slice.

'I'm fine,' Jay snarled as he gathered up the crumbs and rammed the four-day-old bagel in the toaster. 'I hurt my knee, not my fingers.'

Grayson raised both hands and stepped back. He resumed his position at the end of the countertop. His fingers drummed on the granite until Jay longed to take a stab at them as well. Grayson wore an Armani suit, custom-made shoes and a Rolex. Although it was lunch time, Jay had just managed to pull on a filthy T-shirt and boxers before his brother's unexpected arrival.

Hell, he had no right to complain. It was Grayson's kitchen and he had every right to be in it. Even though Grayson owned several apartments around the country, his hectic work schedule meant he barely had time to visit any of them. Grayson had offered Jay the new apartment rent free, but he probably would be pissed if he ended up with chipped and bloodstained countertops courtesy of his loser brother.

Jay jerked his head at Grayson. 'There's beer in the refrigerator, go help yourself.' He pretended to watch the bagel as Grayson strolled across to the opposite wall and opened the huge stainless steel door.

'You're right, there is beer. But I don't see anything else.'

Jay drew in a steadying breath. 'I haven't had much time to shop. I only got out a week ago. I'm used to people bringing me food on trays.' His older brother had an annoying habit of trying to treat him like, well, like a younger brother. He didn't need this crap at the moment. He needed a bed to sleep in, beer to drink and the ability to lick his wounds in private.

Grayson returned with two frosted bottles and put one on the counter in front of Jay. 'I'm not going to ask whether you should be drinking, what with all those pills you still have to take.'

Jay glared at him. 'Good, because it's none of your fucking business.'

He wondered if that would be enough to make Grayson walk out. He didn't want to deal with his wealthy, successful, oh-so-perfect brother at the moment. It would be nice to wallow in his own failure. True, if it wasn't for Grayson he wouldn't have a place to live or any ability to pay his huge hospital bills. The PBR fund had taken care of most of the costs of the surgery but he still had to pay the rest.

Two months of intense physical therapy at the rehab center hadn't come cheap either. He still had a long way to go before his knee was fully functional. If it ever was . . .

He chased that thought away with a long swig of beer. Grayson continued to stare at him.

'I know this is tough for you, Jay. But if you don't stop taking cheap shots at me I'm going to rearrange your pretty-boy face, permanently.'

Jay gave him a reluctant smile. 'I'm not a very good patient, am I?'

'You're a pain in the ass.' Grayson finished off his beer and went to get another. Jay poked the toaster and extracted the two bagel halves. He held one up to Grayson who wrinkled his fastidious nose.

'I'm not eating that, and neither are you.' He picked up the phone. 'The great thing about having this apartment in the hotel is that they have room service. If you don't want to cook, just get them to send something up and charge it.'

Jay waited as, without consulting him, Grayson ordered cheeseburgers, fries and soda for two. At least he hadn't ordered him milk. Grayson put down the phone with a satisfied expression and turned to Jay. 'Now what?'

Jay poked his charred bagel. 'I can't afford room service.' Jeez, now he sounded like a whining ungrateful teenager.

Grayson rubbed a hand over his unshaven cheek. He sounded tired. 'Let's not get into this again. I'm not hurting for money. Just charge it. We can sort out the details when you're on your feet again.'

Jay wanted to laugh at the apt cliché. 'And when do you think that will be?'

His brother met his gaze dead on. 'I don't know. Do you?'

Jay was the first to look away. His chances of being a

world-class bull rider were gone. Realistically, he knew that, but it was hard to imagine a world not shaped around the rodeo. The traveling, the brief sexual encounters, the loyalty of the other riders. It was all he'd known, all he'd ever wanted since he'd left school at sixteen.

'What the hell am I supposed to do?'

The question escaped him before he realized it.

'You'll find something. And if you need my help, you know where to find me.' Grayson's cell rang and he checked the number. 'I've got to take this.' He punched a button and made his way across the kitchen and back into the entrance hall. 'Yeah.'

Jay abandoned the still smoldering bagel and carefully lowered himself off the high stool. He grabbed the walking stick propped up against the counter and made his way over to the black leather couch in the den. Grayson's decorator had used muted tones of gray and brown in the starkly furnished apartment. The décor suited Jay's mood.

He settled himself on the couch and turned on the big-screen TV, muting the sound for Grayson's convenience. The view beyond the TV across San Francisco was foggy as usual and even though he had one of the most expensive views of the city he couldn't see much. The new Ritz-Carlton Club apartments in the old Chronicle building on Market were highly sought after and way out of Jay's financial reach. Perhaps he should ask Grayson if he owned an apartment somewhere flat, in the Midwest, instead of amongst all these hills.

Restlessly, he flicked through the channels. If he had to move, he wouldn't have to go back and see Dr Helen Kinsale again. He glanced at his watch, checked the date. His next appointment was at the end of the month. He was expecting her to give him the bad news. News he already knew in his head but was trying to ignore.

He realized he'd left his beer on the counter and weighed getting up and fetching it against remaining on the couch. No more bull riding or rodeo ever. At thirty, he'd have to find a new career.

Grayson's terse replies on the phone got louder. Jay wondered if he was talking to their father. Beau Turner was on his fifth wife now, having gotten rid of the rest when they failed to meet his exacting standards. That is, when they reached 25 or had a kid.

Jay gazed longingly over at his beer. Asking Grayson for help was hard enough; crawling back to his daddy and asking for a job was too horrific to contemplate. Grayson might be earning a fortune as their father's right-hand man but he looked stressed and unhappy. Jay couldn't see himself in a suit or working in an office. He'd have to find something to do that allowed him to be outside or he'd shoot himself.

Grayson returned, his expression grim. 'That was dear old Beau. He's wondering why I'm not in the office.'

'Did you tell him you were doing charity work? He'd probably like that. Good for the company image.'

Grayson swung around and pointed his finger straight at Jay. 'Don't you start. Sometimes . . .' He let the sentence hang in the air as he walked across to stare out the window.

Jay watched him carefully. He'd never seen his confident brother so rattled. 'What?'

The buzzer sounded and Grayson replaced his phone in his pocket and took out his wallet. 'Great, here's our lunch. Stay there. I'll get it.'

Jay breathed in the heavenly scent of fried onions and

ketchup and realized how hungry he was. Grayson sat opposite him on a matching leather recliner and passed him the hamburger. Silence fell as they both dug in.

Eventually, even though he knew his brother was waiting, Jay had to look up. Grayson set down his glass of soda on the coffee table with a decisive thump.

'Look, Jay,' he said abruptly, 'the apartment is yours for as long as you need it. If I'm in town, I'll call and see if you want me to visit. Otherwise I'll stay away.'

Jay didn't bother to correct him. He knew he should tell his brother he was welcome anytime but it wasn't true. There was too much rivalry, too much history between them for their relationship to ever run smoothly.

'And don't worry about money either. I've arranged for an allowance to be deposited in your bank for as long as you want it.'

'You don't have to do that. I'll be OK.'

Grayson shook his head. 'I don't want you to be just OK. I want you to use the time and the money to decide what you want to do with your life. If you decide to go to college, do it. If you want to spend a year traveling the world, do it.'

Jay fixed his gaze on Grayson. 'More to the point, why are you doing this?'

'Maybe because I never got the chance.'

Jay frowned. There it was again, that crack in the perfect veneer of Grayson's life. The sense that everything wasn't going as well as it seemed. It was so much easier to hate his brother when he was in full-fledged successful businessman mode rather than when he was like this. For a second he was tempted to ask what was wrong.

'Whatever you do, make sure you keep up with the physical therapy and your hospital appointments,' Grayson added. 'You're still seeing Helen Kinsale, aren't you?'

Ah, that was better. Jay relaxed. Grayson was back into his usual big brother lecturing style.

'I'm not stupid, Grayson. I'm not going to blow it.'

He'd even brave the chilly smiles of Dr Kinsale if it meant he'd recover more quickly. To give the woman her due, she had performed the surgery that had saved his kneecap so he should be grateful.

She was easy on the eye as well. Tall and slim. Just the type of woman he loved, except she'd treated him like dirt since the first time they'd met. He was never exactly sure what he'd done to annoy her but she definitely wasn't his biggest fan.

As Grayson gathered the dirty plates, his cell rang again. This time he ignored it.

'Just concentrate on getting better, Jay. The rest of it will fall into place.' He dumped the dishes in the sink. 'And leave a list of groceries out for the cleaning service. I'll make sure they pick up what you need.'

The phone rang again. This time Grayson turned it off and headed for the door.

Jay struggled to his feet and limped after him. 'Hey, Grayson, I do appreciate what you've done for me.'

His brother grinned, transforming his normally stern face. 'See? That wasn't so hard to spit out, was it?'

Jay reluctantly smiled back. 'I'll call you.'

'You won't, but I'll call you.' He punched Jay's arm. 'Take care of yourself, little brother.'

Jay waited until he heard the hum of the elevator taking his brother down to street level before he went back into the apartment. He stared at the soundless images of the Flagstaff rodeo on the big screen. Of course, he'd automatically selected the channel that showed all the PBR and NRCA events.

He gripped the back of the couch until his fingers hurt. He was a thirty-year-old has-been, a washed-up cowboy with nothing to show for twelve years of effort except a few gold belt buckles and a closet full of sponsored clothing he no longer had the right to wear.

After finishing his beer he stared at the refrigerator. He had two choices: drink the rest of the beers or do his physical therapy exercises. He stumbled over to the fridge and flung open the door. Eight bottles sat in lonely splendor on the shelf. Enough to get him wasted.

He grabbed the whole lot and pictured Dr Kinsale sneering at his lack of will power. Hell, she'd expect him to drink the beer so why should he disappoint her?

As he opened the first bottle he gave the good doctor a salute. No doubt she was sitting in some fancy restaurant with a rich guy fawning over her. No beer for her. Only the finest of champagne. He pictured her small mouth sipping daintily at the bubbles. Pictured her lips around his cock . . .

He choked on his beer and half of it dribbled down the front of his T-shirt. Where the hell had that image come from? He glared at the bottle. Perhaps Grayson had a point about not mixing alcohol with painkillers. If Dr Doom ever got her mouth around his most prized possession, she'd probably bite it off.

He rubbed a hand over the front of his boxers where his cock had grown hard. He frowned down at his lap. 'Don't you have any standards? I said she'd probably castrate you.'

With a sigh, he put the rest of the beer back and

headed for the couch. Naturally, Grayson had all the TV channels you could buy. He'd finish his beer, watch some porn and persuade his cock to forget about Dr Helen ever getting within a mile of him.

Chapter Two

Helen Kinsale took a deep breath and picked up the phone. 'Hi, Lisa, this is Dr Kinsale. Could you put me through to Mr Dempsey, please?'

Fingernails drumming, she endured the brief spurt of syrupy automated music until Simon Dempsey came on the line. Even though he couldn't see her, she still found herself manufacturing a smile.

'Simon? It's Helen. Something's come up at work. I'm not going to be able to get away this weekend after all.'

She held the phone away as the whining and recriminations began. Work was such a convenient excuse with so many variables. Her ex-husband had taught her that. He'd used the tired old excuse for years while he carried on his petty affairs with various hospital personnel.

She examined her French manicure as Simon continued to talk. Not that she was planning on having an affair. She was using the hackneyed excuse to get out of an unpromising relationship, not indulge in a new one. Simon Dempsey had been a mistake from the first. He was too opinionated, too old and did nothing for her sexually.

She waited for him to draw a breath and cut in. 'I'm sorry you feel that way, Simon. And yes, I agree, women who put their careers ahead of their personal relationships are such bitches, aren't they?'

She scratched over his phone number with her pen until it disappeared in a black inky mess. 'Absolutely, no future for us. No need to call me ever again, forget you ever knew me. Goodbye.'

She put down the phone with a satisfied smirk. Any man who called her a career-minded bitch deserved to be dumped. Simon's attitude reminded her of her ex. David had been furious when she refused to use her contacts to advance his medical career at the expense of her own. Of course, he'd paid her back when he divorced her, but after three years, she was finally able to see his treachery as a good thing.

Her phone buzzed. She glanced at the number before she picked it up, just in case Mr Dempsey had decided to call back and say all the clever things he'd meant to say during their first go-around. But it was only Nancy, the head nurse at the outpatients' clinic.

'Dr Kinsale, just thought you should know the Sundance Kid is here.'

Helen groaned. When would Nancy get tired of that old joke?

'Thanks, Nancy. I'll be there in a moment.'

Just her luck. Her last patient of the day was one of the most irritating male specimens she had ever operated on: Jay Turner, Robert Redford lookalike and soon to be ex-rodeo star. She'd managed to fix his shattered knee but, despite months of intense rehabilitation and therapy, he'd never be able to compete professionally again.

Today was the day she had to break that particular piece of news to him. She knew he wasn't going to be happy. Successful sportsmen tended to have alpha personalities and egos to match. Jay Turner was no exception.

With a sigh, she got up and buttoned herself into a

clean white coat. She located his chart on her desk and tucked it under her arm. Might as well get it over with.

Jay Turner looked completely out of his element in the prim confines of the blue and pink wallpapered examination room. He sat on the side of the examining table, arms folded across his broad chest, bare legs crossed at the ankles. Even though he wore one of the unappealing paper hospital gowns, her stomach gave its usual odd leap at the sight of his long muscled legs and handsome face. Like most cowboys, he looked incomplete without his hat. To conceal her instinctive feminine approval, she always tried extra hard to keep him at a distance.

'Mr Turner. It's good to see you again.'

He didn't get up and she didn't offer her hand. He slowly inclined his head an inch. Up close, she could see the new lines pain had engraved on his face. His chart said he'd lost weight.

'Could you lie back for me?'

He stretched out, arms by his sides, fists clenched. Helen carefully examined his right knee. Like most bull riders, his skin was studded with the reminders of previous injuries. The new surgical scars would fade over time but the damage within would always be there. She touched his skin, felt his tremor of response as she probed his reconstructed patella.

'We'll get another X-ray, just to be sure, but I think overall, it's healed up nicely.'

She turned to write something on his chart. He sat up and slowly lowered his legs to the ground. 'Are you going to do the X-ray now or can I go?'

She glanced up and found him standing too close to her. His aftershave held the scent of lemons. 'You can get the X-ray done anytime in the next week but I would still like to talk to you after you get dressed.'

He frowned and glanced at his watch. 'OK, I'll wait.'

Helen bristled at his grudging tone. She was the doctor with the demanding schedule. What else did he have to do today?

'Oh wow, I didn't realize you were so busy, thanks for making time for me.'

As soon as she said it she regretted her sarcasm. What was it about Jay Turner that made her want to behave like a shrew? He was too pretty, too arrogant and too ... too much for her to deal with in such a small space.

'You're welcome.'

His slow grin was meant to irritate her. Did he think she'd fall to her knees and beg his pardon just because he had a smile like that? She deliberately stood up taller.

He gestured at his clothes. 'I'll put these on then.' Still holding her gaze, he reached behind his neck and tugged at the strings that held the gown together. Turning his back, he gave her a glorious view of his naked body from shoulder to heel. She barely resisted an uncharacteristic urge to bite his ass just to see if it was as firm as it looked.

She knew from experience that horse riding gave cowboys a head start when it came to making love. Stamina, lower body strength, abs like steel ...

Jay Turner cleared his throat and she forced her gaze away from his body.

'I'll go and order that X-ray. I'll be back in a minute.' Her voice sounded too high-pitched.

She rushed out of the room before she could react to the sound of his hospital gown hitting the floor. Why did her hormones have to decide to get all excited now? Jay was her patient. He was five years younger than her. She was obliged by her medical oath to treat him with respect.

After walking a few steps, she stared down at her blank prescription pad. She wanted to grab his ass and hang on as he thrust inside her. She wanted to lick the sweat off his muscled biceps and comb her fingers through his thick corn-colored hair.

She realized she was standing in the middle of the hall, pen poised over her pad. What was wrong with her? That wasn't how she felt at all. She disliked him, didn't she? The only consolation was that he certainly didn't seem too keen on her. Even if he noticed her salivating over his ass, she had nothing to worry about.

After scribbling her signature on the prescription she turned back toward the room. She even knocked on the door just to make sure she didn't have to witness any more of his delectable body.

He'd resumed his position on the exam table, booted feet planted firmly on the floor. He wore jeans and a faded blue T-shirt which matched his eyes. Helen took the only chair and opened her file. She'd learnt that the best way to deliver bad news was to do it fast.

'Your knee has healed well. The new cartilage implants, combined with the strengthened patella, should make normal movement possible.' She concentrated her gaze on his face. 'If you were Mr Average, you would probably not notice much difference in your activity and ability level. But for a professional athlete, the damage is far more serious.'

He folded his arms, his face impassive, and nodded for her to go on.

'Your knee will not hold up if you attempt to ride in any professional rodeo events, including bull riding.'

'Are you saying I have to stop competing?'

'I'm saying that if you do decide to compete and you get injured, you will risk your future ability to walk normally again. There are only so many times a knee can be rebuilt, Mr Turner.'

A muscle twitched in his cheek. 'And if I won't take your advice?'

She handed him a copy of a letter from the PBR sports medicine team. 'Obviously, you are welcome to seek another opinion. I've already talked to Dr T and his team. They agree with me. In fact, you don't have to come and see me anymore after this. You can continue to see Dr T.'

He studied the letter. It trembled slightly in his hand as he held it out in front of him.

'In time, and with continued therapy, I believe you will be able to ride a horse again and manage most ranch work.'

He handed her back the letter. 'Is that supposed to make me feel better?'

'No, I don't think anything I say will do that.' She held his gaze, saw the mingled anguish and anger before he blinked them away. 'I'm sorry, Mr Turner. I wish things were different.'

He shrugged. 'Aren't you going to say I told you so?'

Helen stood up, the file crushed to her chest. 'You're a grown man. You made your own decisions.'

He slid off the gurney. 'If I'd listened to you a year ago and stayed away for a few more months to heal up, I might have avoided this.'

She hesitated. 'We don't know that. You were just unlucky. It happens sometimes.' She remembered to hand him the prescription and half-turned to the door. 'If you could get this done in the next few days I can schedule a new appointment. When you've had time to think things through, we can discuss how to proceed with the transfer of your treatment to the sports medicine team.'

He smiled, the cocky glint back in his eyes. 'If I was a horse, you would've had the pleasure of putting me out of my misery back in the Arco Arena. No need to see me ever again.'

Helen turned fully toward him and held her ground. 'If you are unhappy with the care I've given you, Mr Turner...'

He held up his hand and took a step toward her. 'That's not what I said. I reckon you have the balls to put a horse down. You're one hell of a frightening woman.'

He took another step closer and she felt her temper rise. Great, another man who felt he had the right to make unflattering comments on her character just because she had proven to be correct. She realized she was backed up against the door.

'I could put an animal out of its misery if I had to. Are you suggesting I'm unfeminine, that a real woman wouldn't dream of dirtying her hands like that?' She clutched her files like a shield as he loomed over her. 'Real women can do anything they put their minds to.'

He smiled and her stomach did that peculiar flip. She stiffened as he reached out and touched her full lower lip with his callused thumb.

'Who shoved the stick up your ass that makes you think you're so damned perfect?'

She tried to laugh. 'I'm not perfect. You've never liked me because I didn't immediately lie down and worship you.'

He repeated the subtle caress. 'Hell, I wouldn't want

23

you lying down yet. On your knees would be good enough to start with.'

Helen glared at him, waiting for the anger simmering inside her to explode. But he was her patient. He'd just received devastating news and this was obviously his way of dealing with it. She had to remember that.

'You should go.'

'Why? Am I scaring you? Are most of the guys you date too intimidated to cross you?' He leant in and brushed her mouth with his own. 'I've had a lot of leisure time recently and I've been dreaming about doing this.'

Before she could do more than take a quick indignant breath, he nipped at her lower lip and thrust his tongue into her mouth. She expected him to be angry but he kissed with a slow thoroughness that weakened her resistance. Within a few seconds, her hand was buried in his thick hair, holding him close.

When he drew back, she was panting. His big body held her pinned against the door. She could feel the heat of his erection against her stomach. Nancy laughed in the hall just outside the door. All she had to do was scream and someone would hear her.

'Let me go.'

Jay shook his head. 'I haven't finished yet.' His mouth returned to hers and he began his slow torturous kisses again. His hips rocked gently forward until she wanted to climb him and press herself against the warm inviting bulge in his jeans.

She couldn't seem to stop kissing him back. Her body was on fire and her knees were trembling. She'd never felt like this before. No man had ever been so disrespectful, so insistent and so devastatingly male.

He broke off the kiss and stared down at her. 'You see? That's what you needed – a bit of heat to melt all that ice. Now we just need to work on getting that stick out of your ass and putting my cock there instead.'

She stared into his eyes. Oh God, all she could think about was him bending over her naked body, cock poised to penetrate her aching flesh.

She thumped on his chest and he stepped back. The papers from her files were strewn around their feet like confetti. She couldn't stop watching him as he wiped her lipstick from his mouth and smoothed a hand over the front of his jeans. Shouldn't she be screaming sexual abuse? Shouldn't she be doing anything rather than watch him absently caress his erect cock?

'You should go.'

He turned to pick up his jacket and his Stetson. 'I'll go if you'll have dinner with me tonight.'

'Are you serious?'

He grinned. 'Why not? We seem to be getting along so well.'

She scrabbled on the floor to retrieve her papers. Did he think she was too much of a coward to take him up on his offer? After her ex-husband's betrayal, she'd promised herself she would never back down from another man.

'OK, I'll think about it,' she said, standing up.

He went still, his hat in his hand. She fought a smile. Had he assumed she would refuse? What would he do now that she'd called his bluff?

'Great.' He continued putting on his jacket and placed his Stetson on his head.

She frowned. 'I'm not going to bed with you.'

'On a first date?' He grinned. 'That would be tacky, and tacky definitely isn't your style. I'll wait for you in the lobby. What time do you get off?'

'Six.' She automatically formed the words before her brain caught up with her. 'But I haven't said I'm definitely coming ...'

'You'll be coming all right.' He took her by the shoulders and moved her gently to one side. When the door shut quietly behind him, she still hadn't managed to move.

Chapter Three

Jay studied the clock over the elevators in the pristine lobby. It was almost six. Would Dr Know-it-all come down and face him or was she already creeping down the back stairs and heading for the parking lot? After leaving her office he'd had his X-ray taken and got a coffee from the nearest Starbucks before returning to the hospital.

Her news about his injured knee hadn't hurt as much as he'd anticipated. After all, he'd had several months to get used to the idea. Subconsciously, he'd known the moment the bull stamped on him that he was done. Maybe it was better to have it all out in the open and finally deal with it. He snorted. *Yeah, it was that simple, right?*

He automatically checked his new cellphone and realized it wouldn't help. Of course there were no messages; he hadn't given anyone his new number yet. She wasn't a coward. He reckoned that if she didn't want to go out with him, she'd come and tell him herself. The rational part of him wondered what the hell he'd asked her out for anyway. The purely male part wanted to touch her again in a more primitive way.

Kissing her had turned out to be an unexpectedly erotic experience. She'd tasted so good he'd had a hard time letting her go. Beneath that ice was pure fire. He could sense it with every male cell in his body.

The elevator chimed and he looked up to see Dr Helen

approaching him. She'd taken off her white coat and wore a simple blue pants suit and green blouse. Her blonde hair lay in soft waves around her shoulders.

Jay almost swallowed his tongue. She always looked so calm and in control. He had an absurd desire to kiss her until her hair was mussed and her body wrapped around his.

He got to his feet and touched the brim of his hat. 'See, I knew you'd show up. Are you ready to go?'

She stared up at him, her blue eyes untroubled by the difference in their height and the way he deliberately crowded her personal space.

She jangled her keys. 'Do you have a car or shall I drive?'

'I usually use BART when I'm in the city, so I reckon I'll have to put up with your driving.'

'I'm a good driver. I've never had a ticket in my life.'

He followed her back into the elevator and down to the garages below the building. 'Now why doesn't that surprise me?'

'Because you think I'm a goody two-shoes.' She shifted her purse higher on her shoulder as the doors opened.

'I bet you were a cheerleader too.'

She stopped beside a new silver BMW convertible and hit the button on her key. 'Nope, too plain and too poor.'

He raised his eyebrows as he carefully slid into the passenger seat, inhaling the luxurious scent of new leather and her unique spicy perfume. She didn't seem too plain or poor now. And did he really want to know her personal history? He'd always avoided that trap with the women he'd slept with on the rodeo tour. Too afraid of them getting up close and personal and starting to expect things from him.

He leant back in his seat as Dr Kinsale reversed smoothly out of the parking space and headed toward the exit. She spared him a glance as they approached the barrier. 'Where are we going?'

'The Ritz-Carlton on Stockton and California.'

She kept staring at him until he had to grin. 'What's up? Did you think I'd take you to Burger King?' He enjoyed the way color flooded her cheeks. 'We can go there if you'd rather.'

She swung into the flow of traffic and immediately came to a dead stop. 'I'm just surprised you managed to get a reservation at such short notice.'

Jay pretended to look out the window. Dr Kinsale didn't need to know that being a resident in the Ritz-Carlton Club on Market, even if it was courtesy of his brother, came with a few attached benefits such as priority dinner reservations in any of their hotels.

Despite the traffic, it wasn't long before they approached the imposing entrance of the hotel. A valet whisked away the car and they were ushered into the cool luxury of the restaurant.

Dr Kinsale took off her sunglasses and stared at his jeans.

'Will they let you in wearing those?'

He shrugged as they approached the reservations desk. 'I sure hope so. I've already sacrificed one pair of jeans for your benefit. I'm not planning on losing these.'

The maître d' looked down his long nose as Jay approached him and didn't smile. He obviously felt the same way about jeans as the good doctor did.

'Good evening, sir. Do you have a reservation?'

Jay smiled. 'I sure do. Turner. Two for six-thirty.' His smile disappeared as the guy ostentatiously ran his finger over the page.

'Are you sure about that?' His gaze lingered on Jay's faded T-shirt. 'Perhaps somewhere less formal might suit you better. There are several fast-food restaurants nearby.'

Jay stepped in front of Helen, took out his wallet and flicked the Ritz-Carlton Club card Grayson had given him onto the open reservations book.

A flush spread over the man's face. 'Of course, sir. Please come in, madam.' His bad French accent miraculously disappeared. He turned to bow to Dr Kinsale. 'We'll have our best table ready for you in just an instant.'

Jay picked up the card and didn't move. He waited until the guy stopped blabbering and turned back to face him. 'What's your name?'

'It's Foster, sir, Charles Foster.'

Jay nodded as he took Dr Kinsale's arm. 'I'll be sure to mention you when I let the hotel know about the service here.'

He thought he heard a choke of laughter and looked down to see Dr Kinsale struggling not to smile. He might be the black sheep of the Turner clan but he'd been around powerful men long enough to know how to deal with bad service.

By the time they were seated and Mr Foster had practically prostrated himself at his feet, Jay had recovered his equanimity.

Dr Kinsale gave him a suspicious look.

'What did you do to make him seat us so fast?'

He shrugged. 'I dunno, doc. Perhaps he recognized me. He's just the type to be a big PBR fan.'

She smiled as she unfolded her napkin. 'Somehow I doubt that.' She sipped at her lemon-flavored water. 'Can we drop the "doc"? My name's Helen.'

'And mine's Jay. To be honest, calling you "doc" reminds me of all the painful hours I've spent in hospital this year.'

Her expression changed. 'It makes me remember all the painful hours I've spent there, too.'

He raised an eyebrow. 'I would've thought you loved it. Being the hero in the white coat who comes along and saves everyone.'

'Like the guy in the white cowboy hat?'

He found himself grinning at her. 'That guy no longer exists. I believe he got run out of town by Clint Eastwood.'

The waiter arrived to take their order and Jay took the opportunity to study Dr Helen up close. She had the severe kind of beauty that kept men at a distance. He wondered how it must feel to be a woman men wanted. Was that why she looked so remote? Was it a deliberate ploy to put horny men like him off?

He knew where he wanted her. Naked and in his bed. But how was he going to persuade her it was a good idea? He wasn't even sure it was himself. She wasn't the kind of woman you could fuck and forget. What did he have to offer her that a million other men didn't?

Helen finished her fourth glass of Chardonnay and placed it carefully on the linen tablecloth. She didn't normally drink much on a date but, to her surprise, Jay Turner had proved a relaxed and attentive dinner companion. He'd asked a bunch of questions that actually made sense and then listened to her answers without using them as a springboard to talk about himself.

He sat back, one arm draped over the back of his chair, his attention fixed firmly on her face. 'So how come you were free this weekend? I assumed you'd be the kind of woman who had only to snap her fingers to get a date.'

She sighed and rested her chin in one hand. She felt oddly lightheaded and chatty. 'I dumped a guy this morning. I was supposed to spend a weekend away with him and I realized I couldn't stand the thought of it.'

His gray eyes crinkled with amusement. 'Why?'

'Because he was too old, too rich and too respectful of me.'

'I would've thought you'd like that.'

She held his gaze. 'I thought I would too, but I'm bored. I've spent my whole life making men bow down to me. At work and in my personal life. I'm fed up of being in charge. I want something different.'

He sat forward and took her hand. 'Is that why you agreed to have dinner with me?'

She stared at him. Was it? If only her brain was working properly instead of fizzing with sexual excitement like a teenager's. 'You've never treated me like a fragile glass ornament.'

'That's because I want to fuck you and I know glass breaks.'

'You want me?' She stroked his thumb, which then curled possessively over her fingers. To her distant surprise she was too relaxed to resent his blunt statement. Her whole body heated in a lustful rush. 'I thought you hated me.'

He laughed. 'Hell, I thought I did too, but now I realize I was looking at it from completely the wrong angle.'

The waiter brought their coffee but Jay didn't release her hand. 'If you're serious about this, I'd like to make you an offer.'

Helen couldn't resist stroking his lower lip. He shuddered and turned the caress back on her by sucking her thumb into his mouth.

'What offer is that?' She sounded breathy. She never sounded breathy.

'I want to be your lover, but there are certain conditions attached that you have to agree to up front.'

He smiled at her with such sexual promise that she felt her panties flood with moisture.

'I've only had a few glasses of wine. I'm perfectly capable of making a decision now.'

He shook his head. 'I'll tell you what I want and then I'll give you the night to think it over. It's better that way.'

Helen took a deep breath. Her whole body hummed with excitement and anticipation. All the years of being responsible, of being the boss, suddenly seemed meaningless.

'Tell me what you have in mind.'

He studied their joined hands before looking back up at her. 'It's simple really. You promise to give up sexual control to me. You do what I say, when I say it. No arguing, no pleading, no changing your mind unless you walk right away from me and never come back.'

She gazed into his eyes, realizing he was serious.

'How do I know you won't hurt me?'

His fingers tightened over hers. 'Don't you know that in the right circumstances pain can also be pleasurable?

As I said, if you agree to this, you're going to have to trust me with your body completely.'

She shivered, imagining what he might have planned for her. Squeezed her thighs tightly together against the aching tension building between her legs.

'OK, I want to think about it.'

He brought her fingers to his mouth and kissed them. 'I'd offer to drive you home, but you're the one with the car.'

She smiled at him. 'I'll drop you if you want.'

He shook his head as he scribbled his name on the check and got to his feet. 'There's no need. I can walk from here. My doctor says it's good for me.'

He stood with her at the hotel entrance while the valet retrieved her car. Soft tendrils of fog from the bay floated overhead, caught in the gathering darkness. She noticed he still favored his uninjured leg. She touched his arm.

'You don't have to wait. I'll be fine. I'll call you tomorrow.'

'No, you won't.'

She glared up at him. 'Even if I decide not to take up your offer, I will still call you.'

He bit back a grin. 'That's good to know, but it's not what I meant. I changed my cell today. You don't have my new number.'

She fussed around in her purse until she found a pen and one of her business cards. 'Write it down for me then and we'll have no more misunderstandings.'

'Yes, doc, whatever you say, doc.'

He handed her back the card and she slipped it into her pocket. The valet appeared with her car from underground parking. 'I'll call you.'

He dipped his head and kissed her, only his mouth in

contact with hers. He kept kissing her until the valet's voice dissolved into a meaningless blur. If he could make her feel like this with a simple touch of his lips, what would his lovemaking be like?

When he finally raised his head, her knees were shaking.

He touched her swollen lips. 'Call me,' he said.

Chapter Four

Helen's alarm clock went off with all the fury of an atomic bomb. In her haste to stop the noise, she knocked the clock to the floor and had to lean over the edge of the mattress and scrabble around to find it. She groaned as blood roared into her skull, fueled by the alcohol she'd consumed on the previous night.

By the time she silenced the clock, her head was pounding. She lay still, the clock clasped to her breasts, and tried to open her eyes. Dammit, she'd had four glasses of wine, not four bottles. Images of Jay Turner's erotic kisses flooded her mind and made her blood rush to other sensitive parts of her body. She slid a hand between her legs and cupped herself. Had he really suggested she give up sexual control to him? She squeezed her thighs together against the rush of heat. He'd done her a favor by refusing to accept her answer last night. In her drunken state, she feared she would've jumped at the chance.

Jay Turner had surprised her, something which didn't happen very often these days. Despite his macho cowboy image, he'd treated her like an intelligent woman. A woman he wanted to fuck, yes, but at least he hadn't underestimated her understanding.

Helen groaned as her cat, Tiger, jumped onto her stomach and started to knead the quilt. Twenty pounds of warm feline was too much to deal with at seven in the morning. Tiger purred loudly, canceling out the subdued roar of traffic outside her window. She rubbed Tiger's wet nose and his purring intensified. It was rare for her to have a day off. If the hospital called, she'd go in, but she hoped it wouldn't happen. A day to herself was too precious.

Of course, she'd promised to call Jay and give him an answer. She shivered as her feet hit the floor. Perhaps a day alone to contemplate her decision was just what she needed.

In the shower, she closed her eyes and relived the previous hours spent with Jay, from his unexpected and highly erotic kiss in her office to his subtle goodnight kiss after dinner. How was he able to see past her calm exterior and know that she liked her sex with an edge to it? He'd kissed her like he knew exactly what she wanted.

She ran her tongue over her lips and caught the scent of orange from her shower gel. Her sex life in the last ten years had been as controlled as her career. She sighed as her nipples hardened. When had she last allowed a man to tell her what to do in bed?

Tiger's cross face appeared at the glass door to the shower, his mouth wide open in a silent meow. He liked to be fed on time and would have no compunction in herding her toward the kitchen if she didn't move fast enough. When had she become a slave to her cat?

'What am I going to eat?' She glanced down at Tiger who had his face buried in his bowl. 'It's OK for you, but there's no human food here. I cleared everything out for my weekend away.'

Tiger managed a quick scowl in her direction before he resumed eating. Helen glanced at her purse, which sat on the countertop. She would have to head down to the local convenience store and get a few essentials if she was going to make it through the weekend.

She grabbed her keys and purse and headed for the door. 'I'll be back soon, Tiger, don't worry.'

Her hand was on the door when it opened in her face. With a stifled screech, she dropped her keys on the carpet. 'Oh my God, Carol. You scared me half to death!'

Her best friend grinned at her. She wore a black leather jacket, black pants and an open-necked crimson shirt. Her dark hair hung to her waist and framed an oval face and pink cheeks.

'Hey, you scared me too! I just came by to check on Tiger. Aren't you supposed to be off somewhere with scowling Simon?'

Helen bent to pick up her keys. 'I decided not to go.'

'About time you came to your senses. He was completely wrong for you.'

'You're telling me that now?'

Carol dumped her bags on the table. 'You know the rules, honey. If your friend's going out with a dork, wait until she works it out for herself. Hell, I was just happy to see you going out with anyone with a pulse.'

'That's not fair. I go out a lot.'

'First dates, maybe, but when do you ever go beyond that?'

'It's not my fault I'm choosy.' Helen beckoned imperiously. 'Hand it over.'

With a resigned sigh, Carol gave up her large takeout coffee and Helen gulped at it gratefully. Carol owned a thriving deli and coffee shop in Little Italy. Her coffee beans were organic, hand-roasted and always delicious.

'There's choosy and then there's you,' said Carol. 'Dr Perfect, looking for Mr Right.'

Helen handed back the empty cup. 'You're right.'

Carol opened her mouth and then shut it again. 'What did you say?'

'I said you're right. I've decided I've been dating the wrong kind of men and that I need to add a little variety into my life.'

Carol pretended to stagger and sat down in the nearest chair, her hand clasped to her heart. 'Are you kidding me?'

'Nope. I realized I was bored with men like Simon. That's why I cancelled our weekend together.'

Tiger materialized and wound his way around Carol's outstretched legs. His pitiful cries filled the room. She bent to pet him.

'Didn't you feed the poor guy? He sounds as if he's starving.'

Helen poked Tiger's wobbly spare tire with her toe. 'He's acting. I fed him five minutes ago.'

Carol waved her hand in front of her nose. 'I'll say you did. He stinks of tuna.' She pointed at Helen's keys. 'Are you going somewhere?'

'I need food. I didn't buy anything except cat food and I don't think Tiger will share.'

Carol got to her feet. 'Well, how about I come with you and we can discuss your amazing revelation over a plate of waffles and maple syrup?'

Helen realized her mouth was watering. 'OK, you're on and I'm buying.'

'So are you going to go out with him?'

Helen dipped her sourdough toast in her egg. 'He didn't exactly ask me to go out with him. He asked me if

I was interested in playing a weird kind of sexual game, with him as the boss.'

She shivered as she thought of his intent gray eyes and the strength of his fingers closing over hers.

'And are you?'

Helen sighed as her appetite deserted her. 'I don't know. I said I wanted to meet a different kind of guy, but, Jay Turner? He was one of my patients. I'm not even sure if it's ethical.'

'Is he hot?'

Helen nodded.

'Then screw ethical, screw Jay Turner instead.' Carol's voice rose with each word, causing a lull in conversation around their table.

'But what if he turns out to be a complete deviant?'

'What if he doesn't?' Carol finished Helen's toast and wiped the crumbs away with her napkin. 'You've known him for years, right? Have you ever heard any gossip about him?'

Helen bit her lip. She'd heard plenty from other female members of the rodeo circuit. Most of it concerning the pleasing size of Jay's cock and the amazing things he could do with it. 'Only the good stuff.'

Carol patted her hand. 'As long as you take your cell with you and make sure he doesn't drive you out to any abandoned cemeteries or lonely ranch houses, you'll be fine.'

'I want to say yes to him but I'm afraid of what will happen. Am I crazy?'

'Nope, you're just human. I've known you a long time, sweetie, and I know why you're afraid. But you're all grown up now. You won't make the same mistakes again.'

Helen planted her elbows on the table. 'With two failed marriages behind me, you'd think I might've learnt something by now.'

'You've learnt what you don't want, haven't you?'

Helen studied her friend over the rim of her coffee cup. Carol's face was full of concern. 'At seventeen, I swore I'd never go near another cowboy and here I am contemplating going out with a professional of the alpha variety.'

She usually tried to forget the early years she'd shared with Carol in California's central valley. It was easy to pretend that part of her life had been some kind of dream and that she'd only really found herself when she moved to the city and met David. She'd lied so much about her past that she'd almost forgotten where the truth lay.

'I'm tired of being the ice queen, Carol. I'm tired of being so careful of every word I say.'

'Then go out with Jay Turner. Live a little.'

Helen met Carol's eyes and smiled. 'I think I will.'

'Hi, it's Helen.'

'Hey, doc.' Jay's slow drawl held a hint of a smile.

Carol, who was sitting across from Helen, grinned and gave her the thumbs-up sign. Suddenly Helen was right back in junior high. She closed her eyes as the silence lengthened. Her nerves were stretched taut with anticipation.

'I was calling to see if you wanted to have dinner with me tonight,' she said finally.

'Yeah, I'd like that. Where would you like to meet?'

'How about in front of the Ferry Building, by the clock tower at six? We can make plans from there.'

Another pause while he seemed to consider her words. 'Great, I'll be there.'

Helen let out her breath. 'OK, I'll look forward to it. Bye.' She started to hang up and then realized he was still speaking. 'Sorry, Jay, I missed that.'

'I asked you if you had an answer for me yet.'

This time it was her turn to hesitate. She glanced over at Carol, who was still making encouraging faces at her. 'Can we talk about it when we meet?'

He chuckled, the sound low and intimate. 'You still worried that I'm going to do something bad to you?'

'I like bad.'

After her provocative comment, Helen stifled a groan. Carol wasn't helping much. She was laughing so hard she had to put her hand over her mouth. The silence on the other end of the phone was so prolonged she wondered if Jay had deserted her.

'Then make sure you aren't wearing any panties tonight. I'm going to want to touch you.' He disconnected, leaving Helen staring at the phone. Carol clicked her fingers in front of her face.

'What did he say?'

'He told me not to wear any panties.'

Carol started to laugh. 'God, from the expression on your face, I thought he'd told you to turn up naked.'

Helen stared at her. 'Carol, he expects me to do what he says. I can't remember the last time a man ordered me to do anything quite so tacky.'

Even as she protested, she knew her body was readying itself. The thought of being available to him in public was incredibly arousing. She smiled at her friend. 'And the thing is, I can't wait.'

Chapter Five

Helen checked her image in the mirror. Blue silk blouse, tight black boot-cut pants and spiked-heel boots. Although Jay had said no panties, he hadn't said she should wear a skirt. She wasn't prepared to make it that easy for him. Would he be amused or would he take offense? And if he was mad at her, what exactly would he do? She considered the pile of clothes on her bed. Perhaps she should put on a skirt after all...

Cross at her surprising desire to placate Jay, she stuck her tongue out at the cat. 'I'm not changing, Tiger. You can beg me all you like but I'm not about to roll over and play nice.'

Tiger yawned and settled deeper into the nest of clothes. By the time she removed him and all his fur from another outfit, she'd be later than ever. It was already past six and she was supposed to be there by now. She took her jacket and beaded purse from the back of the chair and headed for the front door. She blew the cat a kiss.

'Don't wait up for me, Tiger!'

Jay would just have to make the best of it.

Jay pushed his hands deep into the pockets of his denim jacket and checked the illuminated face of the Ferry Building clock. Helen was late and the wind was picking up from the bay. After half an hour of pacing, his knee was beginning to ache. Dammit, she was a doctor.

Didn't she know how bad it was for him to stand around?

'Jay? I'm so sorry I'm late. Is your leg OK?'

He turned around to find her studying his cowboy boots. Her face was flushed and her blonde hair was escaping from its tight ponytail. She looked good enough to eat, yet her expression was all business.

'My knee's fine, thanks. Remember, you're not my doctor this evening, you're my date.' He tried to smile down at her, his gaze running over her leather jacket, her black spiked boots and her pants ... He placed a finger under her chin. 'I thought I said no panties.'

Her bright smile didn't waver. 'You did.'

He drew her closer, one hand cupping her buttocks.

'See? No VPL.'

He squeezed hard and brought her tight up against his thighs. 'Is that some kind of new cellulite women get?'

She shivered as his mouth grazed hers. 'No visible panty line. That's because I've no panties on.'

He bit down on her ear lobe, making her jump. 'And how am I supposed to believe that when you're wearing pants and I can't touch you?'

She looked up at him. 'You didn't say anything about what else I wore.'

He bit back a smile at her innocent expression. 'I'll have to remember to be more specific next time, won't I?'

He stepped away from her and took her hand. 'Well, that messes up our dinner plans. Looks like we'll have to do a little shopping first.'

She pulled on his hand until he stopped moving. 'Why?'

'So you can get yourself a skirt.'

She opened her mouth and then shut it again, color rising on her cheeks.

Jay smiled slowly. 'That's right, darlin'. Remember who's the boss.'

'But I haven't agreed to anything yet, have I?'

He leant back against the railing and drew her close, fitting her body against his. 'You've agreed. You might not have said the words, but you wouldn't be here if you weren't interested.'

She raised her chin to stare at him. Her piercing blue eyes reminded him of a Siberian husky. 'Perhaps I'm only interested in one night with you. Perhaps I've decided that you're the one who should be on his knees begging me to touch him.'

At her words, his groin tightened and he slid his hand around her hips to press her against his hardening cock. 'That's not what I'm offering. If you want a guy to adore you on his knees, call that jerk you were supposed to stay the weekend with.'

She squirmed in his grip and he held her even tighter.

'You need to be fucked good and hard until you're so sated that you can't move. You need a man who can make you so hot that you'll agree to have sex wherever or whenever he wants it.' He bent his head and kissed her hard on the mouth until she leant into him. 'Tell me I'm wrong.'

She touched his lips, outlining them with the tip of her finger. His cock butted at the fly of his jeans like an untrained colt.

'I can't.'

Jay closed his eyes. Had he gone too far? Something

about her made him want to explore the depths of his darkest desires. He wasn't sure why but he'd thought she felt the same.

'Then go home.' He forced himself to withdraw from their embrace.

'That's not what I meant. I can't deny that I want some excitement in my love life.'

He let out his breath as a slow tide of relief laced with lust flooded his system. 'Then let's move on.'

'Do you still want me to go and buy a skirt?'

He allowed his gaze to travel over her from head to toe. 'No, I always enjoy a challenge.'

Jay took her hand and tucked it into the crook of his elbow. In a vain attempt to cool down, she took a few deep breaths of the sea air. Her attempt to slow her libido seemed fruitless. Ever since he'd uttered the word 'fuck', she'd wanted to strip naked and shout 'Yes please!'

She pointed toward the corner of Market. 'There's a great restaurant here, or the revolving one at the top of the Hyatt Regency.'

'Let's try the Hyatt.'

They didn't talk for the rest of the walk. Helen let Jay set a pace that was comfortable for him. At first his gait was a little awkward. She felt bad about him standing waiting for her for so long but she knew he wouldn't appreciate her mentioning it. Like most macho men, he probably hated to be seen as weak.

She wasn't in a rush. The feel of his big body alongside hers and his warm citrus scent made her want to rub her face against his chest and purr like a cat in heat.

The elevator was empty. Jay barely waited until the doors closed before he had her pressed against the wall, his face shadowed by the brim of his cowboy hat, his mouth demanding entrance to hers. She moaned as he slid a finger between two buttons on her silk blouse, bypassed her bra and unerringly located her right nipple.

He teased the point until it ached and then turned his attention to the other one. By the time the elevator chimed, both her nipples were visible through the silk of her blouse. Jay stood back and stared at her. Her gaze fell to his jeans and the swell of his erection and she shivered.

'Don't worry. You'll be down on your knees taking my cock into your mouth soon.'

Her sex softened and cream flooded her pussy. With no panties, she wondered if he could smell the dampness he'd aroused. His smile told her he knew damn well what he'd done. For a second she regretted not wearing a skirt. He was right. It would've made things so much easier.

He ushered her into the restaurant, the palm of his hand placed firmly in the small of her back. Helen glanced around the lobby. Even this early on a Friday night, the restaurant hummed with conversation. In the gathering dusk, the views over the bay and the city were spectacular. While they waited for the reservations clerk to finish with another customer, Jay slid his hand down until his middle finger delved between her butt cheeks. He rubbed on the seam of her pants, pressing the soft fabric into the gathering wetness, stimulating her clit.

As the pressure increased, Helen kept her gaze fixed in front of her. Was it possible to have an orgasm from just being stroked? She wasn't too keen to test the theory in the lobby of a public restaurant, but when she tried to move away, Jay brought his arm around her hips and held her exactly where he wanted her.

She let Jay talk to the maître d', his matter-of-fact tone at odds with his continual stroking and the storm of feeling he was creating low in her stomach. When he took her hand and led her toward the bar area, she almost stumbled, her knees felt so weak.

He found them seats at the bar and settled his large frame on the small steel stool with athletic ease. Helen managed to order a martini and then found herself simply staring at Jay's face.

He held up his beer. 'Here's to us.'

She tried to smile. 'We're a couple now?'

He grinned, that slow lazy smile which screamed danger. 'If we want to be. Or what do you prefer? Fuck buddy? Friends with benefits?'

She shuddered. 'Anything sounds better than couple.'

He leant forward until their heads were almost touching. 'I like coupling.'

She took a sip of her drink. 'You are incorrigible.'

'What the hell does that mean?'

Helen raised an eyebrow. 'Don't pretend you don't know. I've been reading your file. Among the papers was your school record.'

He shrugged and drank half his beer. 'I was just dumb enough to bail out of school at sixteen. I wanted to be a cowboy.'

Helen could sympathize. She knew all about being stupid at sixteen. 'A cowboy with an IQ of a hundred and forty.'

'So?'

'So don't pretend to be stupid.'

He caught her hand and pressed it to the front of his jeans. 'I may not be too smart but I'm good with my hands.' He gave her an exaggerated wink. 'And other parts of my anatomy.'

She deliberately dug her nails into the fabric until he caught his breath. 'Why do you turn every conversation back to sex?'

He took her hand and placed it firmly back in her lap. 'Because when I'm with you, it's all I can think about.'

Helen forgot to breathe as he held her gaze.

'I keep wishing you'd worn that skirt because right now I'd have my hand between your thighs and I'd be circling your clit with the tip of my finger, feeling your cream on my skin, hoping to make you come right in front of everyone.'

Her hand tightened around her martini glass. She couldn't look away from the storm gray of his eyes. The last time she'd felt this overloaded with sexual desire had been in her teens. And look where that had led her – straight into marriage.

'Jay –'

His attention shifted to a presence over her shoulder as the maître d' announced their table was ready. Helen tried to shake off the sensation of being caught in a gradually tightening sensual trap. She wasn't sixteen anymore. She was quite capable of calling a halt to the proceedings whenever she wanted to.

Jay waited until she sat down at the window table and then followed suit, sitting alongside her, edging his chair closer. He stretched out his booted feet until they touched hers.

'What were you going to say before the guy interrupted us?'

Helen stared at him. What could she say? Stop turning

me on? Stop making me think of rumpled sheets and sweaty bodies and sex that goes on for days? She dropped her gaze to the cutlery on the table and rearranged it into a neat square. Jay reached out and trapped her hand under his.

'Helen, if we're going to have sex together – and we are going to have sex together – how about we try for a little honesty between us as well?'

'I thought this was all about fantasy.' She forced herself to meet his gaze. His smile made her feel even more off-kilter.

'Hell, yeah, but being honest about your fantasies isn't easy sometimes, is it?' He gripped her hand, his thumb stroking over her knuckles. 'Some of the things I'd like to do to you are strictly not PC, but that doesn't stop me fantasizing about them. And if I dare to share them with you, I risk giving offense or grossing you out.'

'What kind of things would you like to do to me?' Helen cursed her inner slut, who seemed to have taken control of her mouth.

He groaned. 'That's not a fair question. We're about to eat.'

She fluttered her eyelashes at him. 'You were the one insisting on honesty.'

'Tell me what you were going to say before we were interrupted and I'll be as honest as you like.'

Helen paused as their server arrived and took their order. Could she explain her tangled feelings? Was there any chance he might understand?

'I'm confused.'

'About what?'

'About all this.' Helen stared at their clasped hands. 'I

wanted something different in my life but I'm not sure if I can handle how you make me feel.'

'How do I make you feel?'

She took a deep breath. 'Out of control.' She winced as his fingers tightened over hers.

'And being in control is very important to you, isn't it?'

'Yes,' she whispered.

He smiled and dropped his hand onto her thigh, which was covered by the thick tablecloth. 'How about I give you no choice? How about I take control and you can't do a damn thing about it?'

His fingers worked at the zipper of her pants. She shuddered as he cupped her mound. 'I'm going to keep my hand right here while we eat and there's nothing you can do to stop me.'

Helen bit down on her lip and glanced around the restaurant. It was fairly quiet in their area and the lighting was dim. Would anyone notice that her dinner date had his hand stuck down her pants? And what if they did?

She jumped as the waiter returned with their appetizers. He didn't seem to notice how close Jay was sitting to her or that anything was amiss.

'Helen, eat.'

She instantly picked up her fork. Jay seemed to be managing his crab cakes just fine with one hand. She wanted to squirm against the heavy possessive weight of his palm against her heated wet flesh. He flexed his strong callused fingers. Fingers that were used to wrestling with a bucking bull or mastering a green horse.

'I like the feel of my hand between your legs. If it was up to me, I'd always have it there, just to show that you belonged to me.'

'Is that one of the non-PC thoughts you were referring to? Twenty-first century women don't belong to anyone.'

'Yeah, that's one of them, all right. If it were up to me, you'd be permanently naked and available to me twenty-four seven.' He shifted closer until his thigh touched hers. 'Of course, you might get a bit cold.'

'Wow, you are so thoughtful for a man with domination fantasies. Maybe you'd let me wear a thong bikini occasionally.'

He gave her a considering look. 'Nope, too many strings to get in the way. I'd just fuck you a lot. That would keep you warm, or even better, I'd keep you sitting on my cock.'

Helen found she couldn't eat another bite as she imagined being naked and available for this man, just waiting for him to fill her with his cock.

Jay groaned and adjusted his fingers in her slippery wetness. 'You see, your body is honest even if you can't be. Your pussy would love to be fucked like that.'

Helen stood up so suddenly her chair almost fell over. 'I've got to go to the bathroom.'

Jay only just managed to rip his hand out of her pants before she was moving away from him. Holding her purse in front of her, she made her way as quickly as possible to the restroom.

She almost didn't recognize herself in the mirror of the luxurious bathroom. Her face was flushed, her eyes wide with desire. Helen stumbled into the largest cubicle and collapsed onto the toilet seat. She rested her elbows on her knees, her hands on the side of her head and rocked back and forth.

'Oh God...' She wanted him so badly it was like a physical pain. Did he sense that from her? Every time he talked about fucking her, about *taking her*, it was as if he'd stepped into the most private part of her imagination and read her darkest fantasies.

She tensed at the soft knock on the door. Jay's scuffed brown cowboy boots showed under the gap.

'Helen, let me in.'

She opened the door and he stepped inside, immediately filling the small space. She watched as he relocked the door and faced her.

'Are you OK?'

She nodded, too afraid to open her mouth in case she begged him to touch her. He reached for her wrists and held them together in one of his big hands.

'Don't worry, I'll take care of you.'

In one deft motion, he turned her until her hands were pressed against the cream-tiled wall opposite the toilet. All she could see were the tiles. All she could feel was the slight pressure of his grip on her wrists. He stood behind her, his soft breath stirring the hairs at the nape of her neck.

Helen closed her eyes as he kissed her ear lobe and then bit down on it.

'Keep your hands on the wall and don't turn around, OK?'

She tried to control her breathing as he unfastened her pants and pushed them down to her thighs, exposing her ass and her pussy. He slid one booted foot between hers, widening the gap between her legs until the tight fabric of her pants stopped further movement.

'You see how easy it is to do what you are told?'

He stepped closer until his body leant into hers, the buckle of his belt cold against her heated skin. She shivered as he stroked her hip and then cupped her mound. 'Of course I'd like it if you didn't do what I said as well. It would give me an excuse to put you over my knee and spank you.'

His thumb circled her clit and she jumped. 'Has anyone ever spanked you before?'

'Not since I was about six.'

'I told you my thoughts weren't PC. I'd love to spank you until your cheeks were red and then fuck you hard. I like to imagine you going to work the next day and not being able to sit down because every time you did you remembered the feel of my hand heating your skin.'

In desperate need of relief, Helen pushed her hips back against his groin. She could feel how hard he was. He groaned and pinched her clit. She bent her head until her brow rested on her outstretched hands. Now she could see his fingers buried between her legs.

'Please . . .' God, was that her whimpering?

'What do you want, Helen?'

Beneath her arousal, anger stirred. He knew, the arrogant bastard, he knew what she wanted. Did he expect her to beg? She had to force the words out between her teeth.

'You're supposed to be in charge, aren't you? Don't you know?'

'Hell yeah, I know.'

She gasped as he pushed all four of his fingers deep inside her, widening her so quickly she thought she couldn't take anymore. He thumbed her clit as he worked his fingers in and out. She leant into the wall, rising on her tiptoes as he led her toward a climax.

Her scream echoed around the bathroom until he abruptly cut it off with his hand over her mouth. She bit into his flesh as the aftershocks continued to dance through her. He kept his fingers inside her, his thumb lingering over her clit.

'Is this honest enough for you? I want to fuck you hard and fast and then slow and steady. I want to tie you up and make you beg; I want to fill every part of you with my come and then do it again and again until we're both too tired to move.'

Helen barely registered his possessive words as she struggled to come down from the best orgasm of her life. The roughness in his voice made her squirm against his fingers, wanting more, needing more. He let out his breath.

'Dammit, our dinner will be getting cold.'

He stepped away from her. With all the composure she could muster, she checked that her blouse was buttoned, tucked it into her pants and did them up. He watched her, a slight smile on his face, and one thumb tracing the bulge of his cock in his jeans.

'We haven't finished yet. You know that, right?'

'Of course, fair's fair.'

'Oh, don't worry about me. I was talking about you.'

She knew she was blushing as she pointed at the door. Would he let her get away with changing the subject? 'How did you manage to get in here without causing a riot?'

He smiled as he eased the lock open and went to wash his hands. 'I asked the maître d' if I could check up on you because you were pregnant and might be throwing up. I also suggested he keep anyone else out.'

She just gaped at him. Such a devious dirty mind behind that handsome exterior. He tipped his hat and opened the outer door. 'Now we've got the appetizer out of the way, let's go eat dinner.'

Chapter Six

Jay studied Helen as he ate his way steadily through his steak. She wasn't eating much, her color was high and she was definitely aware of him. He liked that. He liked the way her body responded when he leant closer to her, the welcoming scent of her sex and her heat.

His cock ached so much that his back teeth hurt. If he wanted to remain sane and in control for the rest of the evening, he needed to take himself in hand. He placed his napkin on the table and got to his feet. Helen looked up at him, her expression guarded.

'I'll be back in a minute. Order me some coffee, will you?'

He managed to stroll to the restroom without whimpering from the tightness of his jeans and locked himself in a stall. He leant up against the wall and carefully eased down his zipper. The hem of his blue denim shirt was soaked in pre-come. His breath exploded through his teeth as he wrapped a hand around his engorged shaft.

The restroom door creaked open and two guys in the middle of a loud conversation about the Super Bowl entered. Jay closed his eyes and concentrated on his cock, glad that the noise they were making would cover any sound he might inadvertently make. He pictured Helen's pussy, imagined easing inside her, her tight channel clenching around him as she came.

He pumped harder, deliberately rough with himself, wanting the same explosion of feelings he'd created in

Helen. As he felt his balls tighten and his come travel up his shaft, he grabbed a handful of paper and caught the stream of liquid as it gushed from him. He gulped in a couple of deep breaths and carefully zipped himself up.

He waited until the guys left before flushing the toilet and leaving the cubicle. Just the thought of Helen sitting there waiting for him made him semi-hard again. He hadn't felt this horny since he was a teenager. Delving beneath that ice-cold exterior to find the sexy woman who existed there was more interesting than anything he had ever attempted before.

He studied his expression in the mirror. Eager didn't even begin to cover it. Helen offered him the opportunity to regain control in one part of his life at least and that thought was intoxicating. Everything suddenly seemed brighter. He couldn't wait to get back out there and start the slow build-up of sexual tension once again.

Despite Helen's protests, Jay scribbled his name on the bill and handed it back to their server with a grin. Grayson probably hadn't intended his generous allowance to be used to wine and dine women, but, hell, he didn't need to know about it.

Helen looked up as he pulled back her chair for her. 'What are you smiling for?'

'I'm thinking about my big brother. He's the real powerhouse in the family.' He put a casual arm around her shoulders, felt her instant response. 'I'm the black sheep, if you haven't already guessed.'

'Now there's a surprise.'

He drew her closer and guided her into the elevator. 'I suppose you were always the golden girl in your family.'

She shrugged and avoided his gaze. 'Not really.'

'I find that hard to believe.'

Her expression was wry and full of some emotion Jay didn't want to identify. He opened the door of the hotel and let her walk past him onto the sidewalk. A salt-tinged breeze from the ocean ruffled her hair. She pushed at the flying strands in a vain attempt to tuck them behind her ear.

He still wanted her. Five minutes of pussy time wasn't enough. He wished he'd had time to lick up all her cream and make her come with just his mouth and tongue.

She took a step backward as if she sensed the lecherous direction of his thoughts. 'Is it time to say goodbye or shall we get a drink somewhere?'

He took a moment to scope out the terrain. He had to touch her before they did anything else. Without speaking, he took her hand and led her back toward the hotel. To one side of the door was a shadowed niche. He backed her up against the wall and kissed her hungrily, his mouth demanding entrance, his hands lifting her against his aroused body.

She responded instantly, her hand in his hair, her mouth hot and eager beneath his. One of her legs curved around his thigh, opening herself to him. He took the invitation, grinding his cock against her pants-covered pussy until he feared he might come in his jeans.

When he finally pulled his mouth away, she was panting and straining against him. 'Jay, come back to my apartment with me.'

He smiled at her husky demanding words. She still wanted to be the boss. 'No.'

She bit down hard on her lip. He instantly wanted to worry the small swollen spot until it bled.

'Remember, we agreed that would be tacky. And you don't do tacky, Helen.'

She took a deep shuddering breath. 'You're right, I don't.'

He kissed her gently on the lips. 'Go home. Call me when you get there, OK?'

Jay walked her back to her car, kissed her once more and waved as she drove away. It wasn't far to her apartment in Pacific Heights and for once the traffic was light. She was surprised to find herself sitting outside her house with no recollection of how she got there.

What had she eaten? She couldn't remember anything except the taste of his mouth. All she could think about was his big hand cupping her sex and the way he'd made her come in the restroom.

She went into her bedroom, where Tiger was still fast asleep in the center of her discarded clothes. With a sigh, she pushed the whole heap onto the floor. Her clinic didn't start until ten in the morning so she had plenty of time to clean up before she left for work.

She sat on the edge of the bed and took off her boots. Her body felt restless and unsatisfied. She half-wished Jay had taken her up on her idiotic suggestion to come home with her. Jay ... She remembered the thrust of his fingers between her legs, the deliberately demanding caress of his thumb on her clit. She'd loved everything he'd done to her.

Her cellphone vibrated in her purse and she rushed to answer it. Sometimes it was the hospital needing her in immediately. She almost dropped the phone when she heard Jay's distinctive drawl.

'Are you home?'

'I was just about to call you.'

'Do you have a speakerphone?'

Helen frowned at her cellphone. 'I do on my main line, why?'

'Because there's something I want to say to you and I want your entire attention when I say it.'

She gripped her cell so tightly it almost popped out of her hand. 'I'll call you back.'

It was difficult to dial the number because her hands were shaking so badly. He picked up before the first dial tone finished.

'Where are you?'

'I'm sitting on my bed.'

'Put me on the speakerphone.'

Helen crawled across to the bedside table and punched the relevant button. Jay's voice sounded louder and more confident as it filled the room.

'Have you started to undress yet?'

A hot tremor of excitement settled in Helen's stomach. 'I've taken my boots off.'

'Good. Take your jacket off next and then wait.' She heard the creak of leather as if he'd shifted his weight or sat down.

She slid out of her jacket and tossed it onto the ever-increasing pile. Tiger was buried underneath and continued to snore undisturbed.

'Where are you, Jay?'

'I'm sitting on my fancy black leather recliner, one foot on the floor, the other on the couch.'

She tried to picture his long lazy form and found it all too easy.

'Take your blouse off for me and then your pants.'

She hurried to comply, grateful to be rid of the restrictions of the material when her body was heating so rapidly. 'I just have my bra on now.'

'Tell me what it looks like.'

She glanced down at her chest. 'It's beige and lacy.'

'Is the lace see-through?'

'No, but it's quite sheer.'

'I bet you can see your nipples through the fabric then, right?'

'Yes.'

'Are they hard?'

'My nipples?'

'Yeah.'

'Of course they are.'

He chuckled. 'Touch them for me, make them harder.'

Helen closed her eyes and stroked her nipples between her finger and thumb. The soft tug made her sex cream.

'What are you thinking about?'

She tugged harder. 'Your mouth on me.'

'Thinking about kissing your breasts has made me hard again. I'm gonna unzip my jeans now and touch my cock.'

She heard the clink of his leather belt as he unbuckled it and the zipper of his jeans.

He groaned. 'Take your bra off, darlin', and cup your breasts for me. Don't stop caressing your nipples though.'

Helen unclipped her bra and gathered her breasts in her hands, enjoying their weight and smooth texture.

'Sit back on the bed and open your legs wide, so that if I was there I could see your pussy.'

She scrambled up the bed and leant back against the headboard, picturing him kneeling between her thighs.

'Are you wet for me?'

She stifled a moan. 'You know I am.'

'Touch yourself, tell me how wet.'

She slowly slid her hand down over her stomach until it rested between her legs. She flicked her aroused clit and shuddered. 'Oh God, I'm soaking.'

'Slide a few fingers inside your pussy. Tell me how it feels.' He sounded hoarse and jerky as if his words matched the movement of his hand on his cock.

'My fingers aren't enough. I'm so wet I can hardly feel them.'

'My cock will fill you up.'

She worked her fingers faster, thumbing her clit as hard as she could.

'I'm going to enjoy watching you turn yourself on like this. But I'm going to enjoy fucking you more. Perhaps I won't have time to get my clothes off, just unzip my jeans and thrust into you until you scream and beg me to make you come.'

Helen arched her hips and brought her other hand down to help stimulate her clit.

'Perhaps you wouldn't even have time to get all those fingers out and I'd fuck you just like that, making you scream even more.'

She could barely concentrate on his words now, her attention focused on her upcoming orgasm. Her fingers were so wet and slippery that all she could do was spread them wide, concentrate on finding her G-spot and hang on.

'Come for me, Helen. I need you to come, now.'

The urgency in his voice echoed the urgency of her need. She climaxed with a scream, heard his hoarse shout echo around the room.

She slowly relaxed her grip on her sex and then wiped her fingers on the bedclothes.

'Was that good, Helen?'

She didn't want to speak. She just wanted to drift to sleep on the haze of pleasure.

His satisfied chuckle echoed around the room. 'I hope that silence means yes. And it's going to get even better. I'll call you tomorrow night.'

She sighed as he disconnected and just managed to crawl under the duvet before she fell asleep.

Jay groaned as he stared down at his now flaccid cock. Dating the doctor was going to kill him. He clicked off the light and resumed his slow walk toward the bathroom. His smile returned. He had plans for his sexy doctor and they would take some thinking about.

He paused in the dining area to survey the pile of purchases he'd made that morning. Grayson would be pleased that his little brother had finally decided to make something of himself, or even more appropriately, make something *for* himself.

The subtle scent of cured leather drifted across to him and he inhaled deeply. His fingers itched to get started but he knew he had to sign up for a few more classes before he felt confident enough to go it alone. Of course his father would call him a fool and a pussy for his new choice of career. Did he care about what his father thought anymore? It was time to find out.

Chapter Seven

'I can't meet with you today, professor. I have patients to see.'

Helen closed her eyes against an impending headache and gripped the phone more tightly. After her intense evening with Jay, her dreams had been filled with such erotic imagery she'd hardly slept.

'Forget about the patients. It is imperative that I see you.'

Helen glanced up to see Nancy, the head nurse, at her door. Nancy raised her eyebrows and pointed at her watch. Helen nodded. She knew she was falling behind and she already had a full schedule.

'How about lunch time? I can meet you for half an hour at one.'

Professor Peter Hart's sigh was so loud, Helen winced. 'Well, I suppose it will have to do. Don't be late.'

Helen took great satisfaction in dropping the receiver into the cradle from a great height. After the debacle of her divorce from David she certainly hadn't expected Peter, her former tutor and mentor, to follow her to another hospital. But here he was, still making her life difficult. Sometimes she hated all the politics and games in her profession, especially those sprung on her at the last minute.

'Sorry, Nancy. That was the boss.'

Nancy wrinkled her pert nose and leant against the door frame. 'I heard. I also heard there are going to be some changes around here.'

Helen sat up. The hospital was a veritable hive of gossip and scandal, and dear Nancy was the queen bee of knowledge.

'Are you going to tell me or leave me to walk into a meeting with Professor Hart unprepared?' Helen got to her feet and picked up the pile of charts Nancy had deposited on her desk.

'I hear his highness is retiring.'

'You're kidding, right?'

Nancy shrugged. 'Nope, that's what they're saying. Apparently, he's received an offer to head up a research unit in the drug company that wants to develop your product.' Her eyes narrowed. 'I thought you'd know all about it.'

Helen stiffened. The rumor that she had slept with her mentor and collaborator wasn't a new one. To some, it was the easiest way to explain her rise to the top of her profession. She'd learnt not to react to the implied insult although it still hurt.

'Working in the private sector sounds right up his alley.'

In her opinion, Peter Hart had become a doctor for all the wrong reasons. He was incredibly political and not above manipulating anyone for his own advantage. Almost from the first, she had regretted asking him to sponsor the necessary academic progress of her new discovery. She'd been too young to see the project through by herself and too ambitious to see the downside of confiding in Peter until it was too late.

Their academic success and the interest from Nifenberg in developing a new, more malleable and resistant plastic for joint implants hadn't stopped him from siding with her ex-husband. After her divorce, Peter had assumed she should be the one to leave her job so that her ex could take over her position in Southern California and continue to advance his career. Despite Peter's considerable charm, and the fact that she did owe him for her academic success, she didn't consider him an ally.

As she made her way down the hall to see her first patient – an elderly woman who'd fractured her arm in three places after slipping in a convenience store – Helen considered Nancy's pointed comments. She couldn't help wondering if she was being considered for promotion. If she was, she'd be the first woman to head the orthopedic department at this particular university hospital.

She wasn't popular though. Her success didn't sit well with many of her peers. They never asked her to go out for a beer with them, play squash or golf. Helen imagined herself in a plush office on the top floor telling her secretary to hold her calls while she went to play a round of golf. She snorted. OK, she didn't play golf but maybe it was time to learn.

She frowned at the faded blue tiles on the floor. Perhaps it would be better to invest in self-defense classes and a Kevlar vest to protect her back. She just remembered to smile before she opened the door to exam room 3 and found Mrs Hutton waiting for her.

'Sit down, Helen.'

Helen took the chair Peter Hart indicated and sat, ankles crossed neatly, hands folded in her lap. Her boss took his seat behind his antique mahogany desk and studied her. He was in his sixties, a suave silver-haired man who looked every inch the consultant. His hands were unlined, his nails buffed to perfection. She wondered how long it was since he'd actually touched a patient.

'Thank you for fitting me into your busy schedule, doctor.'

Helen ignored the hint of sarcasm and simply smiled. He dropped his gaze to his gold pen and doodled something on his blotter. Helen refused to let him rattle her. He was notorious for his long silences. Years ago she'd learnt not to rush into speech and make a fool of herself. He cleared his throat.

'I was wondering if you've heard any rumors about my future here.'

Helen raised her eyebrows. 'Rumors?'

'That I'm about to retire.'

'There are always rumors, Peter.'

He smiled, displaying a flash of perfectly aligned teeth. 'That's true and, in this case, they might be right. I've received a very interesting offer from our drug company to head up the development of our little plastic gadget.'

She shrugged. 'It's hardly my drug company or my gadget. You were the one to take my idea and turn it into something commercial.'

She'd come to regret her decision to take the formula to her former mentor. But she'd been too ambitious to understand the implications of what she'd done and how far Peter Hart's influence could take her half-formed concept and turn it into a project that the drug companies would fight over.

Peter seemed taken aback by the directness of her response but she knew it was an act. He must've expected her to be upfront. She'd long suspected he didn't like female doctors after he insisted her ex-husband's job was more important than hers.

'As your name is also on the academic paper that proposed this new formula, it would seem odd if you weren't involved in any decisions regarding the patenting of this product, wouldn't it?' His gaze was sharp and considering. 'It would also seem odd if you weren't considered for my job. Many people believe that I've groomed you to be my successor.'

Fucked me, rather. Her involvement would also give the gossipmongers more ammunition for their assumptions about how she had slept her way to the top. Peter had never come out and actually denied he was her lover. He seemed to relish the idea.

He watched her closely and she hoped her expression gave nothing away. 'You would recommend me as your successor?'

He laughed gently. 'Oh no, that's not allowed anymore, but I'll certainly suggest your name to the search committee. It would benefit Nifenberg to have a direct link with you, here, in the field, as it were. If you were appointed, they might be prepared to offer a substantial grant to the hospital for further research.'

Helen frowned. 'The position will have to be posted, won't it?' Recruiting a candidate from within an existing team could be difficult. An outside candidate might be able to bring new funding and new academic status to the hospital and these days that was vital for the future of any teaching facility. Despite Peter's comments, Helen knew that nepotism and favoritism were alive and well at every single medical institution in the country. 'When will I have to make the decision to enter the race?'

He dropped his pen. 'Are you suggesting you might not want the job after all? You would be the youngest female orthopedic department head in the country.'

Helen got to her feet. 'I'm just asking when the job will be available so that I can make a reasoned decision.'

Peter stood up too, his gaze cool. 'I'll make sure they notify you through the official channels. It shouldn't be more than a week or so.'

She nodded. 'I appreciate you thinking of me, Peter, and I'll certainly do my best to impress the selection committee if I decide to go forward.'

'I thought better of you, Helen. I thought your ambition had no limits.'

She paused at the door but decided not to answer him. In the last few years she'd learnt that ambition and material success were no substitute for her sense of honor. Before he could repeat his remark, she shut the door and headed into the outer office. Peter's secretary, Clarice Hill, gave her a friendly wave which almost stopped Helen in her tracks. Clarice normally treated her with complete contempt. Perhaps she was worried Helen would be her new boss. Helen made sure to smile extra sweetly as she passed by. If she got the job, Clarice would be out on her ear five seconds later.

At least Peter had been brief. Helen glanced at her watch. She had fifteen minutes to get something to eat before she needed to be back at her clinic. Sometimes she wished her job was less stressful but when she helped a patient like Mrs Hutton regain function of her arm, it made it all seem worthwhile.

The vending machine obligingly coughed up a BLT sandwich, which Helen took back to her desk. Five sticky notes now adorned her phone. Three of them said to call

Carol. Dammit, she'd forgotten to put her cell on again. Helen unwrapped her sandwich and took a bite. Her years as a resident had left her with a cast-iron stomach and the ability to eat anything that stood still long enough to be devoured.

But today she had to force herself to eat. Did she *want* a promotion? After the series of academic papers she had co-authored with Professor Hart while still in training, she'd become something of a celebrity within the medical community. Some had openly doubted that a young attractive woman could possibly have come up with the idea for the new implant plastic formula by herself.

She stopped chewing. And those doubters would be right. Not that the gossip was correct. The idea hadn't come from Professor Hart either. Helen stared at her sandwich as the old familiar guilt swamped her. She should have contacted Robert Grant and told him what she'd done long ago.

She dialed Carol's business number and continued to munch the slightly soggy bread and greasy bacon without complaint. She swallowed quickly as Carol picked up.

'Hi, what's up?'

'Professor Hart is thinking about retiring and he wants me to apply for his job.'

'Oh wow. That's good, right?'

Helen swallowed a lump of sandwich. 'I'm not sure. Can you come over tonight?'

Carol chuckled. 'Of course I can. That's why I called you earlier. Your cell was off. I'm waiting for all the gory details of your date.'

'What date?'

'You mean you didn't go?'

Helen grinned at Carol's outraged tone. 'I went. It just

slipped my mind. Or maybe I'm just messing with your head.'

'Very funny. I won't be bringing that pie I made for you now.'

Helen's mouth watered and she glanced down at the sad remains of her sandwich. 'You made pie? From scratch?'

'Buttermilk pie.'

'Did I ever tell you that you are the smartest and prettiest person I have ever known?'

'Good try, girlfriend. See you later.'

Helen dumped the rest of the sandwich in the trash. If Carol was bringing pie, she needed to pace herself.

Jay walked through the entrance hall of the community college, his booted feet echoing in the silence. Despite the so-called digital age, the notice boards were covered in a million colored flyers that flapped and rustled every time someone opened the door. The place stank of spoilt milk, sweat and fresh paint. A pimpled kid passed him and gave him a look of complete disdain. It probably wasn't usual to see a real live cowboy in such a suburban setting. Or else he simply looked too damn old.

Where the hell was he supposed to go? He spotted a window labeled OFFICE and headed toward it. A small gray-haired woman eyed him suspiciously. He tried a reassuring smile but she didn't respond.

'Hi, I've come to see Rob Wilton.'

Her gaze never left his. 'He's probably in his classroom. Why are you asking me and why do you want to see him?'

Jay frowned. 'I want to take his class. This looked like a good place to ask where to find him.'

She gave a little huff and studied the list in her hand. 'And who did you say you are?'

He touched the brim of his hat. 'I'm Jay Turner.' She stared at him again until he began to feel uncomfortable. 'Ma'am, is Mr Wilton here?'

'I've seen you before somewhere. On TV.'

'It's possible.' Well hell, who would've thought the old dear was a rodeo fan?

She clicked her fingers in his face. 'What have you done?'

'Do you mean on TV?'

'No, what crime? What did you do?' She grabbed the phone. 'I know the hotline number off by heart.'

Jay pushed the brim of his hat back with one finger and tried not to laugh. 'What show do you think I've been on?'

'*America's Most Wanted*, I'd say. Now tell me what you did. I have pepper spray in my purse and I'm not afraid to use it.'

'The only TV show I'm on is for rodeo cowboys.' He gestured at the phone. 'Now you can go ahead and check me out but it would be much easier if you just let me go see Mr Wilton. If I'm that desperate a criminal, I'm sure the police won't mind waiting an hour.'

She glared at him, her lips pursed. 'I'll call him. He's in Room one hundred and four, down the hall, turn left and go up the stairs.'

Jay straightened up. 'Thank you.'

He tried not to laugh as he followed her directions. It wasn't the first time he'd been mistaken for someone else on TV. It seemed that even if your face was well known, people needed to see you in your familiar setting.

Maybe if he'd ridden his horse into the building she might have gotten it.

Jay stopped walking. Shit, for the first time in his life he didn't own a horse and he couldn't even ride. A sharp pang of longing took his breath away. God, he missed the rodeo so much. He forced himself to keep going. This was his new life, his choice of how best to move forward.

'Come in.'

He opened the door and found Rob Wilton sitting at a workbench. He was younger than Jay had anticipated, probably in his mid-forties. His black hair was starting to silver at the temples and his gaze was friendly and open. Against the wall sat an ancient industrial-strength Singer sewing machine and several sets of lasts. Leatherwork in various stages of completion cluttered the worktops and spilt out of the cupboards. The familiar tang of freshly cut leather tugged at Jay's senses. He smiled and held out his hand.

'Hi, I'm Jay Turner.'

Rob returned his handshake with interest and gestured to a stool alongside him. 'I hear from Mrs Rettle that I should watch my back.'

Jay smiled. 'She thought she'd seen me on TV and that must mean I was dangerous.'

'Yup, she was all set to call the police after she finished talking to me, so don't be surprised if there's a reception committee waiting for you when you leave.'

'As long as it isn't a lynching party, I'll be OK.'

Rob sat back and studied Jay's face. 'Thing is, you do look kind of familiar.'

Jay's stomach tightened. 'Don't say Butch Cassidy and the Sundance Kid, or I'll definitely have to leave.'

Rob laughed. 'You get that a lot, do you?' He shook his head. 'Nope, can't see it myself but you are familiar.'

Jay forced a smile. 'I was on the rodeo circuit for a fair few years.'

Rob slapped his hand on the worktop. 'That's right! Jay Turner. You were all set up to become world champion a few years ago. What happened with that?'

Jay's hand slid down to his right knee. 'I got hurt. That's what happened.'

'It's a tough old business.' Rob shook his head. 'I make boots for some of the guys on the tour and, jeez, some of them are going to pay for their moment in the spotlight for the rest of their lives.'

Jay shrugged. 'It's part of the deal.'

'But no one expects to get sidelined before they want to go, right?'

Jay tensed but there was no sympathy in Rob's voice, only a friendly interest. He met Rob's gaze head-on.

'I've been told I have no chance to compete at a professional level again and yeah, it sucks. Now I just have to figure out what I want to do for the rest of my life.'

'And you think that might be making cowboy boots?'

Jay picked up a scrap of tan leather from the worktop and smoothed it between his finger and thumb. 'I've always loved working with leather. My grandfather made his own boots and I used to sit and watch him for hours. On the rodeo circuit I got used to fixing my gear and gained some skill along the way.'

Rob nodded. 'Yeah, sometimes the best way to learn is on the job.'

'I suppose it is but I always wanted to learn properly. I

figured I'd take it up when I retired.' He cracked a smile. 'I got my wish sooner than I expected and started doing more complex leatherwork at the physical rehab place in Oregon.' He shrugged. 'They told me I had to do something or they were going to force me to learn how to crochet.'

Rob chuckled and slapped his hand on the worktop.

Jay put the scrap of tanned calfskin down. 'That's why I'm here. I've always been fascinated by the history of cowboy boots and I want to make mine special and unique. I heard you were the best teacher on the West Coast.'

'Thanks for the compliment.' Rob sat forward. 'I can teach you. I have an adult class in the evenings you can join and, if you like it, we can take it from there.' Rob got to his feet and went to his desk, then returned with his business card. 'Leave me your details and if you're connected to the web, you can enroll online. It's real easy.'

Jay stood too and realized that Rob was almost the same height as him.

'Thanks for seeing me.'

'It was a pleasure. Watch out for the cops on the way out.'

Jay grinned as he made his way back down the hall. He already liked Rob Wilton's no-nonsense attitude. It suited him just fine. He was going to be treated just like any other guy and judged on his skill rather than for how long he could sit on a bull. After months of uncertainty he realized it was a challenge he was more than ready to take.

He remembered to wave at Mrs Rettle as he left the building but she only scowled at him. He had to give her credit. Dealing with young adults all day certainly hadn't dampened her dander. It might've made her a little paranoid, but, hell, teenagers were tough.

He tipped the brim of his hat back to stare up at the clear blue sky. Life was definitely getting better. He had the opportunity to embark on a new career and the delight of dating Dr Helen. His pulse quickened as he thought of her. He'd call her tonight and see when he could meet her again.

Chapter Eight

'So what's the problem? I thought you'd jump at the chance to take Peter Hart's job.'

Helen put down her spoon and stared regretfully at the crust of her second piece of pie. 'That's exactly what he said.'

Carol put her elbows on the table and her chin in her hands. 'So you don't want to be the youngest department head in the country?'

'I'm not sure. Hospitals are strange places. Most people imagine that the people who work there are saints and heroes, but they're not. They're just as ambitious and greedy as the rest of corporate America.'

'That's never stopped you from achieving what you want before.'

'I know, but this time it feels different.' Helen sighed. 'And I'm not well liked.'

'Because everyone assumes that as an attractive young thing, you simply batted your long eyelashes at Professor Hart to get your name on that academic paper.' Carol pointed her spoon at Helen, a militant sparkle in her brown eyes. 'But you know that's not true. You were the one who brought the idea to him!'

'I really wish I hadn't.'

'That's stupid. You wouldn't be in the position you are in today if you hadn't made that decision.'

Helen smiled. 'Exactly.' She'd never told Carol about

the drunken night she'd spent with Robert and the birth of the brilliant idea. She'd never told anyone.

'You'd prefer to be stuck in a small hospital still being treated like a drone?'

'I'm not sure anymore.'

Carol reached across the table and took Helen's hand. 'What's up, sweetie? Do you want to give it all up and make babies? Are you having a midlife crisis?'

'Babies?' Helen snorted at the very idea. 'It's more of a crisis of confidence. I'm not sure I want to get into this race and expose myself to all the gossip and backbiting again. It's taken me three years to be grudgingly accepted at this hospital. If I go ahead, I'm going to cause friction within the team.'

The phone rang and Helen reached across to pick it up.

'Helen.'

'Jay.'

'How's your day been?'

'Complicated. How about you?'

He chuckled. 'Good enough. I was wondering what your plans are for the week?'

Helen glanced across at Carol who was making kissing sounds. 'I have a late clinic tomorrow and I'm on call this weekend.'

'Damn. How about we meet up on Wednesday then?'

'Sounds good to me. Where?'

'The lounge bar of the Ritz-Carlton Club on Market?'

Helen raised her eyebrows. 'Are you sure we're allowed in there? I heard it was for residents only.'

'It'll be OK. If anyone asks, just give them my name.'

'Great. I'll be there at six.'

'Helen.'

'Yes, Jay?'

'Wear a skirt this time.'

She put down the phone to find Carol staring at her.

'He's a man of few words, your cowboy, isn't he?'

'Most cowboys are.'

'When you talked to him, your face went all soft and gooey.'

Helen picked up the remains of the pie and got up. 'That's because he relaxes me.'

'I bet he does.'

Carol stacked the bowls in the dishwasher and poured two cups of coffee from the waiting pot. 'Tell me about your date. It must've been good if you're going out with him again.'

Helen took the cup of coffee and made her way into the cozy family room. The walls were cream, the thick carpet a dark chocolate brown which made her feel warm and secure. She settled into her favorite spot in the corner of the red velvet couch and tucked her legs under her. Carol sat at the other end, coffee cup balanced on her denim-clad knee.

'I enjoyed myself. He's still a pain in the ass but he was ... interesting.'

'Interesting. What the heck does that mean?'

'He made me feel like a horny teenager.'

'Holy shit. I remember what you were like back then and you were bad.'

'I'll take that as a compliment. I didn't think I'd feel that way so fast, though.'

Carol sat up, almost spilling her coffee. 'Did you sleep with him?'

Helen squirmed in her seat. 'Not through lack of trying on my part. After turning me on way past the point of no return, he turned me down. He said it would be tacky.'

Carol laughed so hard that Helen began to laugh too.

'Oh my God, that's priceless. The ice queen frozen out by the rodeo star.'

'He gives good phone sex, too.'

Carol just stared at her, her mouth forming a big 'o'. 'You had phone sex?'

'We did.'

'And you're going to have real sex with him pretty soon, right?'

'I believe that's the plan.'

Carol held up her cup. 'Here's to you, girlfriend. I never thought I'd see the day you moved into the digital world.'

Helen leant forward and clinked her cup against Carol's. She knew Carol would expect more details when she and Jay had sex. Normally they shared their experiences over breakfast, a kind of hysterical post-sex mortem. For the first time she wasn't sure if she wanted to share. Her relationship with Jay was already darker and far more intense than anything she'd experienced before.

Helen finished her coffee. With all the current stress in her professional life, she could use some down time with Jay. Giving him control of her sex life might prove more beneficial than she could possibly imagine.

Jay winced as he added another Band-Aid to the two that already adorned his left hand. He'd forgotten how sharp leather-cutting blades could be. During class, he'd been concentrating so hard he hadn't realized he was bleeding until Rob Wilton pointed it out to him.

He'd made a good start on his new pair of boots. The paper pattern was cut, most of the leather pieces for the top were ready to go, and he'd stretched the wet vamps and linings over the crimpboard to dry before he attached them to the boot tops. Only another forty steps to go and he'd be done.

He glanced at the clock. Helen should be on her way to the lounge bar on the ground floor of his building by now. He hoped she was wearing a skirt. His fingers itched to sink into her pussy again.

She'd sounded tense on the phone. He wondered what was happening in her world to make her feel that way and immediately tried to banish the thought. He'd always steered away from getting involved in his lovers' personal lives.

His phone trilled and he checked the number. It was the community college. Had he filled in his forms wrong or something? Had Mrs Rettle finally contacted the police?

To his surprise it was Rob.

'Hey, I was looking at your work this evening. You've made a great start on those cowboy boots. Once I'd cleaned up all the blood, I was impressed.'

Jay found himself smiling. 'Thanks.'

'Well, I wanted you to know that you're good and you're quick without sacrificing quality. I'll have to set you some more challenging tasks next time I see you.'

'I'll be back on Thursday, if I haven't bled to death.'

Rob's laugh echoed down the phone. 'Great, I look forward to it.'

Jay hung up, still grinning like an idiot. He felt like a teenager who'd just gotten to first base. He'd been worried that the skill he'd acquired over the years wouldn't be good enough for Rob's class. It was nice to be proven wrong occasionally. He picked up his hat and put on his favorite cowboy boots. His evening was getting better and better.

Helen sat on a high stool at the bar chatting happily to the bartender. Soft piano music filled the shadowed well-designed lounge. Jay paused in the entrance to admire her profile. She was wearing her blonde hair down tonight and a soft cream blouse and patterned black skirt. Her pantyhose were black. He hoped they were stockings. He wouldn't put it past her to confound him with yet another barrier to reaching her pussy. He reminded himself to be even more specific next time.

She turned as he approached and smiled. It gave him a warm feeling in his gut to see her welcome.

'Hi, Helen.' He bent to kiss her cheek, inhaling her soft rose perfume and her warmth.

'Hi, Jay.' She grabbed his wrist and frowned. 'What happened to your hand?'

He stared down at her slim fingers, so pale against the roughness of his tanned skin. 'Do you ever stop being a doctor?'

'Nope, I don't think I do.' She examined his flesh, turning his hand over in hers to check his palm. 'What did you do? Try to cook something too advanced?'

He tried to pull his hand away but her grip was surprisingly strong. He wasn't sure he was ready to share his new potential career with her yet.

'I cut myself with a knife. Now can we get back to the sex?'

She glared at him and pushed his hand away. 'I apologize for being concerned about you. I forgot that our agreement doesn't go beyond what *you* want.'

He let out his breath. 'I just hate being fussed over,

OK?' He gestured at the bartender who lingered beside Helen. 'Do you want a drink?'

She opened her beaded black purse with a decided snap. 'I'm buying. What would you like?'

He glared right back at her. 'I'll have a beer.' So much for a great evening. Every time he saw her, he had to work his way back beneath the prickles to the real woman he wanted to fuck. He slid onto the bar stool beside her. When his beer arrived he drained it in one gulp. Helen sipped at her martini, one elegant foot crossed over the other.

'So, are you wearing pantyhose?' he asked bluntly.

She put her glass on the bar with a decided thump. 'What?'

'I said, are you wearing pantyhose.'

She met his gaze, her pale eyes narrowed. 'What is it with you? Are you really such an insensitive jerk?'

He pressed a hand to his heart. 'Me? Insensitive? Where the hell did that come from?'

'You are rude, crude and totally obsessive in your single-minded pursuit of sex.'

'Hey, you were rude right back. And as for the sex, of course I'm single-minded, I'm a guy. I've been planning what I'm going to do to you since I left you last weekend.'

She closed her mouth and a faint flush of pink heated her cheeks. Damn she was easy. Emboldened, he leant forward and covered her hand with his own.

'If you come up to my apartment, I'll show you how I cut my hand.'

She swallowed, her fingers moving restlessly under his. 'I'm not sure if I'm ready to see your apartment yet. This is only our second date.'

He grinned. 'Hell, you tried to get me into bed on our first one.'

She snatched her hand away. 'Trust you to bring that up. I regretted it the moment I said it.'

He held her gaze. 'Yeah, right. You didn't miss me stripping you naked and sinking my cock into you at all, did you? You didn't miss me going down on you and making you come with my mouth and fingers, either?'

She leant into him, her breathing uneven. 'Damn you, Jay Turner. Don't do this to me in public.'

He slid his hand onto her knee and up her thigh. 'What? Turn you on? It's too late, honey. I bet when I touch your pussy, you'll already be wet for me.' Sometimes he couldn't believe the words that came out of his mouth or that he had the nerve to say them to Dr Helen. He winked at her. 'I promise to behave myself.'

'I don't believe that for a minute.'

She studied him for a long moment and finished her drink. 'All right then.' She sighed. 'Show me your apartment.'

His satisfied smile should have made her wary but it only served to add more heat to her slow-gathering arousal. He was right, she was already wet and ready for him. As soon as he stood next to her she wanted to touch him, to feel the warmth of his skin under her hands, to have him wrap his arms around her and hold her close. Was she really that easy?

After she paid the bill, he slid off the seat and held out his hand.

'Come on. It's not far.'

Bemused, she allowed him to lead her to the bank of elevators. Inside the elevator, he slid a card into the slot.

'You live here?'

'Yeah.'

She frowned as he leant back against the wall and watched the floor numbers fly by. This was one of the most expensive places to live in the city. 'Are you sure?'

His eyebrows rose. 'Yeah.'

The elevator pinged on the top floor and opened onto a wide lobby with two doors. Jay slid his card through the second door and held it open. 'Come on in.'

Helen stepped tentatively into the apartment. Was he squatting? Would she find his furniture consisted of a blow-up mattress and a couple of cardboard cartons?

She moved forward into the huge open space, a symphony of rich dark brown, granite and steel. Definitely not a woman's idea of home. In the center of the room, three black leather couches formed a semicircle facing a huge plasma TV. A modern recliner and a glass coffee table completed the contemporary industrial look. Behind the TV, floor-to-ceiling glass windows revealed a balcony beyond.

'Do you like it?' Jay remained by the door, his arms folded over his chest.

'It's very masculine.'

'My brother's definitely a macho dude, although I doubt he picked out this stuff himself. He has an interior designer to do that crap for him.'

'It's your brother's apartment?'

He walked forward and headed to the kitchen, which took up the rest of the space. 'My half-brother. I have several but Gray's the successful one in the family.'

'I can see that.'

He laughed, the sound harsh. 'I can introduce you if you like. He'd be perfect for you.'

Helen returned his smile with interest. 'Why don't you do that?'

In an instant, he changed direction and crossed the space between them. He put his hands on her shoulders. 'Because you're mine and I don't share.'

She raised her head to look him in the eye. His gaze held a possessive glint that should've made her mad but simply made her hot. It would be so easy just to give in and let him ravish her.

He turned her around, his hands steady at her waist. 'Have you seen the view?' He guided her back toward the floor-to-ceiling windows that lined the fourth wall of the penthouse. She gasped as the city came into view beneath her, the bay in the distance, the ferry lights dancing on the water.

'Wow, it's fabulous.'

His hands slid up to cover her breasts. 'Yeah, it's great.' He started unbuttoning her blouse. She didn't stop him. She rested her hands on the glass, palms flat against the cold surface as he unhooked her bra. His fingers closed on her nipples and he squeezed them hard.

'I like this view better though. Your tits in my hands, your nipples hardening between my fingers.'

She looked down as he continued to fondle her breasts, his big muscular body pressing her closer to the glass. Their reflections were so intertwined she couldn't separate them. She felt the heat and strength of his erection prod her buttocks.

'Can anyone see us up here?'

He nuzzled her neck and then licked it. 'I hope so.'

His hands slid down her arms and undid the cuffs of her blouse. It fell to the floor, followed by her bra. He made an appreciative noise low in his throat as he caressed her naked skin. 'I didn't have time to spend on your breasts before so now I'm going to make it up to them.'

He turned her in his arms until her back hit the glass window. He lowered his head and licked her right breast. She gasped as his mouth tugged at her nipple bringing it to a hard aching point. She forgot the cold glass as he warmed her with his mouth and tongue; she drove her hand into his thick hair and pushed his face closer to her breasts.

When he pulled away she was shaking. He held her gaze and slid his hand over her flat belly toward her skirt.

'Pantyhose?'

She shook her head and he smiled.

'Good.' He slipped his hand under her skirt and stroked her cream satin thong. 'I like to play here. Licking that narrow strip of satin and lace until you'll be begging me to rip it off and fill you up with my cock.'

She jumped as his palm grazed the fabric over her clit. He rubbed two fingers slowly back and forth until she was wet and angling into his touch. He withdrew his fingers and took a few steps backward until he sat on the recliner. She watched as he smoothed a hand over the bulging front of his jeans.

'I want your mouth on me,' he said.

Helen didn't even stop to consider whether she objected to his tone of command. She liked sucking men's cocks. She always had. There was something about servicing a man that way that made her feel horny and powerful. She loved the sensation of the crown of a man's cock at the back of her throat, the fear that she wouldn't be able to take it all, the exquisite sensation when he finally came.

She knelt between his outstretched thighs and worked the buttons on his jeans. His body was tense, his breathing ragged. She sighed when she revealed his cock. He was just as big as gossip insisted. His thick bulbous crown was already wet with pre-come.

'Suck me, Helen.'

He shoved his jeans further down his thighs. She leant forward and licked him from tip to base. She kept up the little licks until he was dry and a new bubble of pre-come was forming at the top of his shaft. Her naked breasts grazed his jeans, stimulating her already hard nipples. His hands closed over her breasts, pulling her even closer, making his shaft thrust against her lips.

She took him into her mouth in one clean motion. He was long and thick and fit perfectly. He groaned as his cock bumped the back of her throat. She kept swallowing, easing him further down and fighting her gag reflex to take him deep.

'Damn, I won't last long if you keep that up.'

One of his hands left her breast and fisted in her hair as she sucked him hard. He filled her so well that she could feel every slight movement of his cock, the frantic beat of his pulsing blood and the swell and rise of his come. He tasted of leather and cowboy.

She slid her hands around his back, pulling his jeans further down until she could grab his hard ass and keep him close. He tried to move his hips in short sharp jerky movements but was hampered by her tight grip on his shaft.

'Jeez, Helen, let me ...'

She dug her fingernails into his skin as his come exploded into her mouth. She swallowed fast to keep it all down but she didn't mind. It was enough that he was so turned on.

When she sat back, his eyes were closed and his head rested on the back of the recliner.

'I have to tell you, doc, you sure know what to do with a man's cock.'

'So I've been told.'

Helen licked her lips and Jay opened one eye. Before she could move away, he caught her around the waist and swung her up onto the couch, reversing their positions. As soon as her back touched the smooth leather, he caught her wrists in one hand, drew them over her head and crawled between her legs.

She moaned as he bent his head and nuzzled her soaking wet thong with his nose. He released her hands but she left them where he'd placed them. He tongued her clit through the silk and she arched into his mouth, seeking his touch, desperate to be allowed to come.

His fingers worked on the fastenings of her skirt, leaving her in just thigh-high stockings and her thong. She lay still as he studied her, one of his fingers gently brushing her sex.

He pushed her legs wider, opening her to his gaze.

'I like sucking too. And biting and licking.'

He lowered his head and tugged at her thong with his teeth, slipping his tongue under the fabric, each flick an electric shock on her sensitive flesh.

'Please, Jay.'

He didn't bother to answer, his entire attention focused on what he was doing to her sex. He used one finger to hold the thong to one side as he licked her thoroughly from clit to anus. The lush wet sounds of his mouth and his approving murmurs made Helen writhe and buck her hips.

As he slid two fingers inside her, his teeth grazed her clit and she jumped. He pumped his fingers back and forth while continuing to attend to her clit. God, she was so close to coming. If he would only move his fingers a bit faster. She tried to encourage him by rocking her hips but he kept up the slow regular plunge and withdrawal.

Her excitement climbed to another level and she slid her hand down to his head. She almost screamed as he pulled away from her. Her fingers clenched around strands of his blond hair. He looked up at her, his lips wet with her cream, his grin laced with pure lust. Using one finger, he pulled her thong down her legs.

His cock was erect again and thrust toward his navel. He dug a hand in his pocket and pulled out a condom packet.

'Put this on for me, honey. Do it real slow.'

Too turned on to care how she looked, Helen sat up, pushed him onto his back and ripped the snaps of his shirt open to bare his chest. After a short struggle, she threw the shirt behind her. His grin widened as she straddled him and held out her hand for the condom.

'You're a take-charge kind of woman, aren't you?'

'Tonight I am.'

She opened the packet and took her time sliding the thin latex over his straining shaft. His erratic breathing told her how much he enjoyed her attention. She finished covering him and knelt up.

Jay wrapped one hand around the base of his cock, the other rested on Helen's hip. 'Ride me, doc, make me come.'

She allowed the wide crown of his cock to penetrate

her, holding his gaze, making him wait. He felt good. Solid and thick and so hot that she wanted to come immediately.

'Take more.'

His hoarse command made her smile. She bent to kiss his mouth. 'There's no rush. That's the trouble with you youngsters, no staying power.'

He groaned as she used her internal muscles to squeeze the two inches of his cock that were inside her.

'Take all the time you want, darlin. I was only thinking of you.'

He breathed deeply, defining the tight physique of his abs. She allowed herself to sink down further on his shaft. God, he was delicious. She hadn't felt this full since her first few fucks with Cory as a teenager. She slid one hand down between them and stroked the base of his shaft and his balls.

'I didn't get to suck your balls.'

His cock jerked inside her. 'What?'

'I didn't get to lick and suck your balls this time. I'll make it up to you. I love rolling those smooth globes around my tongue.'

'You are a dangerous woman.'

'Only if you scare me.'

His mouth quirked up at one corner. 'I'll bear that in mind when you have the family jewels in your mouth. We wouldn't want you biting off more than you could chew now, would we?'

She sank down fully on his cock and his smile disappeared. He grabbed her hips and rolled her over the side of the recliner. She squeaked as her back hit the suede rug. He was still buried deep inside her, his balls pressed high against her sex.

He reared back and slid his hands under her knees, pulling them up until her ankles were over his shoulders.

'Now let's see who's got stamina.'

At this acute angle there was very little she could do to stop him thrusting hard and deep to her very core. His weight controlled her movement, his hips drove into her without pause, hitting the sweet spot of her clit with every long full stroke.

The intensity of his thrusts and her inability to stop him made her wild. She bucked and fought against him but nothing stopped his fast pace, not even her pleas for him to slow down. Sweat gleamed on his muscled torso as he worked his hips, his intent gaze never leaving her face.

Her climax crashed over her with such intensity that she screamed. He didn't stop pounding into her, leading her to a level of arousal she'd never experienced before. She came again and this time he groaned and climaxed with her, his hips ramming into her as his cock released his come in long pulsing streams.

Helen opened her eyes to find Jay collapsed over her. With a yelp, he rolled off her and lay on his back, staring up at the ceiling.

'Shit.'

Helen couldn't move. Her left knee was lodged perilously close to her left ear. She wondered distantly if she'd ever seen it that close before and whether she'd ever be able to walk again.

Jay reached across and slowly lowered her legs to the ground. 'Well, I think that proves who's got the most stamina.'

'That would be me. I came twice. You only managed it once.'

He chuckled and laid his large warm hand on her belly. 'Hell. Let's call it a draw shall we, and concentrate on getting off this floor.'

Helen tried to move and stifled a whimper. 'I don't think I can.'

Chapter Nine

Jay swore again and carefully got to his knees. His jeans were wedged uncomfortably below his butt. He paused to pull them up and shed the condom. Helen lay on the suede rug, her eyes closed, her skin flushed with arousal. Her legs were still wide open and he could see every inch of her well-fucked well-creamed pussy. His cock twitched and he grimaced.

Damn, his knee hurt. He hadn't planned to put Helen under him and fuck her without mercy. She hadn't complained though. She'd taken every hard thrust and given it right back to him. His shaft thickened again and he fought the temptation to bury himself back inside her until she begged him to do her again.

He grabbed his shirt from the arm of the couch and gave it to Helen. Taking her hand, he hauled her into a sitting position. 'Put this on or I'm going to be inside you again.'

'I wouldn't mind.'

She turned her head to look at him and he tried to ignore the invitation in her gaze.

'My knee would.'

Immediately her expression became all business. 'Do you have an ice pack?'

He wanted to kick himself for drawing her attention to his knee but he nodded in the direction of the freezer. She pushed her arms into his shirtsleeves and got carefully to her feet. He tried not to groan as she bent over the freezer drawer, exposing her naked ass and rumpled stockings to his lustful gaze.

'There's a knee brace in the drawer behind you too. The ice pack fits inside it.'

As carefully as he could he scooted back until he sat against the bottom of the couch, his right leg stretched out in front of him, his left bent at the knee. When Helen applied the ice pack he winced.

'That feels good, in a weird, painful kind of way.'

She knelt beside him and felt around his kneecap, her gaze focused and calm. 'There doesn't seem to be any swelling. You should know not to put too much pressure on it.'

'Well, hell, doc, I wasn't thinking about my knee, I was thinking about fucking you.'

'I shouldn't have been so demanding. I forgot about your knee and I'm supposed to be a doctor.' She continued to touch his leg, strands of her hair drifting across his groin.

He caught her chin in his fingers. 'I'm glad you forgot, and you weren't too demanding. I was the one who turned it into some kind of competition.'

Her laughter warmed his skin. 'You're a guy. Of course you did.' Her fingers lingered on his knee, tracing the scars from the surgery. His cock stiffened as she leant forward and kissed his knee. Damn, there was no way she was going to miss that. It was practically poking her in the eye.

Turning her head, he watched in horrified delight as she licked the crown of his cock with the tip of her tongue. Her eyes were half-closed as if she was trying to guess the mystery flavor.

He slid a hand into her hair. 'Do that again.'

Her tongue made a swirling foray around the exposed head of his cock and then paused to penetrate the oozing slit. He groaned as she continued the little stabbing motion, his body tense with delight.

'Wait,' he groaned. She stopped, her inquiring gaze fixed on his. Retaining his position on the floor, he picked her up until she straddled him, facing his cock. He pushed the shirt up until it exposed her butt.

'What about your knee?'

'Forget my knee. You've already kissed it better. Kiss my cock instead.'

He drew her hips back until her sex was presented to his mouth.

'Do it, Helen.'

He waited until her lips closed over his crown and then licked her clit. He couldn't believe how wet and ready she was for him again. His tongue penetrated her channel and she shuddered, pressing her pussy back into his face until he wallowed in her creamy sex. Not that he minded the sensation. It wasn't a bad way to suffocate.

Her mouth surrounded his shaft, sucking and pulling hard enough to make him writhe. She seemed to know just how he liked it. A touch of roughness and a sense of danger, the fear of her pushing him over the edge or making him beg. In response, he flicked her clit with his tongue until it was as hard and swollen as his cock. He rubbed his chin against her tender flesh until she moved restlessly against him, demanding more, seeking his mouth. As his climax approached, he increased the pressure of his strokes, sucking on her clit as her teeth clamped around the base of his cock and sent them both into release.

He groaned, thrusting his tongue as deep into her

channel as he could while he waited for his cock to stop pulsing. God, she was good with her mouth. For once his cock had been right all along.

Helen sat up, careful not to touch Jay's outstretched right leg. Despite their frantic lovemaking, the ice pack had remained in place. She surreptitiously studied his knee, which appeared to be bearing up well, considering. It took all her energy to crawl off Jay and all her courage to face him. He lay back against the couch, his face relaxed, and a satisfied smirk on his lips. Would he be shocked by her excessive demands? David had always hated it when she'd wanted to be fucked more than once. Eventually she'd stopped asking. She licked her lips and tasted Jay's come. She folded her arms across her breasts. 'I'd just like to say that I don't behave like this with all my patients.'

He opened one eye. 'Only a select few, right? Damn, I'd love to see you turn up for an appointment with me with nothing under your white coat but skin.'

She shivered at the erotic image he presented. He reached out to touch her thigh.

'Be a good doc and help me up, would you?'

She maneuvered him back onto the couch and checked his knee again. While he got settled, she retrieved her clothing and put herself back together. He smiled as she threw him his shirt.

'It looked better on you,' he said.

She studied his muscular chest and abs. His fair hair hardly showed up on his chest but she knew it was there. He hadn't bothered to do up his jeans and his cock was half-erect.

'You might have a point. If it was up to me, I'd confiscate all your shirts.'

His grin was slow and sultry. 'Why, thank you, ma'am. I aim to please.'

Helen avoided his gaze and attempted to smooth the creases out of her skirt. If she didn't concentrate, she'd be running her fingers over his slick skin and hoping for another bout of amazing sex. He was like a drug. Despite her agreement to let him be in control, she had to maintain some standards.

'You promised to show me how you cut your hand.'

He blinked at her and scratched his head. 'I did?' He struggled to his feet, gradually putting weight on his right leg. Helen breathed a sigh of relief when he stepped confidently toward the recessed dining area. He flicked on a light to expose a glass and steel dining table covered in bits of leather. Helen went over, picked up some of the scraps and pressed them to her nose. The scent was intoxicating.

'What are you making?'

His smile was self-deprecating. 'It's going to be a belt, if I ever finish it.' He moved past her and picked up a longer piece of leather.

Helen took it from him, marveling at the intricately woven strands and the rainbow of colors. 'It's beautiful.'

He shrugged, his shoulder brushing hers. 'It's crap.'

Why did he sound so defensive? Did he think she'd find his hobby amusing? She put the belt back on the table and picked up one of the craft knives. 'I can see why you cut yourself. These things are sharp.'

'No sharper than a scalpel, and I don't see you walking around wearing Band Aids.'

'I learnt to take care, just like you will.' She held his gaze, saw the defensiveness in his. 'It's no big deal.'

He took the blade from her hand and placed it carefully

on the table. 'I did some leather work in the rehab place the sports medicine team sent me to.'

'The Beeches, right? They have an excellent reputation.' She stroked the leather belt, reluctant to leave it. 'You obviously have a gift for it.'

'Yeah, right. What kind of man makes his living fooling around with bits of leather?'

'A talented one?'

He turned away from her and walked back into the kitchen. She followed more slowly, watching the rigid set of his shoulders and the way he flung open the refrigerator door. He took out two beers and slammed them onto the granite countertop.

'What else do you make?'

'Cowboy boots.'

He opened the beers, handed her one, and brought the other to his mouth. His throat worked as he swallowed, reminding her of his mouth on her sex. She clenched her fists. The stubborn set of his jaw made her want to punch him real hard.

'And why are you telling me this if it makes you so angry?'

He paused and lowered the bottle to glare at her. 'You asked how I cut my hand.'

'Fine.' She gave him back the beer, marched back over to the couch and grabbed her purse.

Jay watched her, a frown in his eyes. 'Where are you going?'

'Home.'

He put the beers down and wiped the back of his hand over his mouth. 'I thought you were going to stay the night.'

'Well, you thought wrong, didn't you?'

He took a step toward her. 'I don't want you to go.'

'But I'm going anyway.'

'Helen, it's late. It's dangerous out there. Stay here.'

She raised her eyebrows. 'No thanks. I got what I came for.'

'And what was that?'

'Sex and an explanation as to how you cut your hand.'

He folded his arms across his chest. 'That's it?'

'That's all I've been offered. It's been fun. Call me when you get over whatever it is that's making you so mad and maybe we can have a real discussion like a couple of adults.'

'Helen...'

She headed for the door, aware that she wanted to cry but totally unwilling to let Jay know he'd affected her so badly. The door closed behind her and she let out her breath. She'd forgotten their deal was all about sex and didn't include getting close to him. Dammit, the man was as uptight as he claimed she was. How could he move so fast from white-hot passion to completely shutting her out?

The elevator arrived and she stepped in. In the mirrored surfaces she looked emotionally wrecked, her eyes over-bright, her mouth still swollen from Jay's kisses. She smoothed down her hair and straightened her clothes. It wasn't that late and she'd valet parked. Jay believed she was a fragile flower but she was quite capable of getting around the city without putting herself into danger.

As she exited the elevator, she blew her reflection a kiss. Now she was out of his sight, she could function like a normal person again. She shouldn't have let her sexual attraction for him delude her into thinking he wanted any kind of relationship with her. And if Jay wanted to behave like a sulky kid, that was his choice. She didn't have to put up with it, whatever their bargain.

Chapter Ten

'Fuck!'

Jay barely restrained himself from hurling the phone to the polished kitchen floor. He'd tried to call Helen at least ten times and she either wasn't picking up or she didn't want to talk to him. Somehow he guessed it was the latter. He left another terse message and hung up.

He couldn't say he was surprised. He'd managed to turn the best fuck of his life into a disaster. How in the hell had he let himself do that?

He grabbed a bottle of orange juice from the counter and chugged it down, wincing at the slightly bitter taste. It was a new thing for him to actually try to analyze what he'd done wrong. In all his other relationships he'd been happy to let things slide if they didn't work out, but this time it was different. Dr Helen had gotten under his skin.

He tossed the carton in the trash. And why was he so pissed off? Because she'd tried to get to know him, that's why. She'd been interested in his new line of work and he'd frozen up and pushed her away.

The phone rang and he leapt for it.

'Helen?'

'Nope.'

'Oh, damn, it's you, Grayson.'

His brother sighed. 'What's up?'

My cock, permanently since I fucked Dr Helen.

'Not much.'

'Glad to hear you are your usual communicative self.'

'Huh?'

'I'm just checking up on you. I said I would.'

Jay scratched his unshaven chin. 'Hey, Grayson. If you've offended a chick, what do you do to make it up to her?'

The silence was so long Jay started to sweat.

'Let me get this straight. You can't be bothered to answer a civil question and now you're asking for advice?'

'Yeah, you're the big bro. You're supposed to know about these things, right?'

'Right, and I've been such a success with women recently, haven't I?'

Jay set his teeth. Damn, he'd forgotten about Grayson's broken engagement. 'Forget I asked. I'm doing good, see ya.'

'Jay, wait a minute. This "chick" of yours. Is the relationship serious or casual?'

'Sexual.'

'So not very important.'

'Are you kidding?'

'OK, so what did you do?'

Jay glowered at the phone. 'I'm not giving you details so you can get your rocks off. Let's just say, I forgot that women like to communicate.'

'You fell asleep after sex?'

'Hell, no! I . . . I just got pissed when she tried to talk about me.'

Grayson sighed. 'Women.'

'That's exactly it, Grayson. What is that about?'

'I was being sarcastic, dumb ass. So you offended her by not opening up and now you're regretting it.'

'Kind of.'

'Because you'll miss the sex or because you'll miss her?'

Jay sat down heavily on the leather couch and looked out of the window. 'Both,' he muttered.

'I can't hear you.'

'I said, both.'

'And I assume she won't answer her phone.'

'Nope.'

'Do you know where she works? She does have a job?'

'Ha, ha, very funny. Of course she does and yeah, I know where she works.'

'Then you go and buy a big bunch of flowers, meet her after work and prepare to grovel.'

'I'm not getting down on one knee.'

Grayson chuckled. 'You're not proposing, you're just groveling. Tell her you were an idiot and ask her what you can do to put things right.'

'And what if she tells me to fuck off?'

'*Then* you get down on your knees and start begging.'

Helen lifted her chin and opened the door into the staff break room. It had been a tough day filled with difficult patients, barbed comments from her colleagues and unhelpful nursing staff. Several people looked up but no one spoke to her. She knew why. The notice about Professor Hart's resignation had come out and everyone was waiting to see what she was going to do.

'Hey, Wonder Doc. How's it going?'

Helen smiled at one of her few allies, Dr Tara Davies, her favorite ER resident. Tara sat reading the *San Francisco Chronicle*, her big red-stockinged feet planted on the stained coffee table.

'It's going good. How about you?'

Helen settled herself on the worn seat beside Tara and opened her beef sandwich. Two male doctors opposite them immediately moved away. It had been like that all day. As soon as she appeared, all the chattering little groups dispersed. It was hard not to feel paranoid.

Tara's gaze flicked to the departing doctors. 'I guess they don't like beef.'

Helen shrugged. 'Or they don't like me.'

'Now why wouldn't they like you?'

'Because I'm a doctor?'

It was an old joke between them and Helen's spirits lightened. She already knew that both the guys who'd left thought they were better qualified than her. They'd made their contempt of her obvious from day one of her appointment.

'Professor Hart announced his resignation today and now everybody hates me.'

'Not everyone.'

'All right. Everyone except you.'

'I hate you, Helen, but that's because you're smart and blonde, not because you're bound to get that job.'

Helen groaned. 'I suppose that's what everyone thinks.'

'Well, it is kind of expected. You are his protégée.'

'That's one way of putting it. I have a feeling others won't put it so nicely.'

Tara narrowed her eyes. 'It's a bit too late to be worrying about that, isn't it? If you didn't want the hassle, you should've become a nurse.'

'I'd love to be a nurse.' Helen sighed. 'That's what I originally intended to be. It wasn't until some teacher told me I'd never be good enough to be a doctor that I decided.'

'Was it a guy teacher?'

'Strangely enough, it was.' Helen faced Tara. 'And you're right. I got here on my own merits and I deserve the chance to fight my own corner.'

Tara punched her fist in the air. 'That's the spirit, sistah. And if you get to be the first female to head up this department, it makes it that much easier for me to follow in your footsteps.'

'You see me as some kind of seat warmer for you?'

'Absolutely. And I'm sure you'll do a fine job of it.'

Helen stared into Tara's confident brown eyes. Someone had to lead the charge to advance women in medicine. She just wished it didn't have to be her.

'You are going to apply, aren't you?' Tara looked anxious. 'If things are going to change around here, women need to be heard.'

'Of course I'm going to apply.'

God help her. If she didn't, she'd cause more talk than there was already. People would assume she was afraid to take the job without Professor Hart to back her up and she'd never be taken seriously again. Tara was right. Nothing would change unless some woman stepped up and forced things to happen.

'How's Patrick?'

Tara's face softened. 'He's adorable. He said his first word this weekend. Dave and I were so thrilled.'

'What did he say?'

'Dada, of course.' Tara smiled. 'Although after all those hours I spent giving birth to him, you'd think he'd have the decency to say Mama.' She passed Helen two new photos of a grinning bald-headed Patrick waving a rattle.

'I don't know much about babies,' Helen confessed. 'I

moved away from my family when I was young. I don't even know if I have any nieces or nephews.'

Tara's eyebrows rose. 'You don't know?'

'My family's not exactly close.' How could they be after she'd broken their hearts by marrying at sixteen and divorcing a year later? Her mother had never trusted her again. In the end, it had seemed kinder to leave Blossom Creek as quickly as possible and hope they forgot her.

'It wasn't a great idea, having Patrick right in the middle of my training, but we're managing. It's tough but I don't regret it.'

Helen passed the photos back. 'You shouldn't. Someone with intelligence has to populate the Earth.'

'Not you though. You've never wanted kids, have you?'

'I haven't had time. And I certainly haven't met the right man yet.'

She'd always been too busy planning the next stage of her career or manipulating the men in her life to think about having a child. Would Jay want kids? She could just see him tossing a kid on his shoulders and running through the trees like some dreamy ad dad for baby diapers or something. Dammit, she didn't want to think about Jay Turner. He was a complete jerk.

'If you do want a baby, you'll need to think about it soon before those eggs of yours fry or die.'

'You have such a lovely way with words, Tara.' Helen stood up and threw her sandwich wrapper into the trash.

Tara grinned up at her. 'I'll watch your back and let you know any particularly bad gossip, OK?'

'I'd appreciate that, but don't feel you have to get involved. These things have a way of coming back and biting you on the ass.'

'No problem.' Tara slapped her ample behind. 'I've got plenty of that to go around.'

Helen left the room feeling much better than when she had arrived. Only five more patients to see and then she could go home. She also planned to make time to put her name forward for the promotion. It didn't mean she'd take the job if it was offered but it sure as hell sent a message to her colleagues that she wasn't going to be intimidated by their treatment.

With a weary sigh, Helen shut down her computer and got to her feet. It was six-thirty. Her application letter lay in her out-tray and her desk was clear for the first time in months. It occurred to her that she could stay at her desk all night if she wanted to. No one would miss her. No one waited for her to come home to them.

In retrospect, by storming out of Jay's apartment, she'd acted just as childishly as he had. She'd agreed to give him sexual control and then gotten mad when he wouldn't share his personal life with her. That wasn't really fair. She didn't need to know what he planned to do with the rest of his life, only what he planned to do to her in bed.

Was she really so starved for company that she assumed Jay would want to share stuff with her? She hadn't opened up to him, so why had she expected any-thing more from him? Helen rubbed her temples where a headache threatened. He'd lulled her into a false sense of intimacy by revealing his softer side and fooled her into thinking he might be interested in her as a person.

She bit her lip. If she was so desperate to connect, perhaps it was time to try to reconcile with her own family. Would they be able to forgive her or would the old grudges still be fresh and painful? Marrying Cory, an out-of-work cowboy, while still in high school hadn't exactly been smart. But she'd definitely learnt from her mistakes. Cowboys were bad news.

Irritated by her uncharacteristically muddled thoughts, she grabbed her jacket and headed for the elevator. Apart from the cleaning staff, the out-patient building was almost empty. Doors stood open and the sharp smell of disinfectant wafted along the halls. In the distance, the wail of an approaching ambulance set her adrenaline pumping. How many times had she heard that sound and dealt with its consequences? Too many to count. She'd enjoyed her stint in the ER: the endless parade of patients, the controlled panic of the staff and their often gruesome humor.

She opened her eyes as the elevator doors parted to reveal the first-floor lobby.

'Helen?'

At first, all she registered was a big bunch of flowers and a cowboy hat. She punched the down button but he was too quick for her. His booted foot slid between the doors before they closed. He stepped into the car and she backed up until she was pressed against the scratched blue wall.

He lowered the bunch of daisies until she could see his resolute expression.

'My brother said I had to be a man and apologize right to your face.'

She folded her arms over her chest. 'And do you always do what your brother tells you?'

His lips moved in a fraction of a smile. 'Nope.'

'I don't care about your brother, Jay.'

The elevator stopped in the staff parking lot and she pushed past him. She'd barely made it out before he caught up and grabbed hold of her elbow.

'I'm trying to apologize here.'

'For what?'

He shrugged. 'For being a jerk.'

'Great, you've apologized. You can go now.'

She fumbled for her car keys in her purse. His fingers shifted and closed around her wrist.

'You haven't accepted my apology.'

She pulled out of his grasp, keys clutched in her hand. 'I'll think about it, OK? Now will you go?' She turned to open her car door, saw the flowers hit the floor.

'I knew he was wrong,' Jay muttered. 'I knew I should've just handled it my way.'

Furious now, she turned to glare at him. 'Are you still here?'

'I sure am.'

She squeaked as he pulled her into his arms and kissed her hard on the mouth. When she pushed at his chest, he abruptly released her. She faced him, her breath coming out in short angry bursts.

'Don't you understand "no"?'

'You didn't say no. You said go away.'

'They kind of mean the same thing.'

He studied her, his gray eyes clear, his gaze open. 'No, they don't. We had great sex and I ruined it by behaving like a jerk, OK?'

'You ruined it by refusing to talk to me like I was a person with opinions and ideas rather than just a sexual object.'

His mouth took on an obstinate line. 'We have a deal.'

'We *had* a deal. I walked out. Deal over.'

'You really think we're done?'

Helen closed her eyes, feeling his warm impatient breath explode on her cheek.

'I'm not good at sharing personal stuff, all right? I've never stayed around a woman long enough to understand how that works.' He sighed, his strong fingers caressing her skin, weakening her resolve. 'I'm all washed up with the rodeo, I'm trying to find a new life and, yeah, I'm as touchy as hell about it.'

She sighed too. 'I'm not being fair. Some of it is my fault. We agreed it was just about sex. I pushed you into revealing something personal about yourself.'

He caught her hand in his, pressed it to his cheek. 'The weird thing is that it felt good to tell someone what I was doing. It kind of made it real for me.'

She couldn't help but smile back at him.

His gaze intensified. 'Don't walk out on me yet.' He turned his cheek until her trapped fingers brushed his mouth. 'I'm not ready to let you go.'

She shivered at the warm feel of his lips against her skin. 'I can't believe I'm saying this, but I'm not ready to let you go either.'

He slid his hand into her hair and aligned their mouths. His kiss was as possessive as his stare. Helen allowed herself to sink into his arms and enjoy his touch. She missed a man's arms around her. She missed having somewhere to lay her head. Damn it, what was the matter with her? She'd never needed a man. Why start now? Thinking about her family had made her vulnerable and unsure. His kiss intensified and she forgot about her concerns as he pressed her against the side of the car. He made her so hot she wanted to strip off her clothes and take him deep inside her.

The clank of the elevator machinery forced her to open her eyes.

'Jay, someone's coming.'

'Yeah, and unfortunately it's not one of us.' He straightened slowly and released her, his expression rueful.

She gestured at her car. 'Can I drop you somewhere?'

After a quick glance at his watch, he nodded. 'That would be great. I have a class at seven.'

Helen opened her car door just in time to see one of her male colleagues approaching. She managed a cool nod and then dove inside the car. Had Dr Baker seen her and Jay? She knew how easily the hospital gossip mill started up and Dr B was definitely capable of grinding those wheels.

While Jay struggled with his seat belt, she maneuvered the car toward the exit, only letting out her breath when they cleared the last barrier.

'Hey, slow down, you almost hit that delivery guy.'

Helen flicked an irritated glance at him. 'Don't tell me how to drive. My ex-husband did that.'

'And is that why he's your ex?'

'No.'

'No?'

The lights changed and they inched forward only to stop again.

'Didn't we just agree to keep our personal lives out of this affair?' Helen asked.

'I sure didn't.'

Helen found she was grinding her teeth.

'Come on, spill,' Jay said.

She revved the engine as the lights changed and shot forward, making Jay slam his hand against the dashboard. 'My ex-husband was a complete prick. And like most pricks he couldn't keep out of women's panties.'

'He cheated on you?'

This time she risked a glance at him.

'Why the hell would anyone cheat on you?' he asked.

'Thanks for the boost to my ego, but he's a man. That's all there is to it.'

'Not all men cheat.'

'Just most of them, which makes it extra hard for a woman to find one who doesn't.'

'When I get married I'm not going to cheat.'

Helen gave him a small superior smile. 'That's what they all say.'

His hand dropped onto her knee. 'Honey, you sure are a bitter and disillusioned woman.'

She turned right at the next light and realized she had no idea where they were headed.

'Seeing as we're not likely to get married, Jay, I'll leave you to your delusions.'

He chuckled and squeezed her knee. 'If you're set on taking me to my evening class, you need to head for the Cow Palace. The college is close by.'

The navigation system bleeped. 'I think I know how to get there, but punch in the address and then I'll be sure.'

He worked out how to use her car's system with a speed that astounded her. She still wasn't quite sure how to use it sometimes. The traffic grid in San Francisco wasn't exactly straightforward. When the route was set, she was relieved to see that they were going the right way.

'How long is the class?'

'A couple of hours and then a bit more if you need it.

Rob, the guy who runs it, pretty much gives me all the access I need.'

'This is for your leatherwork?'

'Yeah.'

'I'm looking forward to seeing more of your work someday.' He had no idea how much the scent of leather, the feel of it against her skin, turned her on.

He turned to smile at her. 'And I might just let you do that.'

'See? We can make progress if we both try.' Helen winced, wishing she sounded less like an old schoolmarm.

'I can see you Thursday night if that works.'

Helen turned into the college parking lot and stopped the car. 'I think that's OK.' She took a deep breath. 'Would you like to come over to my place?'

He unbuckled his seat belt and studied her. She closed her eyes as he brushed her cheek with his fingertip.

'You look tired,' Jay said.

She barely resisted the urge to dump all her problems in his lap. 'It's been a tough day.'

He leant in to kiss her. The citrus scent of his after-shave stole through her senses making her ache.

'Damn, I wish I still had my truck. If I did, I'd be inside you now.'

She glanced down at the narrow console between their seats. 'This probably isn't the best car for sex.'

'I'd manage if I had to but I'd appreciate a bit more room to fuck you properly.' He bit down slowly on her ear. 'Thanks for the ride. Go home and get some sleep. You'll need it.'

He kissed her again, this time more intensely. She

responded with a deep need of her own. At that moment, she wanted to beg him to come back home, sleep in her bed and hold her tight. It was difficult to release him.

'Have a good class and see you Thursday.'

She almost pushed him out of the car. Jay stood where she'd left him mouthing something as she drove away. She was halfway home before she realized he had no idea where she lived.

Chapter Eleven

'I hear you've got yourself a new man.'

Although she knew Nancy was standing by the door, Helen didn't bother to look up from her paperwork.

'Dr Baker said he saw some guy in your car yesterday.'

'Did he really?' Helen kept her tone even, her head bent over her work.

'I also heard you've applied for Professor Hart's job.'

'And?'

Nancy cleared her throat. 'You won't get it, you know.'

'Why's that?'

'Because everyone knows exactly how you got to be so successful so young.'

Helen raised her head to look Nancy directly in the eyes. 'You have a problem with a woman using her brain?'

Nancy crossed her arms over her ample chest. 'I have a problem with women doctors who think they are better than everyone else.'

Helen got to her feet. 'Then let's hope I don't get the job because I'd sure hate to lose you.'

'What's that supposed to mean?'

'Only that if I do succeed, you probably wouldn't feel comfortable working under me. I'd make sure you got a great reference though.' *Not.*

She smiled brightly at Nancy as she moved past her. At least she knew where Nancy's loyalties lay and they definitely weren't with her. So much for female unity in the workforce. Fueled with rage, she continued down the hall until she found herself staring at the main notice board. There was a new sheet of paper on the top right-hand corner headed 'Initial candidates'.

An all too familiar name caught her eye and she moved closer to confirm her suspicions. There it was: Dr David Campion, orthopedic surgeon extraordinaire. Her second husband and, in her opinion, an even bigger loser than her first, although most people considered him a raging success.

Would David ever stop competing with her? She hadn't realized how obsessed he was about coming out on top until after their marriage, when he'd expected her to give way to him both professionally and emotionally. For Helen, the final straw had come when he'd sabotaged her application to head up the department they both worked for. He'd sent a supposedly private email revealing she was trying to get pregnant to the entire department and the selection committee.

Of course he had apologized profusely and insisted it was a mistake but it undermined her enough to let him receive the promotion in her stead and then insist on her resignation. It hadn't helped when she realized the email was actually about his latest mistress who really was pregnant and eager to move into Helen's house.

There were four other names on the list, most of whom she recognized. Two of them were current colleagues, the guys who had walked out on her and Tara yesterday at lunch time. Helen stored the information in her head until she could get home and research the rest.

When she returned to her desk, Nancy had disappeared. A single white envelope addressed in Professor Hart's handwriting lay in her in-tray.

'Dear Dr Kinsale. Thank you for your application for

the position of department head. The faculty would like to invite you to an informal drinks evening at the doctors' lounge to meet the other candidates and the selection committee on Friday at six. Please RSVP.'

Helen stared at the professor's almost illegible handwriting. This would be the first opportunity for the candidates to get a good look at each other and start staking their claims. Helen sighed. The thought of being trapped in the same room as her ex was almost enough to make her regret her decision to enter the race.

Perhaps David wouldn't be able to make it. His new wife, Carrie-Ann, was very possessive and apparently pregnant with their second child. Helen scolded herself for her cowardly attitude. She'd decided three years ago that she wasn't going to let David manipulate her anymore. Going to the drinks evening was a good way of showing how much she'd grown and how little she needed him.

She picked up the phone to call Jay. He answered on the fourth ring.

'I forgot to tell you where I lived,' she said.

'I know.' He chuckled, the sound warming her even through the static.

'I don't actually live at the hospital, you know, despite what a lot of my patients think.'

'You don't? Wait a sec, I'll get a pen. OK, go ahead.'

She recited her address, made certain he knew his way to Pacific Heights and hung up. She smiled at Professor Hart's letter and emailed a reply. By the time Friday evening rolled along, she should be looking just fine and dandy after all that sex with Jay. That would show her ex just how much better her life was without him.

* * *

Jay paid off the cab and checked the address one more time. He should have expected Dr Helen to live somewhere fancy. The much-photographed Victorian houses of Pacific Heights suited her perfectly. Classy, yeah, but with a distinctly quirky personality. He mounted the stone steps and pressed the third bell.

'Come on up, Jay.'

He smiled as the door buzzed and then pushed it open. Helen sounded breathless. Was she as excited to see him as he was to see her? He'd been walking around with a perpetual hard-on ever since they'd had sex. It was almost like being a teenager again but this time he had more to look forward to than a copy of *Playboy* and his fist.

Helen opened the door to her second-floor apartment and he stepped inside. He paused briefly to admire the evening sun as it streamed in through a large bay window at the front of the room, allowing a view of the San Francisco hills and colorful house fronts.

'Nice place, Dr Helen.'

She shrugged. 'I like it.'

She wore a simple green T-shirt and khaki Capri pants. Her toenails were painted dark red. Jay reached out and drew her close for a long, lingering kiss. She sighed into his mouth, her fingers entwining in his hair. He kissed her more deeply, his blood heating, his cock swelling against her flat stomach.

'Pants again.'

She shivered as he slid his hand down her back and below the waistband of her pants. His fingers caught in the string of her panties and he tugged on the fabric.

'Take them off.'

He released her long enough to watch her shimmy out

of her pants leaving her in her T-shirt and tiny green satin panties. She licked her lips; her nipples poked through the soft cotton of her top. Did she even have a bra on?

'T-shirt too.'

She pulled that over her head, messing her hair until it waved around her shoulders. No bra. She kept her gaze fixed on his. He liked that. Slowly, he unbuckled his belt and drew the leather free. Her eyes flicked to his belt.

'Come here.'

She walked toward him until her breasts brushed the front of his shirt. One-handed, he unbuttoned his jeans and let his erection spring free. He worked a condom over his heated flesh. Her nipples tightened and he smelt her arousal. He ran a hand down his aching wet shaft.

'I need to fuck, right now. No foreplay, no kissing, just hard and fast.'

Her pupils dilated and she reached for him. With a growl, he picked her up, his cock brushing the triangle of satin that covered her clit. Her legs encircled his hips, pressing her wet heat against the underside of his straining shaft. He backed her up to the nearest wall.

He slid his fingers between them to push her panties to one side and thrust into her, penetrating her tightness until he could go no further. As he pumped into her, her fingers dug into his shoulders, driving him on, and her heels pressed into his ass keeping him firmly inside.

He fucked her hard, rubbing her clit in time to his thrusts, determined to make her come with him. When he felt the first quiver of her climax, he worked her faster, slamming his cock into her welcoming warmth until he had to come or his balls would explode.

They came together and he closed his eyes at the

intensity of the sensations roaring through him. Helen's legs relaxed around him and he allowed them to slide to the floor. He opened his eyes to find her staring up at him.

'I knew I wouldn't hurt you.' He touched her lip with the finger he'd used on her clit. 'You were already wet and ready for me, weren't you?' His cock jerked inside her as she licked his fingertip. 'Did you touch yourself? Did you get yourself hot for me?'

She bit his finger as he slid out of her.

'I like to think that you did, although according to our deal, your body belongs to me and I should really be giving you permission.' He grinned as she drew in a sharp breath and pressed his hand over her lips. 'Uh-oh, darlin'. Don't be shooting your mouth off. I don't want to have to get mad at you.'

Over the top of his hand, her blue eyes snapped murder.

Without releasing her, he leant down and picked up his leather belt. 'How about I put you over my knee? We'll call it a round dozen if you promise to ask me nicely next time you want to play with yourself.' He paused to catch her reaction, realized her entire attention was fixed on his leather belt. Lust and dark excitement stirred deep in his belly. He lowered his voice. 'You like the sound of that, yeah?' He looped the belt in his fist and brought it up to caress her throat, then slid the soft leather down toward her breasts. Her nipples puckered as he rubbed the belt over them. Her breathing shortened to soft pants and he took his hand away from her mouth.

'Yeah, you do, don't you?'

* * *

Helen couldn't take her gaze off the leather as it caressed her breasts. A bitter-sweet memory of Cory fucking her dressed only in his chaps made her shudder. She always associated the smell of leather with sex.

Jay slid the belt lower, rubbing it over her stomach. Mesmerized, she waited to see what he would do next.

'Take off your panties and open your legs.'

She did what he said, couldn't stop herself and didn't want to stop herself. Her panties hit the floor. He opened his hand and allowed the belt to fall in one straight line. It slapped against her mound, the leather warm and supple. Her clit started to throb and her sex creamed.

'Let's try this before I spank you.'

He slid the buckle end of the belt back through the first loop of his jeans to anchor it. Reaching behind her, he drew the rest of the belt between her legs, the leather flat against her soaking wet sex. He wound the excess around his left hand and pressed his fist into the small of her back.

'Look down, Helen.'

His right hand moved to cover the belt buckle, protecting her skin. He moved in close, tightening the leather as he went, until she felt her clit start to pulse with the friction and pressure. She was caught between his body and the wall, her sex covered by the leather band, her heart thumping so hard she thought she might die. He looped another circle of belt around his left hand, bringing her up on tiptoe.

'Yeah, that's right. I want my belt soaked in your cream, honey.' He bent his head, sucked her nipple into his mouth and moved his hips, dragging the leather back and forth over her sex. Helen couldn't stop moaning as the pressure built.

She almost screamed as he raised his head to stare into her eyes.

'I want your mouth around my cock when you come.'

He released some of the leather loops and guided her down to her knees. He shoved his jeans down to his hips, maintaining the link to her sex even as he discarded the used condom. He sat heavily on the couch.

'Hard, Helen. I want it hard.'

She wanted to do him like that too. She'd never allowed herself to be rough with a man before but she was beyond that now. Jay had pushed all the right buttons and allowed her to experience some of her wildest fantasies. It was only right that she should give as good as she was getting.

He groaned as she grazed his shaft with her teeth and then sucked at the swollen crown. His left hand continued to move the belt between her legs, slippery now with her juices. She sucked harder, using her tongue for every long rough pull on his shaft. Her climax slammed into her, and she set her teeth into the base of his cock keeping him deep in her throat as she came. His come flooded her mouth and she swallowed in time to each heavy spurt.

In the small of her back, his left hand clenched and released the belt freeing her aching over-sensitized sex. He reached down and pulled her over his lap, facedown. She shuddered as the leather belt danced over her butt.

'Next time you feel like playing with yourself, call me.'

She struggled to breathe as his fingers delved between her butt cheeks. 'You don't own me.' She jumped as the leather smacked against her skin twice. His hand returned, smoothing the pain away.

'I own this pussy.'

'That's ridiculous.'

Two more sharp cracks of the leather made her writhe, mingling pain with pleasure, making her want more.

'Just tell me you won't do it again without permission and I'll let you go.'

Helen pressed her lips together.

'Nothing to say?'

She tensed as he slid two long fingers into her anus.

'I'd like to fuck your ass now. My cock thrusting into all this warm sensitized flesh.' He added two more fingers making her gasp. 'I bet you'd come so hard they'd hear you screaming on the Bay Bridge.'

He tapped her with the belt four more times.

She bit down on her lip, enjoying the additional small pain as he continued to play with her ass and caress her hot butt cheeks.

'I know why you're not speaking, Helen.'

She closed her eyes.

'Because you like what I'm doing too much, don't you?'

Was she brave enough to admit it for the first time in her life? His fingers stilled.

'If you don't answer me, I'll stop.'

'All right. Yes.'

'Yes, what?'

'I like what you are doing to me.'

Her breath hissed out as he turned her over and pulled his fingers out of her ass. His eyes were narrowed, his face taut with passion. He kissed her, his mouth grinding against hers. When he finally raised his head he was grinning. 'Hell, I like it too.'

She grabbed hold of his hair, kissed him back, her body still craving his touch. He groaned as she bit down on his bottom lip.

'Slow down, honey. I'm not nineteen any more and I've got this banged-up knee.'

Helen nipped his lip again and then drew back. 'There's nothing wrong with your knee. I happen to know it was fixed by an outstanding surgeon.'

He tucked a strand of her hair behind her ear and reached down to stroke his cock. 'Give me a minute and I'll be ready for you again.'

As her sexual high faded, Helen felt cold. When had she turned into such a demanding, perverted . . . slut? She wriggled off his lap and wrapped her arms around her waist.

'How about I get you a drink and then we can shower?'

Jay made no effort to move, his attention fixed on her face, his expression puzzled. 'Only if you shower with me.'

'I have soda, juice, beer or coffee. Which would you prefer?' She scurried into the small kitchen, aware of her nakedness, unwilling to cover herself while Jay watched her so intently.

'Soda would be great,' he called after her.

She opened the refrigerator and located two cans of 7-Up. She pressed one to her hot face enjoying the icy chill that shot through her.

'Thanks, darlin'.'

Jay took the other can from her hand making her jump. She hadn't heard him come up behind her. The rough cloth of his unbuttoned jeans brushed against her bare behind and she shivered. His large hand cupped her left cheek and squeezed.

'Still stings, yeah?' he asked.

Helen couldn't look at him. Had she really let him tan her hide with his belt?

'Don't turn away from me, Helen.'

She faced him, chin held high and he met her gaze.

'What's up, honey?'

She shrugged. 'I'm just not quite comfortable with how I behaved.'

He placed his soda on the tiled worktop and considered her. 'I can appreciate that.'

'I'm not saying you made me do anything I didn't want to do, just that . . .'

'You didn't know you were going to let me use my belt on you.'

She nodded, too confused to speak.

He sighed. 'Hell, I didn't know that was going to happen either but I don't regret it.' He met her eyes. 'How about you?'

'I don't regret it. It was . . . liberating.'

'It was damned sexy.' He closed the gap between them and drew her into his arms. 'You'll be thinking of me tomorrow whenever you sit down.'

Helen relaxed against him, her head resting on his shoulder. It sure was a unique way to help her ignore her ex. She smiled.

'What's so funny?'

'I have to go to a drinks party tomorrow evening.'

'And?'

'My ex-husband will be there.'

'Should I be worried about that?'

'No, I told you, he's an asshole.'

His fingers probed between her ass cheeks. 'Nothing wrong with assholes.'

'OK, prick, then.'

He took her hand and pressed it against his rapidly hardening shaft. 'Nothing wrong with pricks either.'

She squeezed him gently. 'In the right place, of course.'

'Of course.' His fingers continued to caress her. 'So why do you have to go to this party?'

She sighed. 'Do you really want to know?'

'Yeah, I do.' He moved her hand away from his cock and held it behind her back.

'I'm being considered for a promotion to department head. This drinks evening is for all the candidates to meet the faculty.'

Jay released her and leant back against the countertop. 'I've watched *ER* for years and been in a few hospitals myself. Aren't you a bit young to be a department head?'

Helen tried to look dignified, difficult when you are naked. 'It's complicated. Let's just say I'm advanced for my age.'

'OK, I'll buy that. So your ex is going for the same job?'

'Him and four other guys.'

'And do you think you'll get it?'

She took a deep breath. 'I'm not sure.' She opened her soda and drained the can. 'Can we talk about something else?'

Jay grinned. 'Sure.' He ran a hand over his now erect cock. 'I want you on that cold countertop, me standing between your legs fucking you. How does that sound?'

She could only nod as her body stirred to life. She'd never met a man who matched and anticipated her sexual needs so well before. It was exhilarating. He picked her up and placed her on the white-tiled surface. She winced as her butt touched the cold tile.

Jay rolled on a condom and pushed her legs wide. He

took her ankles and planted her feet on the countertop too.

'Yeah, honey, you're already wet for me.' He slid one finger inside her making her moan. 'Tomorrow, when you're at the drinks party, I want you to think about my cock driving into you and how I make you come.'

'I'll think about you every time I have to look at David, my ex's smug face.'

'Do that.' He thumbed her clit and then rubbed the tip of his sheathed cock over her. 'Did he fuck you like this? Did he tan your backside and make you wild?'

'Do you think I would've divorced him if he had?'

He grinned as he slid the crown of his cock inside her. 'I bet he had no idea what to do with you, did he? You must've masturbated a lot.'

She tried to arch her hips to draw more of him inside her. 'He thought I was oversexed.'

His grip on her thigh tightened as he shoved himself home. 'Honey, the man was a fool. You're just perfect the way you are.'

Chapter Twelve

'I want to see your bedroom.' Jay stripped off the used condom and lifted Helen off the countertop. Her knees wobbled and she leant into him, grabbing his arm for support.

'The shower's in there, too, so it's on our way.'

Now that he wasn't consumed with lust, Jay realized that her apartment was not at all how he'd expected it to be. 'Your place is nice, doc.'

'You already said that.'

He put his arms around her shoulders and allowed her to lead him down the narrow hall. 'No, I mean it. It's very warm and inviting.'

She glanced up at him. 'Not like me at all, you mean?'

He paused at the door of the bedroom. The walls were covered in a lush rose print and the bed was a four poster with crisp white and lace covers. God, he was looking forward to having her in that bed, her legs spread wide on those smooth sheets. He cupped her breast and she immediately moved closer to him. 'It's like you. The inside you no one gets to see. The lush red of your nipples and your pussy –' He stopped abruptly. *Shit*. Helen was staring at him. He tried a grin. 'Forget I said that. I must've have watched too many afternoon soap operas while I was recovering.'

She came up on tiptoe and kissed him, her mouth soft against his, her body pressing into him. Despite its recent activity, his cock responded to the feel of her in his arms.

He was slightly sore but that only added to his excitement.

His hand slid down over her ass and she shivered; her hips rolled against his making him even harder.

'Help me take off my jeans,' he said.

She was quick to undress him, her hands moving with a speed and assurance that spoke of long hours in the ER. He'd fucked her twice and he hadn't even taken off his cowboy boots. When he was naked, he faced her again, loving the way she stared at his cock and body.

'I want you again on that bed, before we shower.'

For once she didn't argue, just climbed up on the bed after him and waited. He scooted back until his butt hit the headboard and spread his legs.

'Your turn to ride me. Fast or slow, whatever you like. I'm easy.'

She climbed on top of him, her sex warm against the underside of his cock. He pulled on her nipples with his finger and thumb, drawing them out into stiff peaks.

'Do you have another condom?'

Her question made him tear his gaze away from her breasts to her face. It was hard to think when the warmth and wetness of her pussy was settled over his groin.

'We've used all the ones I brought. Do you have any?'

She pointed at the bedside table drawer.

'In there, look in there.'

He reached into the drawer, drew out a vibrator and then a pack of condoms. He studied the pink plastic cock, comparing it to his own heated flesh. 'It's not big enough for you, darlin'. We need to get you one that really makes you come hard like mine.'

She sniffed, still magnificent even in her naked skin. 'It's standard length. It's perfectly adequate.'

He raised an eyebrow. 'You're not talking about my cock, are you?'

She studied his growing erection. 'I'd say you were slightly above average.'

He took her hand and wrapped it around the base of his shaft. 'Well above average, and you'd be right. Somewhere between eight and nine inches, depending on the pussy.'

She took her hand away. 'Sometimes you are so crude.'

'I'm a guy. We know these things. For you, I'm definitely a ten, don't you think?' He put the vibrator back in the drawer and shook a condom out of the box. His shaft was sensitive as hell as she worked the condom over it. He couldn't remember the last time he'd had so much sex in such a short space of time. His body didn't know whether to shout for joy or whimper in shock.

He gripped his shaft at the base, guiding the thick crown away from his belly. 'Ride me, Helen. Fuck my cock.'

She rose up on her knees and positioned herself over him. He tensed as she slowly lowered herself until her pussy grazed his knuckles. She gasped. He released his cock, allowing her to swallow him up.

'Are you sore?' Jay asked.

She nodded, her expression hidden from him as she stared down to where their bodies were joined. He reached between them, flicked her clit, making her jump.

'Do you want me to stop?'

He already knew what she wanted, but he had a perverse desire to hear her say it. She was like him. The rough edginess of their lovemaking a completely unexpected turn-on for them both. He fingered her swollen clit again and she moaned.

'Jay, I'll come if you keep that up.'

'And that's a problem? You can come as many times as you want, honey. I'll stick with you.' He squeezed her clit harder now. 'And then I'll make you come again and again until you think you can't do it anymore. But you will, because I'll give you no choice.' He gritted his teeth as her sex clenched around his shaft in a sudden pulsing wave. Yeah, she was turned on all right. She circled her hips in a helpless, fast tempo. He could only grab them and hold on as he came too, much faster than he'd anticipated but still so fucking good that he wanted to shout her name to the skies.

She collapsed over him and he slid out of her. She sighed and buried her face deeper against his shoulder. Jay put his arms around her and held her close. Five minutes to relax and then a shower . . .

A loud gurgling noise woke Helen. It was followed by the wailing of a starving cat. She opened one eye and realized that her mattress had developed a swath of fair chest hair and a fine set of abs. She sat up carefully, trying not to disturb Jay. How long had they slept? It couldn't be the next morning, could it?

She located the clock, saw with a burst of relief that is was only just past nine and still quite light outside.

'Can we put off the shower and focus on food?'

Jay's gravelly voice in her ear made her jump. 'Of course we can.'

She tried to roll away from him and found their legs entangled. His erect cock brushed against her thigh and she moved quickly off the bed. She hadn't had this much sex in years. Instinctively she knew that if she didn't get out of bed pretty damn quick, she'd be under him again.

Her muscles protested as she thrust her arms into a dressing gown and hurried toward the kitchen. Tiger immediately entwined himself around her legs, almost tripping her up in his frantic attempts to attract her notice. She found a box of opened cat food and filled up his bowl. Without sparing her a single glance, Tiger launched himself at the food and started to eat.

'That's one fat cat you have there.'

Helen stared at Jay, who had managed to pull on his jeans but not button them. God, he looked like every teenage girl's sexual fantasy come to life lounging at the end of her countertop.

'Tiger is not fat. He's just big boned.'

'Bones wobble like that?'

Helen tried to stare him down but found herself fighting a smile. 'He's a very important part of my family. If he doesn't approve, I'll have to stop seeing you.'

His answering smile disappeared. 'Does he like canned tuna?'

She nodded.

'I'll bring him a few cans next time I come over. I've never liked it myself but my brother loves the stuff.'

'Your brother who owns the penthouse?'

'Yeah, that's the one.' His gaze strayed around the kitchen and adjoining family room. 'I don't see any pictures.'

Helen crossed her arms. 'Of what?'

'Of your family. Most women have a million cute photos on their walls.'

'Well, I don't.'

'Don't have pictures or don't have a family?'

She held his gaze before shrugging. 'My family doesn't approve of me.'

'Why the hell not? You're a fricking doctor. My father would be over the moon if I was anything remotely as qualified.'

Helen busied herself with the coffee and got out some mugs. She also took the opportunity to place the lasagne Carol had made for their belated dinner in the microwave. 'I left home when I was eighteen.'

'You did?'

'I did.'

He regarded her seriously. 'They kicked you out?'

'I chose to leave. I made some mistakes. It was kind of a mutual decision.'

She tensed, waiting to see what he'd make of that. The coffee perked and she automatically handed him a mug.

'And yet you still managed to become a doctor?'

'Yes.'

He held up his mug. 'Well, good for you. That showed 'em, didn't it?'

'You did much the same thing.'

His smile died. 'I didn't make the grade, doc. I was a fool.'

'You were one of the top ten rodeo stars in the country. Don't you think that makes you a success?'

'At what? Staying on a fucking bull for eight seconds?'

'It's an amazing talent, Jay. Don't put yourself down. How many guys try to achieve what you mastered and fail?'

He gazed into his coffee mug. 'Perhaps it would've been better if I'd failed earlier and done something useful with my life.'

'You're not exactly old. You have plenty of time to start something new.' Helen reached forward to stroke his arm and he flinched away from her.

'Don't feel sorry for me, Helen. I can't deal with that right now.'

She stepped back and pulled her robe closer around her breasts. 'Trust me. I don't feel sorry for you. I'll go and put the shower on. It takes a minute to warm up.'

She grabbed her coffee and retreated back down the hall. The unmade bed smelt of sex and Jay. She resisted the urge to change the sheets and headed for the bathroom. Her bare feet sunk into the soft pink carpet. Not the most sensible floor covering for a bathroom but the most luxurious for her often overtired feet.

At least this time she'd remembered not to push him too far. As soon as he'd backed off, she'd let him. Of course, he'd also learnt more about her past than any man she'd dated since her divorce. She opened the glass door and turned on the shower. Had she hoped to get him to talk by revealing something personal about herself? If so, it hadn't worked.

Steam billowed from the shower and she decided to start without him. For all she knew, he might have gathered his belongings and left. The lasagne would take a while to reheat and after all that activity she was hungry enough to eat it all if Jay wasn't there.

She closed her eyes and allowed the scalding water to drift over her head. The door clicked open and a cold draft of air announced Jay's arrival as he fitted his large frame into the narrow shower.

'Give me the sponge.'

He took it from her hand and started soaping her breasts. She luxuriated in his touch as he carefully tended to her. Water slid over his hard muscled chest and sculptured abs as he moved around her. She licked his warm skin and he sighed, his erect cock brushed her thigh.

'I'm still not too good at this sharing crap, am I?' he said.

'Not very, but then I'm pretty bad at it myself.'

He bent to kiss her nipple, his tongue swirling around the soap bubbles to expose the glistening red tip. 'My cock's sore and yet I still fucking want to be inside you.'

She took his hand and guided it between her legs. 'If it makes you feel any better, it's the same for me.' He slid one long finger inside her and she shivered.

'I haven't done a fraction of the things I want to do to you yet.' His soft murmur made her heart rate increase. 'When can I see you again?'

'How about Sunday?'

'Yeah, that sounds good. You can tell me how it went with the dickless wonder.'

She slid her hand around his muscled biceps. 'He never satisfied me. He always made me feel like a slut for wanting more.'

Damn, where had that come from? Was she trying to make him feel sorry for her? She ducked her head to stare at their entwined feet. He caught her chin.

'Don't hide from me.' His gray eyes were intense and focused on her face. 'I've never met a woman who could keep up with me sexually before.'

She had to smile. Now he looked as embarrassed as she felt. She placed a hand over his chest, felt the hammer of his accelerated heartbeat.

'I don't know how far I can go yet.'

His slow smile was breathtaking. 'Well, honey, we'll just have to find out.'

Chapter Thirteen

Even though she was bored to tears, Helen kept smiling. The drinks party was the same as any other faculty event she was forced to attend. A whole series of ass-lickers trying to outdo each other while simultaneously fawning over the professor. In some ways it was worse because the prize was so much bigger.

The small conference room was a bland brown shell, that reeked of coffee and stale food. The wine was warm and cheap and half a box of cheese crackers scattered over a dozen small plates didn't really count as cocktail snacks. But she'd done her duty and spoken to all the search committee. She glanced at her watch and headed stealthily toward the door. Surely no one would notice if she left.

'Helen, my dear.'

With a barely suppressed sigh, she turned and faced her two least favorite men in the universe: Professor Hart and her ex-husband, David Campion. She inclined her head.

'Peter. David.'

'You look very professional tonight, Helen.' David's smile was as proprietary as the professor's.

'I try to fit in the best I can.' She glanced down at her black pants suit and crisp white blouse. The only thing missing for her to blend in completely was a tie – oh, and a penis. She'd learnt early on that anything too feminine was frowned upon. In the early days if they'd sold a fragrance made out of testosterone she'd probably have tried that too.

Peter Hart put his arm around her and she tried not to shudder.

'Helen is always professional, David. That's why she is such a valued member of my team.'

Peter squeezed her hard before walking across the room to accost another candidate.

David's gaze sharpened. 'I hope you'll contribute just as well to my team when I accept the position of department head.'

'You think I'd work for you?' Helen raised her eyebrows. 'And I didn't know you've already got the job.' She glanced around the room. 'Have you told anyone else that this evening is a complete waste of time? I wish I'd known. There are much better things I'd rather be doing.'

'Really? Like what?'

She thought about Jay's body moving over her, the slick taste of his sweat and his come.

David's fingers clenched on the plastic stem of his glass of cheap Chardonnay. 'We all know I'm going to get the job, Helen. It's just a matter of time.'

'I admire your confidence. But I wouldn't be so sure you'll succeed.'

'Why, because you think you've got it all sewn up?' His smile was ugly. 'Not every man thinks with his dick.'

She let her gaze stray to the front of his well-cut black pants. 'Are you sure about that? It always seems to work well for you.' She turned away but he caught her arm and pulled her into the corner.

'Sleeping your way into a job isn't going to work this time.'

Helen went still. 'This time?'

'Sweetheart, everyone knows you only married me to advance your career and then turned me over when the professor made you a better offer.'

Helen drilled her fingernails into his wrist until he released her arm.

'Number one, don't call me sweetheart. Number two, you're the guy who sucks whatever he has to to get promoted, not me.' She looked him right in the eyes. 'If you spread any trash about me this time, I'm not going to take it like I did before. I'm not married to you anymore and I'll fight you on every word.'

He backed off, hands held high. 'Calm down, baby. There's no need to get so emotional. I was hoping you'd be able to deal with this situation in a professional manner but I suppose your jealousy has to come out somewhere.'

Helen struggled to breathe. 'My jealousy of you?' She laughed in his face. 'I'm more jealous of that potted plant over there than I am of you.'

He took her hand, his palm moist and warm. 'It's OK. I know it must be hard for you seeing Carrie-Ann having my babies and sharing my life.'

She immediately broke free, wiping her palm on her jacket. 'It's not. Honestly, she's welcome to you. Our past has nothing to do with this present job opportunity. I promise I'll treat you exactly the same way I treat all the other candidates – with professional respect.'

'If that's how you want to play it, fair enough.' He pressed his hand to his heart. 'Only I'll know how much you are crying inside.'

Her hand fisted as she stared at his smooth unlined forehead. He never listened to her. He had his own crazy little world running inside his head and he lived it to the fullest. She'd never been able to get through to him and he hadn't really wanted to get to know her. God, she wanted to get away. Jay knew more about who she was and what she needed than David ever would.

Reaching forward, she shook David's hand.

'I hope Carrie-Ann is well and that I'll finally get to meet her with her clothes on.' She could tell from David's blank stare that he'd completely missed her reference to her first encounter with Carrie-Ann, naked and on top of David in Helen's study.

'Oh right, Carrie-Ann. You'll get to meet her sooner than you think. I've arranged with Professor Hart for all the candidates and the search committee to come and barbecue with us this Sunday.'

'In LA?'

'I've bought a house in the Oakland Hills area.'

'Wow, you are confident you'll get the job, aren't you?'

He held her gaze. 'I'm the best candidate, Helen. You know that.'

Helen couldn't bring herself to speak so she compromised by nodding and inched toward the door.

'I'll send you an email with the directions, baby. And, don't worry, you can bring a friend with you.'

'Boyfriend?'

David smiled indulgently. 'No pressure. You can bring one of your girl friends instead, although I think that makes you the only candidate without a partner.'

'Fine. I'll do that.'

Helen turned sharply on her high heels and headed out the door before she gave in to the impulse to leap on David's back and rip his artfully highlighted hair out by the handful. How dare he be so ... She stared at the set

of doors in front of her, willing them to magically part
... so ... David?

The sterile white hospital hall felt cool after the stuffy
room. Why had she expected him to be different? Just
because she'd moved on didn't mean he had to. What
puzzled her most was how no one else seemed to see
through his charm to the shallow selfish individual
underneath.

Helen dug into her purse for her keys and opened the
car door. Inside the car, she rested her hot forehead on
the steering wheel. When she first met David, he'd been
so charming and attentive she had not seen his flaws.
She knew he was cold-blooded about his career and at
first that had turned her on. She wanted a man who was
as ruthless in the pursuit of what he wanted as she was.
He also had class and money, things she aspired to and
wanted to learn how to use.

She had believed they were alike and would conquer
their profession together. Too busy with her own career,
she hadn't realized what a two-faced bastard he was
until she caught him exchanging dirty emails with one
of the nurses from the hospital. They'd only been married
six months.

Helen lifted her head and stared out of the windshield.
Suddenly it was hard to breathe. Stupid fool that she
was, she'd given him more chances, and every time he'd
proved her trust in him was a mistake. It wasn't surprising that she hadn't let any man get close to her for years.
So how come she wanted to speak to Jay?

She fumbled for her cellphone and found his number.
'Yeah?'

She swallowed hard. 'It's Helen.'

'What's up, honey?'

'I'm finished at the party.'

Silence hummed along the line. In the background, she caught the faint sound of male voices laughing. She gripped the phone more tightly.

'Can I come over?'

'Sure you can. I'm at college but I'll meet you there. Ask the concierge to let you in, OK?'

She let out a breath she hadn't realized she'd been holding. 'Thank you, Jay.'

'Nothing to thank me for. I'm the one who got lucky.' He paused. 'Do something for me, would you? Leave your clothes by the door and be ready, naked in my bed.'

'I can do that.'

'Then I'll be as quick as I can.'

Jay's apartment was in darkness. Helen stood by the door, listening to the lonely hum of the refrigerator punctuated by the blare of horns from the street below. Flashes of light reflected from the city beneath the vast windows struck the chrome furniture in a random arcing pattern. The place smelt of cleaning supplies and burnt toast.

Unhurriedly, Helen stepped out of her clothes and left them by the door. She felt so much better without the constriction of the boring black suit. Feeling guilty, she'd called Carol and asked her to feed Tiger. Carol had been more than delighted to help and had even kept the questions to the minimum.

Jay's bedroom door was open and she tiptoed in. Judging from the professional corners on the bed sheets, he definitely had a cleaning service. She clicked on the two lamps by the bed and then headed into Jay's walk-in closet. A light snapped on as she entered, making her jump.

In one corner of the closet hung several western-style shirts and a few pairs of tattered jeans. Three polished pairs of old cowboy boots sat on the shelf, two on the floor. The rest of the oak cabinetry held an amazing array of men's business suits, casual wear and shoes of every color. Helen checked the label in the first suit and found it was Armani. Somehow she doubted the immaculate rows of clothes belonged to Jay. They must belong to his mysterious, rich elder brother.

Jay smiled as he stepped over the neat pile of Helen's clothes and followed the trail of light into his bedroom. The lamps were on but there was no sign of her. He smoothed a hand over his jeans as his impatient cock stirred and lengthened.

Where was she?

A slight noise in the closet diverted his attention away from the bed. He stepped inside and found Helen rubbing her cheek against one of his brother's suits. His gut twisted.

'You were supposed to be on my bed.'

Helen dropped the sleeve of the jacket and brought her hand to her chest.

'Jay, you startled me.'

He strolled toward her, his gaze on her face. 'Naked and on the bed. If I remember right.'

Her nipples tightened as his possessive gaze swept her body. Even naked, she looked so right standing among his brother's possessions. He could easily imagine them together.

'I'm here, aren't I?'

Blood rushed straight to his cock, making him painfully aroused. 'Yeah, but you're not on my bed.'

She flushed, the color staining her breasts and her cheeks. 'Does it really matter?'

He didn't bother to reply. He simply unbuckled his belt, watched her gaze lower and took his time drawing it through the loops. She turned away from him and retreated to the far end of the closet, where his own pathetic clothes were stored. She sniffed at one of his shirts, brought the fabric to her lips.

'I like your scent, better. It's like smelling a barn.'

He came up behind her and used the belt like a lasso, dropping it over her head and tightening it slowly around her neck. She went still, her face still buried in his shirt.

'I don't like to be kept waiting.' He yanked hard on the belt until she was pulled back against his chest. 'You're supposed to do exactly what I say.'

'And if I don't?'

'Then I'll have to put you over my knee and remind you.'

She shivered and the delicate sensation rippled through his skin. He angled his head and kissed her hard, his tongue grazing her lips until she yielded and let him in.

Before she could recover from the kiss, he tugged on the belt and led her into the bedroom. He sat on the bed, pulled her over his knee.

'Do you want to apologize and tell me that you should've been on the bed, legs wide open, waiting for me to fill you with my cock?'

'No.'

He smiled down at her exposed ass and brought his hand down hard on her skin four times, the sound loud in the silence.

'Are you sure?'

No answer this time, although the scent of her arousal rose to swamp his senses. Four more slaps and she began to shift on his lap. He let her slide between his legs until her knees hit the floor.

'Suck my cock.'

She unzipped his jeans, drew him out in her hand and bent her blonde head.

'Ah,' Jay sighed as she took him into her mouth. 'That's good. Do it again.'

He waited until he couldn't last another second and tugged on the leather belt still wrapped around her neck. 'Get on the bed.'

She released his cock and scrambled up onto the bed, her breathing as rushed as his, her body flushed with her arousal. He retained his grip on the belt and brought her close for a kiss, tasted pre-come on her lips mixed with the wet heat of her mouth.

He guided her down onto the bed, her ass sticking up in the air just how he wanted it. It took him only a second to sheathe his cock in a condom. Her cheeks were still a little red from his slaps. He squeezed them, heard her catch her breath as he gathered her hips into his hands and surged forward with his cock. She was already wet for him but it was a tight fit. He worked himself deeper, rocking into her until he could go no further.

'Hard, Jay, please. Do it hard.'

His cock swelled as she whispered his name. He was so damned ready to oblige her. Fucking her fast and hard was definitely one of his favorite things to do. She moaned as he pistoned in and out and grew wetter and easier for his thrusts. He increased his speed as he felt his come travel up his shaft.

She gasped as he slid his hand around her hip and found her clit; he worked her hard with his thumb, determined to make her climax right alongside him. When she started to buck underneath him, he let go, filling her with hot spurts of his come, his hips pinned to hers as she continued to milk his suddenly sensitive cock.

He relaxed over her, his face buried in the curve of her neck. He lazily traced the line between her skin and his leather belt with his tongue. 'Was that hard enough for you, darlin'?' The only answer was a muffled groan. He closed his teeth on her throat and she shuddered. Rolling off her, he unbuckled his belt from around her neck. A soft red stripe marred her skin. He touched it with his fingers. 'Hell, I got carried away.'

She reached up to feel her throat. 'It doesn't hurt.'

He kissed her fingers. 'Really?'

'Jay, I liked it. I liked you controlling me that way.'

He stared into her eyes. Christ, he'd liked it too. What was up with him and this woman? Who was controlling who? 'Why did you want to come over here tonight?' he asked her.

She closed her eyes, shutting him out for a moment before refocusing. 'Because I wanted to be with you.'

'For the sex?'

'For everything that you give me.'

Shit, she sounded way too serious for his comfort level. He levered himself away from her and onto his back. Tried to sound relaxed, although he didn't think she would buy it.

'I don't have much to give anybody. If you want more

than a good fucking, you'd be better off with my big bro.'

She sat up and pushed her blonde hair away from her face. 'Why are you constantly trying to set me up with your brother? If he's as perfect as you say, don't you think he's able to pick his own girlfriends?'

Jay refused to meet her gaze. 'He has everything a woman could want: good looks, charm and money.'

Helen got off the bed and stood staring down at him, arms folded over her chest. 'Don't you understand me at all? I've had all those things; I've married all those things. Can't you see that I just want . . .'

Her words petered out, and with an exasperated sigh she turned on her heel. Jay counted to five and then couldn't stop himself following after her. She was already by the door, buttoning herself up into a prim white blouse and black pants.

He held out his hands, palms up. 'Don't do this again.'

She didn't look at him.

'Don't waltz out of here without explaining yourself.'

'There's nothing to explain. You made me feel stupid for coming over here. And God knows why I did. I was obviously deluding myself.'

Jay set his teeth. 'About what?' She looked at him and he caught the glint of tears in her eyes. *Shit.*

'About what we give each other,' she said.

Double shit.

'You see? You have no idea what I'm even talking about, do you?' She finished buttoning her blouse and started to shrug on her jacket. Hell, he didn't want her to go. Time to cowboy up.

'Listen, I've never fucked a woman like you before.'

'A doctor, you mean?'

'No, a woman who likes sex, just like I like it.' Jesus, he sure was an articulate slob.

'And how is that?'

He stepped closer, touched the mark around her neck where his belt had been with his finger. 'A little edgy, a little rough.'

She swallowed hard and finally met his gaze. 'That's what I came here for. The chance to be myself.'

He smiled at her, drew her into his arms. 'See? We communicated. No need to run away from me again.' He nipped her throat. 'You keep doing it and maybe I'll have to tie you to my bed.'

Her breathing shortened. 'You wouldn't do that. Would you?'

His erect cock brushed her thigh. 'If I had to make sure you stayed put, hell yeah.'

Helen stared at him, her thoughts in chaos. No one had ever turned her on like this. Why the hell was she wearing clothes when Jay was naked and ready to give her his all? She licked her lips. 'I'm not sure if I'd let you do that to me, Jay.'

He unzipped her pants, slid his fingers inside her pussy. 'You'd let me, honey. You're wet just thinking about it.'

He worked his fingers in and out until she was moaning and moving against his hand. When he slowly withdrew them, she could only open her eyes and stare up at him. His smile was deliciously dark.

'Stay there, sugar. I'm going to get some clothes on and we're going to do a little shopping.'

She checked her watch. 'But it's almost ten. Most stores will be shut.'

He winked at her. 'Not the kind we're going to.'

* * *

The shopfront was blacked out and the area they walked through was decidedly rough. Steam rose from the man-hole covers and blended with the stench of warm rotting garbage. Helen baulked as Jay placed his hand in the small of her back and steered her gently but firmly through the door. As her eyes adjusted to the light, she realized they weren't alone. Several guys and one lone woman stood leafing through a wall of magazines and books.

Even from her spot by the door, she could see that some of the literature wasn't quite her style. Big-breasted women dressed in chains and straddling motorcycles had never been her thing.

She dug Jay hard in the ribs with her elbow. 'Why exactly are we here?'

'You'll see.'

He took her hand and marched her deeper into the store. The second room was lined with paraphernalia she recognized but had never seen so openly displayed. One wall was devoted to whips and floggers, the second to vibrators. A third held every kind of lubricant and sexual aid a dedicated man and woman might ever need.

After a few minutes, when all Helen could do was gape, a smartly dressed woman approached.

'Hi, can I help you find anything?'

Helen looked pointedly up at Jay.

'Yeah, cuffs,' he replied.

The woman pointed to the bottom right-hand corner of the third wall. 'Here you go. We have all kinds, from fun to furry to serious metal.'

'Thank you, ma'am.' Jay sauntered across to the crowded wall display, Helen's hand held firmly in his. 'What kind do you like, honey?'

Helen whipped her hand out of his grasp. 'I do not *like* any of them.'

Jay picked up a pair of pink fuzzy cuffs and held them out to her. 'You're such a liar.'

Helen met his lazy stare head on. 'Really.'

'Yeah, really, 'cos when I've got your wrists locked into a pair of these and you're tied to my bed, you know you're going to love it.'

Her gaze dropped to the cuffs. 'How do you get them off?'

His eyebrows rose. 'How do I get you off? Well, first I'll kiss your nipples until they're all nice and hard for me and then I'll lick your pussy –'

Helen grabbed his hand and dug her nails in. 'I said how do you get the handcuffs off?'

'Oh, right.' He pulled at the pink cuff. 'This kind have Velcro. They are real simple to undo.' He bent down to study the other sets which were closer to the floor. 'Hey, I think I've found the perfect pair.'

Before she could see what he was doing, he turned her around and pointed her at the door.

'I'll just go and get these. Go wait over there.'

Helen retraced her steps past the helpful sales assistant and back to the front of the shop. There were only a couple of people still viewing the magazines. Helen tried to pretend that she didn't give a damn about what other people read, but somehow her deeply buried Central Valley roots were still shocked.

Jay reappeared with a pink carrier bag and a wicked smile. 'Ready to go, honey?'

Helen nodded and hightailed it out of the shop as fast as she could. Were her cheeks really that warm or was she imagining it? As they walked back to the apartment building, through the deserted streets, she noticed Jay grinning. 'What's so funny?'

He tucked her hand in the crook of his arm, patted it and gave her a sidelong glance. 'You've never been in a place like that before, have you?'

'Of course I have!' Helen kept walking, her gaze fixed firmly on the filthy oil-stained sidewalk.

'Yeah, right.' He drew his finger over her cheek. 'You're blushing like a schoolgirl.'

'Am not.'

'Are too.'

Her lips twitched in a vain attempt to suppress a smile. 'OK, I haven't actually been in a shop like that, but I have seen all those ... things.'

'Really.'

She stopped walking to stare up at him. 'I worked in an ER department, remember. You wouldn't believe where people stick things and then can't get them out again.'

His answering smile was slow in coming but breathtaking enough to make her melt. He kissed the top of her head. 'OK, you win this one.' He put his arm around her shoulders and drew her close. 'Let's go home. I want to play.'

Chapter Fourteen

'Let's eat.'

Helen swung around to stare at Jay. 'Now?' God, she was dying to see what he had in that bag and he wanted to eat?

'A man has to keep his strength up.' He strolled into the kitchen and opened the huge Viking refrigerator. 'I know there's some chicken in here somewhere.'

With a sigh and a last wistful look back at the bedroom, Helen sat on one of the bar stools by the high granite countertop.

'You hungry, doc?'

She licked her lips and eyed the perfection of his denim-clad ass, the only part of him she could see.

'I'll have something if you are.'

He emerged from the cavernous refrigerator, a plateful of chicken sandwiches wrapped in Cling Wrap in his hand.

Helen raised her eyebrows. 'Is that a new kind of appliance that makes the sandwiches for you?'

He shrugged as he placed them on the table. 'Nope, it's the magic of room service. My brother introduced me to it and now I'm addicted.' He returned to the fridge and took out two beers. 'Here you go.'

Helen looked pointedly around the kitchen. 'Don't you have plates or napkins?'

He scratched his chin. 'Sure, somewhere. Take a look, knock yourself out.'

She started opening cupboards and retrieved some fine white china and glasses.

By the time she sat back down, Jay had already finished his first sandwich and was starting on another. Helen pushed a plate in front of him and he grunted his thanks. She slowly ate one sandwich, taking her time, enjoying watching him eat and not bother to talk to her.

He pointed at the glass. 'What's that for?'

'Your beer.'

'Only wussies use a glass. Anyway, I've already drunk it.' He leered at her. 'I'm in a hurry, honey. How about you?'

Holding his eyes, Helen picked up her beer and brought it to her lips. His gaze intensified as she slowly swallowed. She couldn't quite manage the whole bottle but the effect was worth it. Jay had forgotten the remaining sandwich and was totally focused on her. She put it down and wiped her mouth against the back of her hand.

'I'm ready whenever you are, "honey".'

She squeaked as he closed in on her and swung her up into his arms. She pretended to struggle, but realized she really liked feeling so helpless and feminine. God, she hoped his knee was OK.

He kicked the door shut behind them and deposited her on the middle of the bed. She lay there looking up at him, admiring the intensity of his expression as he studied her body. He stripped off his blue-checked shirt, each snap distinct in the silence.

She kept still when he bent over her, removed her clothes and tossed them onto the floor. He knelt between her thighs, the seams of his jeans rubbing against her soft skin.

'Stay right there.'

He got off the bed leaving her feeling cold without the heat of his body close to hers. When he returned she heard the rustling of paper and plastic being ripped apart. She didn't dare turn her head to see exactly what he was doing.

The mattress dipped as he climbed back on the bed and straddled her. In his hand was a pair of sturdy-looking leather cuffs. Helen's mouth went dry. He smiled, brushed her erect nipples with the cuffs and then touched the cuffs against her mouth.

'You like them, don't you?'

Helen nodded as the smell of the leather invaded her senses.

'I knew you would. You're going to love being under me, unable to stop me doing anything I want because your wrists are trapped inside these.'

The rip of Velcro surprised her. She'd imagined these cuffs would have buckles on them. She watched carefully as Jay wrapped them around her wrists. He produced a braided piece of leather and looped it through the metal headboard.

'Now all I have to do is clip the ends of the braid onto the cuffs and we're set.' He smiled down at her, the heavy bulge of his cock pressing on her stomach. 'Last chance to run, Helen. Last chance to tell me no.'

She bit her lip as he clipped the cuffs to the braid and drew her arms above her head.

'Try to get out now, darlin'.'

She tried to bring her wrists down and couldn't. As she continued to test the resistance of the leather, it bit into her skin. Jay bent his head and kissed her hard on the mouth, his teeth nipping at her tongue and lips.

'How does it feel, being at my mercy?'

She shivered as he bit gently on her ear lobe.

'Not talking, huh? Don't worry, you'll be begging and screaming soon, I guarantee it.'

He slid his mouth down from her throat to her breasts and latched onto her nipple, pulling hard and fast. His roughness shocked her body into flooding her sex with cream. He turned to her other nipple and she bucked underneath him, her legs opening to cradle his hard thighs and even harder erection. He moved his hips in rhythm to his sucks, the fly of his jeans a heavy presence against her clit.

God, she was so turned on she was going to come just from his mouth. Helen gulped in air as her body spasmed under the weight of his heavy frame. He raised his head, his gray eyes full of lust.

'I love the way you come so fast for me and get so wet.'

He moved off her chest but only headed downward, kissing her stomach and then moving south until his tongue met her clit. She squirmed as he stroked her with his tongue, pushed her hips in his face, blatantly asking to be fucked.

He licked her whole sex, his mouth lingering on her pussy lips, sucking them in, making them swell to reveal the cream pouring out of her. He licked that too, feasting on her like a connoisseur, praising the taste and feel of her until she wanted to scream, grab his head and force him to finish her. When he stopped touching her, Helen opened her eyes. He knelt up and drew something else out of the bag.

'What's that?'

'It's lube.'

'Like you use on a car?'

'Same principle, different result.'

He unscrewed the bottle, tipped it up until his index finger was coated with shiny oil. He brought his finger under Helen's nose.

'It's called Black Leather.'

She sniffed carefully. It did remind her of the scent of a tack room. She shifted on the bed.

'And what do you plan to do with it?'

'Lube us both up.' He tipped the bottle again until all his fingers were coated. Helen shivered as he carefully inserted one long finger into her ass. 'I want you here tonight. I want my cock deep in here.'

He slid another finger in beside the first, widening her with every subtle play of his fingers. She could only writhe helplessly as he worked her.

'Hold on. I want you to see this.'

One-handed, Jay rearranged the pillows and pulled her higher up the bed into a sitting position. He stuck another pillow under her ass, opening her up to him like an erotic offering. Now she could see his fingers working her, the oil glistened as he plunged inside her. Three fingers now and she could feel the stretch. She started to shift about, suddenly uncomfortable with the ever-increasing pressure.

He glanced up at her. 'You're real tight, honey, but I'm working on it.' He smiled. 'Let me give you something else to think about.'

He reached behind him and produced a large plastic vibrator. The head was a lurid purple and the thick rubber shaft at least eight inches long.

Helen licked her lips. 'Jay . . .'

He didn't look at her, his attention fixed on the vibrator as he worked out how to set the controls. A soft hum filled the air and the vibrator began to undulate.

'Hold it for me a sec, darlin' – oh no, you can't, can you?'

'You're not funny, Jay.'

He rested the vibrator against her hip as he used his free hand to locate the bottle of lube and apply it generously to the shaft. Helen swallowed as he positioned the tip of the vibrator against the lips of her sex.

'Think about this while I get you ready for my cock.'

Helen moaned as he gently inserted the vibrator until it could go no further. The soft slow pulse only seemed to emphasize the presence of his fingers buried deep in her ass. She closed her eyes as the sensations mingled and she couldn't separate out the pleasure from the pressure. It was all starting to feel good and driving her toward another climax.

'Yeah, honey, you feel so fine. Work with me here.'

She opened her eyes. The handle of the vibrator rested on the pillow between her outstretched thighs, Jay's hand lay behind it, the oil on his fingers catching the light as he moved them in and out of her.

'Are you ready for my cock? I sure am ready to sink inside you.'

He knelt up, removed his fingers and shucked off his jeans and boots. His shaft was coated in pre-come and straining toward her. He grasped the vibrator but didn't remove it.

'I'm just going to turn you around.'

Her breath whooshed out as he grasped her waist and deftly turned her onto her knees. Her wrists were still held firmly above her head in the leather cuffs.

She tensed as he maneuvered his big body behind hers, one hand still keeping the vibrator buried deep inside her pussy. His thumb slid over her clit and started to stroke her.

Distracted, she didn't feel the first inch of his cock slide into her ass. He rubbed harder, brought her even closer to coming and slid in deeper, rocking his hips to gain each extra inch.

Inside her, the heat of his cock slid against the thrum of the vibrator, increasing the pressure until she wanted to scream.

'Nearly there, honey. Hold on.'

His hoarse words were whispered close to her ear as he curved his body around hers, holding her captive and in place for his complete penetration. Helen let out her breath, felt him slide in deeper and came so hard that she did scream.

Jay groaned and began to move his hips faster. 'Damn it, doc, do that again, come harder.'

He bit down on her shoulder, his balls slapping against her buttocks as he pounded into her. Just how she liked it: hard, fast and on the edge. She came again and his hand fell away from the vibrator, pulling it out, then stuffing all his fingers in her instead.

She couldn't stop coming, or moaning as she felt him climax and the heat of his seed deep inside her. He collapsed over her, his hips still moving as though he never wanted to stop having her.

'Shit, Helen. I think you've killed me.'

He rotated her back onto the bed and rolled away onto his stomach, his head buried in his arms. When she got her breath back, Helen tested the leather cuffs again. She still couldn't open them. She nudged Jay's recumbent form with her knee.

'Can you let me out of these things?'

He came up on one elbow and looked at her. 'Nope.'

Helen tried to glare at him. 'What do you mean, "nope"?'

He flicked her nipple with his fingertip. 'I haven't finished with you yet. I'm going to wash up. When I come back, you'll be here, just waiting for me to fuck you again.'

Helen watched in disbelief as he got off the bed and headed for the bathroom. 'Jay?'

He looked over his shoulder. 'What, honey?'

'You will come back, won't you?'

His smile was pure sex as he shut the bathroom door behind him. Helen wiggled herself into a more comfortable position and began to count backward from a thousand.

Several hours and several bouts of sex later, the sound of the door opening woke Helen from a fitful sleep. She opened one eye to see a man dressed in a business suit peering into the gloom.

'Jay? Are you in here? Jeez, this place stinks like a teenager's jockstrap.'

Helen scrabbled for the sheets as the room was suddenly illuminated. Jay shot bolt upright, shielding Helen.

'Fuck off, Grayson.'

'Sorry, Jay, ma'am. I'll be in the kitchen.'

Jay mumbled something unintelligible as Helen buried her face in the pillows.

'Trust Grayson to barge in as if he owns the place. Shit, he does. I wonder what's eating his ass?'

Helen shut her eyes. 'Oh my God, he knows we've been having sex. How am I going to get out of here without having to look him in the eye?'

Jay turned her toward him until he could see her face. 'Why? Are you ashamed to be here with me or something?'

His abrupt question made her reach out to touch his unshaven cheek.

'No, I'm not. It's just that this was supposed to be our little secret, right?'

His mouth tightened. 'I don't remember agreeing to that. I'm quite happy to show you off to my friends. Maybe you're the one with the problem.'

Helen frantically tried to marshal her thoughts, never very coherent before her first cup of coffee.

'Don't sulk, Jay. I'm perfectly happy to be seen with you.'

'Then prove it. Shower with me and then come meet my brother.'

She met his challenging stare with one of her own.

'OK, I will.'

Jay pulled out a chair at the breakfast table and guided Helen into it. Grayson sat at the other end of the table, his hands wrapped around a mug of steaming black coffee. His shirt was half-unbuttoned and he hadn't shaved. Jay sniffed and caught the unusual scent of hard liquor on his brother's breath.

'What's up, Gray?'

'Hey, sorry for busting in on you guys. I swear I didn't see anything.' Grayson's attempt at a smile was diminished by his bloodshot eyes and the deep lines on his face.

Helen nudged Jay. 'Aren't you going to introduce us?'

Grayson's smile widened. 'Actually, I think we've already met.'

Jay frowned and swiveled around to stare at Helen. 'You didn't say you knew my brother.'

'He does look vaguely familiar.' She pushed her blonde hair out of her eyes.

Jay got two mugs of coffee and plonked one down in front of Helen. Grayson concentrated his considerable attention on Helen until Jay had to grip his coffee mug in an effort not to leap across the table and punch him right in the face.

'You're a doctor, right?'

'Yes, I'm Helen Kinsale.' She held out her hand and Grayson shook it. Helen smiled. Idly, Jay calculated just how fast he could throw his brother over the balcony.

'You're Jay's doctor. I met you in Sacramento just after you'd operated on his knee.'

Jay put his coffee down. 'You came to Sacramento?'

'You probably don't remember. You were in surgery when I arrived and in recovery by the time I left.' Grayson nodded at Helen. 'I knew you were in good hands so I didn't wait around to see you come out of it.'

Jay swallowed hard. 'And you knew I wouldn't be pleased to see you either.'

'There is that.' Grayson refused to meet Jay's gaze. 'And I was in my usual rush to get to another meeting.' He sighed, one hand raking through his thick black hair. 'I'm done with all that.'

'With what? Looking out for me?'

His brother's smile was wry. 'Nope. With the oil company. With Beau. With the whole fucking businessman-of-the-year deal.'

'What the hell is that supposed to mean?' Jay sat down into the seat next to Helen's and stared into his brother's tired face.

'I quit.'

'Shit.' Jay shifted on his seat. 'What did Beau say?'

'What didn't he say? You know how he is. He even had his security detail throw me off the premises before I could collect my stuff.'

Jay sat back and studied Grayson. 'Do you want me to move out?'

'Why? I own this apartment, not Beau.'

'That's why you offered it to me, right? Beau already told me not to come sniffing around looking for some place to live unless I was prepared to come on his payroll.'

Grayson met his gaze. 'Hell, I knew that.'

Helen cleared her throat. 'I think I should go.'

Jay dragged his attention back to her as she rose from her seat.

'It's OK, Dr Kinsale,' Grayson said. 'You haven't heard anything my father won't be broadcasting to the entire world by tomorrow.'

Helen patted Grayson's sleeve. 'Good luck with everything.' She glanced back at Jay. 'I'll call you later, OK?'

Impulsively, Jay drew her into his arms and kissed her hard on the mouth. She relaxed into him, her body molding itself to his. 'OK, doc, you do that and thanks for being so understanding.'

She pinched his cheek and his cock jumped to attention. Her gaze dropped to his jeans and stayed there. 'Bye, Jay.'

He reluctantly released her and watched as she grabbed her things and left the apartment. By the time the door closed, Grayson was engrossed in eating a huge bowl of kids' cereal.

'She's a classy lady.'

Jay grabbed the choco puffs cereal and helped himself to a bowl as well. All that sex had given him an appetite. 'Yeah, she is.'

'Not sure what she's doing with you, though.'

Jay glanced up sharply, just in time to see the hint of a smile on Grayson's lips.

'She's just taking patient aftercare to a whole new level, bro.'

'I liked her the first time I met her and I liked her even more today. She looked hot in those tight black pants.'

Jay pointed his spoon at his brother. 'Keep your filthy hands and your even filthier thoughts away from her or I'll fucking kill you.'

Grayson's spoon remained suspended near his mouth. 'You like her too, then?'

'Yeah. So keep away.'

'What's with the Tarzan act, Jay?'

Jay mumbled something crude through a mouthful of cereal before swallowing. 'Just leave her alone, OK?'

'Will do. I don't have time to be worrying about chasing women at the moment. I have a whole new life to plan.'

Jay wiped his mouth with the back of his hand. 'What are you going to do?'

Grayson smiled. 'Don't worry, little brother. I've got it all planned out. For the last year or so I've been trying to work out why I was so pissed off with everything. There was all that stuff with Anna, but that wasn't the real problem. I realized I just didn't want to end my days sitting in a big old office acting just like Beau.'

'I can understand that.'

'I'm going back to the life I always dreamt of.'

'Which is?'

'Owning a ranch and training horses.'

Jay slowly nodded. Yeah, in some weird cosmic way, it

made sense. As kids, he and Gray had sometimes been allowed to visit Beau's parents on their ranch. God, sometimes he yearned for that life himself. A good horse under him, miles of untamed land to ride over. Shame he might never be able to ride again.

Grayson rubbed his unshaven jaw. 'It's not going to be easy but I'm prepared to make a go of it.'

'It costs a lot of money to set up a ranch and training facility.'

'Hell, the one thing I have is money. I earned enough when I ran my own company and Beau paid me even more for owning my soul.'

Silence fell between them. Jay studied his empty cereal bowl. 'I could help out.' Grayson didn't reply and Jay pretended to shrug. 'Not that you need me or anything.'

He met Gray's eyes and quickly looked away. Shit, this was getting way too emotional. The hint of vulnerability in Gray's expression made him all too human. Jay stood, picked up the bowls and headed for the kitchen sink. He rinsed out the bowls and slotted them haphazardly into the dishwasher.

'Where are you planning on setting up?'

'I've bought a parcel of land in Applegate Valley in Oregon, not far from the California border. There's room for a house and a decent training set-up.'

Jay shut the dishwasher and took his time wiping his hands. 'Are you sure you don't want me out of here?'

'Not until the end of the year at the earliest. The lease is up for renewal then. I'm not sure whether I'll keep this place or not.'

That was fair enough. Six months to get his shit together and move on. A familiar panic spread slowly in his gut and he forced it back. He wasn't going to fall into that pit of despair again. He had prospects, he had a new life.

'Like you said, you could always come and live with me at the ranch. I need a barn manager.'

Jay forced a smile. 'Yeah, you really need a crippled ex-rodeo cowboy around telling everyone about his glory days.'

'I need someone I can trust.'

Jay met Grayson's steady gaze. 'Then I'm not the right guy for you. I still have some stuff to do on my own before I'm ready to take on any more responsibility, especially from a member of my family.'

'Fair enough, but the offer still stands.' Grayson helped himself to another cup of coffee. 'Now tell me what you've been up to.'

Chapter Fifteen

Helen was late. But enduring Nancy's loud comments for being tardy seemed a better alternative to being seen coming into work wearing the same clothes she left in the day before. She'd also had to go home to feed Tiger, who showed his contempt by refusing to acknowledge her presence while still managing to consume the family-sized can of tuna she'd guiltily offered him.

She leant up against the door and sighed. Her desk already had three charts on it. Saturdays were usually busy. She was often called to consult in the ER where, in her opinion, too many kids played too many sports and broke too many bones.

Despite the files on her desk, she went and got some coffee. Her night with Jay hadn't included much sleep. If she didn't start to mainline some caffeine, she suspected even five minutes sitting at her desk would result in her taking a nice long nap.

Her phone rang and she glanced at the caller ID. What did Peter Hart want now?

'Ah, Helen, dear. I just wanted to make sure that you received your invitation to the barbecue at David's house tomorrow. You left the party rather abruptly.'

'I did, but it's OK. David made sure he invited me personally.'

'You are planning on attending, aren't you? It wouldn't look good if you were the only candidate not to show up.'

Helen made a face at the phone. 'I'll be there, although from the way David was talking you'd think he'd already been given the job.'

'That's definitely not the case. In fact, our little drug company was very interested to hear you had applied for the job.'

'Little drug company? Nifenberg is one of the biggest pharmaceutical companies in the world. And by the way, how did they find out about my job application?'

He chuckled. 'Perhaps a little bird told them. Anyway, if you get the job, they are considering offering a substantial grant to the hospital. Wouldn't that be wonderful?'

Helen closed her eyes as visions of a million dollar bills flooded her senses. Money was often the key to promotion, whatever career you decided on. And to a university hospital, money was as vital as supplies of blood and underpaid, overworked student doctors.

'Joel Franken, the vice president of their surgical division is over from Switzerland this weekend. I plan to bring him to the barbecue. Make sure you wear something pretty so that he remembers you.'

'How about a bathing suit? Would that work?'

Peter Hart's laugh was indulgent. 'Now, Helen, I know I can trust you to do the right thing. I'll see you tomorrow.'

Helen slammed down the phone. It took at least five minutes of focused breathing to get the urge to scream out of her system. She studied her fingers, which were splayed out on the desk in front of her. It was vital she had a date for the barbecue. There was no way she was turning up alone so that David could feel sorry for her.

Helen started to smile and picked up the phone again.

Jay was bugging her about including him in her life. Here was the perfect opportunity for him to strut his stuff.

Jay took the old cowboy boot from Grayson and placed it reverently back on the glass shelf in the walk-in closet.

'That's what I want to make. Cowboy boots that last a lifetime.'

'And are pieces of art.'

Jay glanced up at Grayson in surprise. 'Yeah, that's exactly it.'

Grayson's eyebrows rose. 'I'm not a complete philistine, you know.'

'A complete what?'

'Jay, do you do this dumb kid thing with Dr Kinsale?'

'Yup.'

'Does she let you get away with it?'

Jay grinned. 'Nope.'

'I said she was a smart woman.' He punched Jay's shoulder. 'Hey, I have to go. I've got a plane ticket for seven o'clock.'

Jay followed him back into the kitchen. He'd spent four hours telling Gray about his new career. Not once had his brother put him down or laughed. He'd actually been quite helpful, suggesting ways Jay could turn his talent into a profitable business, how to find the markets and use his old connections.

Grayson shut his briefcase. He'd changed into well-pressed jeans and a checked shirt borrowed from Jay. A new black Stetson sat on the countertop beside him.

'Feel free to use my stuff. I don't think I'll be wearing designer suits and handmade shoes where I'm going.'

'Thanks, I'll do that.'

Jay stared guiltily down at his feet. He'd already liberated a pack of new underwear and several pairs of socks from Gray's closet. Of course, he'd intended to replace them, but never had. Now it looked like he'd gotten away with it.

The buzzer sounded and Jay headed for the door and pressed the button.

'Did you call a cab, Grayson?'

'Yeah, but...'

Jay held up a finger. 'Oh shit, the concierge says it's Beau. He wants to come up.'

Grayson shrugged and checked his watch. 'You might as well let him. He's such a tenacious bastard that he'll just keep coming after me until he gets his chance to shout at me again. Why not now?'

Numbly, Jay pressed the buzzer to allow Beau to access the elevators. He left the front door ajar and went to stand shoulder to shoulder with his brother in the kitchen.

'So this is where you've been hiding.'

Beau glowered at Jay as he slammed the door shut behind him. He wore a blue shirt and tie that matched his eyes, khaki pants and an unbuttoned sports jacket over his rapidly expanding gut. His abundant hair was still the same color as Jay's.

'Afternoon, Beau. Are you talking to me or Grayson?'

Beau advanced into the kitchen. 'I'm talking to both of you. You're both cowards.'

Jay shrugged. 'Grayson's hardly that. He's put up with you for years and that takes guts.'

'Or stupidity,' Grayson added, his blue eyes fixed on Beau. Jay bit back a smile.

Beau's dismissive stare swept over Grayson and settled

on Jay. 'I should've known you'd come crawling around Grayson's skirts when you finally figured out your pathetic rodeo career was over.'

'He didn't need to crawl. I offered. He's my brother.'

Beau swung around to face Grayson. 'He's your half-brother. His mother was a weak-willed bitch who drank too much.'

Jay took a step forward. 'Don't say a word about my mother. The only weak thing she did was taking up with you, and, hell, she regretted it for the rest of her life.'

Grayson laid a gentle hand on his arm. 'Don't let him get to you. You know what he's like.'

Jay took a deep breath. This was always his father's way, to come at you like a raging bull and attack everything you held dear.

'You didn't come here to fight with Jay, Beau, so back off.'

Beau exposed his small even teeth in the famous smile that had captivated a football-crazy nation. 'No, I didn't. I came to tell you, you are a fool. But I want to make one last offer before I wash my hands of you.'

Grayson shrugged, his hands in his pockets. 'Offer away. It won't make any difference.'

Jay could only admire his brother. Grayson looked almost relaxed as he leant back against the countertop.

'If you come back and work for me, I'll retire and make you president within a year.'

'Bullshit.'

Beau's face turned an alarming shade of purple. 'Are you calling me a liar?'

'Yeah, I guess I am. The only way you'll stop being president of that company is when you're buried six feet under.'

'How about I put it in writing? Make it all legal?'

Grayson sighed. 'I've worked with your lawyers, they're a bunch of crooks. I wouldn't trust anything they gave me to sign. And I'm just not interested.'

'Not interested in your own family's company? The business I created from nothing and intended to pass on to my firstborn son?'

Grayson straightened up, his expression grim. 'I don't want it, Beau. You tricked me into coming back to work for you once and it was a mistake. I'm not about to be fooled again.' He picked up his Stetson and jammed it on his head. 'I have a plane to catch. Jay, I'll be in touch when I need the rest of my things.' He turned and held out his hand. 'Thanks for today and give my best to the good doctor.'

Jay shook his hand. 'Good luck, bro, you'll need it.'

Grayson picked up his bags, pushed past Beau and headed for the door. Jay couldn't help grinning as the door shut behind him with a final-sounding click.

'Never mind, Beau. I'm sure you'll find another son to carry on your good work. How many kids do you have now? I can't remember.'

Beau's blue eyes narrowed. 'Well, it sure as hell won't be you. You're thirty and you've never done a decent day's work in your life.'

Jay shrugged. 'I've done what I set out to do.'

'Yeah? You set out to be a wannabe, almost-ran loser?'

'I wanted to get away from you and find a life that didn't revolve around your inflated ego.'

Beau shoved past him and opened the refrigerator. He popped open a beer before Jay had time to blink, took a long slug and then slammed the can down on the counter.

'So what are you going to do now that your big brother isn't protecting you?'

'I'm working on it.'

Beau gave a coarse laugh. 'You'd better take those good looks and find yourself a nice older woman who'll pay good money to fuck you.'

Jay got a beer too and saluted his father. 'What a great idea, Beau. I like it. I'll get a T-shirt that says, "Fucks for Food". That should do it.'

His father finished his beer in one more swallow. 'That's always been your problem, boy, you're conceited and lazy just like your mother. You expect everything to be handed to you on a silver platter.'

Jay gripped his beer so hard the sides began to buckle. 'Right, that's me and my mom, gold-diggers through and through.' He met his father's contemptuous stare with one of his own. 'One of these days I'll surprise you.'

Beau readjusted his large gold belt buckle. 'I doubt it. Once a loser, always a loser.' He glanced around the pristine apartment. 'Enjoy your stay here, because when I'm finished with Grayson, you'll be back to sleeping on the streets where you belong.'

'Grayson has his own money. He's not worried about you.'

Beau stopped at the door, his hand wrapped around the handle. 'And you think he'll keep taking care of you?'

Jay crossed his arms over his chest. 'Soon he won't need to.'

'We'll see about that.' Beau pointed a finger at Jay. 'You're a parasite, son, a pretty, useless parasite. You always have been and people don't change.'

Jay strolled toward him, jerked the door open and maneuvered his father outside. Two large bodyguards lounging against the lobby walls immediately came to attention.

'Thanks, Beau. Good to see you as usual. Give my love to step-mom number four, or is it five now? I forget.'

Jay slammed the door and leant against it. God, he hated that man. He closed his eyes and thought of his mother, struggling to keep him fed and clothed as Beau's lawyers tied up her pitifully small child-support payments in pointless appeals and lawsuits.

She'd died when he was fourteen, worn out by the constant pressure to beat her addiction to alcohol and keep them off the streets. During her last days he'd had to sit by her bed and watch his ex-quarterback father on TV, advertising every product under the sun and smiling all the way to the bank.

He made his way back to the kitchen and grabbed another beer. Beau always made him feel so fucking useless. He glanced over at the dining table, where the belt he'd designed for Helen was now finished. Did he really have the talent to start again or was his father right? Would he always be dependent on handouts from his family? He'd had enough of that with his poor mother.

He sat in the big leather recliner and turned on the TV. At least he hadn't punched the guy. Last time they'd met, he'd ended up being manhandled onto the street by one of his father's bodyguards. He'd landed a good solid punch in Beau's smug face before they'd dragged him off, though. He flexed his fist. Boy, it had felt good. But somehow it felt even better to have kept his cool and sent his father away without a scratch. Maybe he was growing up after all.

His cell rang and he checked the number. 'Hey.'

'Jay, I was wondering if you'd like to go out with me tomorrow.'

The sound of Helen's cool, crisp voice made him relax into the soft leather seat. 'Where are we going?'

'A barbecue, so there's no need to dress up, just come as you are.'

'Are you sure about that? I might be naked right now.'

'Are you?'

His body reacted to the slight breathy hitch in her voice. 'Nope, but I could be.'

'Jay, you are incorrigible.'

'Incorra-what?'

'Don't start that again. I'll pick you up about two.'

'Yes, ma'am.'

There was another short pause.

'Jay? The barbecue is for the candidates for my boss's job. Is that still OK?'

'Yeah, that's fine, honey. I'll see you tomorrow.'

It wasn't until he put the phone down that he remembered one of the other candidates was her ex-husband. He smiled at his beer. It would be interesting to meet the bastard who had cheated on the oh-so-perfect Dr Helen face to face and even more interesting to watch how Helen dealt with him. He definitely put his money on his doc.

Chapter Sixteen

Helen smiled as Jay shut the door of his apartment behind him and joined her in the elevator. He wore a new blue shirt, his usual jeans and well-polished cowboy boots. He tipped his brown Stetson back with one finger so that he could look down at her.

'Hey.' He kissed her forehead, his lips warm against her skin. She inhaled the unique scent of young virile cowboy. 'You told me not to dress up.'

'That's right, I did.'

He stroked the silk bow at the back of her neck. 'But you're all fancy.'

'My boss, Professor Hart, told me to look pretty.'

'And do you always do what he says?' Jay leant back against the elevator wall and studied her blue silk halterneck dress. 'And I wouldn't call your choice pretty. It makes my balls ache. I want to rip it off and fuck you hard against the wall.'

Helen nodded. 'I don't do pretty. And thank you. That's exactly the impression I wanted to make.'

His eyebrows rose. 'You want this Professor Hart to fuck you?'

Helen stepped out of the elevator. 'Why not? Everyone already thinks he has.'

He caught her up in the underground parking lot and yanked on her arm, all the amusement gone from his face. 'And have you?'

'Have I what?'

'Fucked him.'

She glared right back at him. 'If I have, it has nothing to do with you. Unless you're one of those men who thinks that any woman who's successful must have slept her way to the top?'

His grip tightened. 'One, I don't share. And two, I don't go around believing sexist crap like that.'

She stamped her foot. 'How can you even put those two sentiments in the same sentence?'

He stared at her for a long moment. 'Wanting to be the only guy in your bed makes me sexist?'

'You can't deny it, Jay. You get a big macho thrill out of being the dominant male.'

'And you don't like it?'

He bent his head, kissed her mouth until she couldn't think straight. When he drew back, she was panting. He rubbed his thumb over her lower lip.

'You like me just the way I am, honey. Don't try to pretend otherwise. If I wanted, I could have you right now up against the side of the car.'

Her nipples tightened as she pictured him thrusting inside her, oblivious to anyone walking through the shadowy parking lot. With a shake of her head, she found her keys and hurried to get into the car. Jay took his time strolling around to the passenger door and settling himself in the seat.

She glanced at his lap; saw the bulge of his erection taut against the worn denim of his jeans. He caught her right hand and pressed it against his cock.

'Jay, I need that hand to start the car.'

'OK, but give it right back.'

Helen started the engine and released the handbrake.

The navigation system sprang to life, indicating her next route change. She headed for the sunlight, all too aware of Jay's presence on her right and the sexual tension that filled the space. Keeping her attention on the road, she dropped her hand back onto his shaft and squeezed, enjoying the way his breath hissed through his teeth.

'Is that good, babe?'

Jay frowned. 'Don't call me "babe". I'm not that much younger than you.' He rolled his hips, increasing the pressure of her hand against his flesh.

'I'm five years older than you. That's a lot.'

'Does it bother you, doc?'

She turned a corner and slotted the car neatly into the right lane for the upcoming freeway entrance. 'Sometimes.'

'I don't even think about it.'

'Well, it's all right for you. No one's going to be calling you a cradle robber, are they?'

He laughed. 'I'm not sixteen. And who's going to do that?'

'We're about to find out.'

He turned toward her. 'You think the folks at this barbecue are going to get onto you about it?'

'Maybe.'

'Then why did you ask me to come?'

Helen gripped the steering wheel more tightly with her left hand. *Why indeed?* 'You were the one complaining I never introduced you to my friends.'

Jay snorted. 'These guys sure don't sound like your friends, doc.'

They sped along the freeway in silence. After a while, she exited and began the long climb up into the Oakland

Hills. Jay turned his attention to the strongly scented eucalyptus and pine trees that edged the roads. She took her hand back to negotiate the sharp twists and turns of the ever-narrowing streets.

'We're here.'

'Shit.'

For once, Helen was in complete agreement with Jay's cursing. The pink and white house, which nestled at the end of a long driveway, must have been at least ten thousand square feet. A large marbled fountain sat in front of the house, surrounded by cars.

'Is this your boss's house?' Jay asked as they got out of the car.

Helen smiled at him as she took his hand and started up the shallow steps. 'Nope, worse.'

He hesitated as the door swung open to reveal David in superbly pressed designer jeans and a pink polo shirt. Sunlight glinted off the bronzed highlights in his perfectly coiffed hair.

'Helen, baby, you came!'

'David.'

Helen stepped back until she bumped up against Jay's chest. 'How come he gets to call you "baby"?' Jay murmured in her ear. Undeterred, David continued to advance, his smile radiant.

'And who's your friend?'

'David, this is Jay Turner.'

'It's a pleasure.' David grasped Jay's hand and shook it. 'Are you one of Helen's little cousins from the valley?'

'He's my boyfriend. You did say I could bring anyone I wanted.'

David's mouth hung open. 'Your boyfriend?'

Helen grabbed Jay's hand. 'Is that a problem?'

'No, of course not.' David winked. 'I'd forgotten your strange attraction to cowboys. Come on in. Peter's already here.'

Jay tugged Helen's hand, pulling her back. 'Don't tell me, that's your ex?'

'How did you guess?'

'I dunno, doc. Perhaps it's his winning personality. The only other person who can make me feel so dumb so fast is my father.'

'It's OK, he does it to me, too. That's one of the reasons I left him.'

He settled his hand in the small of her back and flexed his fingers. She enjoyed the small possessive caress as she followed David through the overly ornate house and into the backyard.

A vine-covered pergola spanned the expanse of the patio, shading the guests. Beyond the tiled barbecue area, a large pool was surrounded by carefully arranged groups of chairs and tables. Helen slid her sunglasses down onto her nose and surveyed the competition. Almost everyone else wore jeans, khakis or shorts. Despite its flashy appearance, her blue silk dress felt cool and natural against her skin.

David returned, towing an obviously pregnant woman. Helen couldn't help but stare at such a perfect example of Hollywood-inspired beauty. Carrie-Ann's hair was long straight and blonde, her breasts pert and high, her legs endless, toned and perfectly tanned. She wore a pink spandex mini-dress that left nothing to the imagination. Even her pregnant belly looked more like a beach ball she'd stuffed up her dress for a joke.

Helen waited for a surge of jealousy but felt nothing. After three years, her feelings for David were definitely dead and buried. She was able to smile broadly at Carrie-Ann and hold out her hand.

'Thanks for inviting us.'

'Oh, I didn't do a thing. It was all David's idea. I mean, of course you're welcome, but . . .'

Carrie-Ann blushed and looked helplessly from Helen to David. Jay stepped forward and touched the brim of his hat.

'Pleasure to meet you, ma'am. I'm Jay Turner.'

Carrie-Ann gave a little squeak and pressed her hands to her mouth.

'Oh my God, you're one of the PBR guys! I just love that show!' She reached forward and touched Jay's thigh. 'How's your knee?'

Helen slid closer to Jay. 'His knee is just fine. I fixed it myself.'

Carrie-Ann's gaze flew to Helen's face. 'That's right, I remember you taking care of him back in Sacramento at the rodeo. I was there with my cousin Tammy.' She shuddered and gripped David's arm. 'It was terrible, babe, the way that bull came down on him.'

'So that's how you met. He's your patient.' David spoke softly as Carrie-Ann continued to question Jay. 'You didn't have to say he was your boyfriend.'

'He is my boyfriend and he's no longer my patient. Is that clear enough for you?'

'Interesting to see what the selection committee will make of that.'

'You're a fine one to talk. Didn't Carrie-Ann come to you for a consultation about a broken finger?'

'Yes, that's right I did.' Carrie-Ann's face broke out into an adoring smile. 'And wasn't I so lucky to meet my most special person in the world?'

'Absolutely.' Helen grabbed Jay's hand. 'How about we get ourselves a drink?'

Jay allowed himself to be steered toward the bar, his hand held firmly in Helen's.

'She seems like a nice gal.'

Helen's expression breathed contempt. 'If you like that kind of thing, and my ex-husband always has.'

Jay signaled the bartender for a beer. 'How in hell did he end up with you, then?'

'That's a good question. I guess it was my fault. At that point in my life, I was looking for someone who was as focused and ambitious as I was. I didn't particularly care whether I actually liked him or not.'

She took her martini and swallowed half of it in one gulp. Jay studied her set expression.

'So what changed?'

'I did. I realized that anyone who was as selfish and focused as I was wasn't really a complete person.'

He held her gaze, saw the sadness in her eyes. 'You seem pretty complete to me.'

She touched her glass to his beer bottle. 'Thank you, Jay.'

He caught her hand and kissed it, realizing he'd meant every word. When had it become so important to defend her, even to herself?

'Helen, so glad that you could make it.'

Jay turned at the sound of another rich, cultivated voice. The guy staring at him was in his early sixties, his expression benevolent.

'Hi, Peter. This is Jay Turner.'

'It's delightful to meet any friend of my dear Helen's. She is such a pleasure to know.'

'She sure is.'

Jay wrapped his arm around Helen's shoulders and hugged her tight. Her smile seemed a little forced so he hugged her even harder.

'Have you had a chance to chat with the other candidates and the search committee yet, Helen? I know Dr Masudo was anxious to have a word with you.'

Jay gave Helen a last squeeze and then released her. He slapped her gently on the butt. 'Why don't you go chat to old Dr Masudo and leave me and Peter to get acquainted?'

Helen's gaze narrowed as she studied him. 'OK. I won't be long.'

Jay watched her walk over to a huddle of men and their wives. The group opened to admit her and he turned back to Peter.

'So what do you do, Jay?'

There it was again, that slight hint of condescension.

'I used to be a rodeo cowboy until I busted up my knee. Now I make cowboy boots and western-style leatherwear.'

To his surprise, it felt good to come out and say what he did, especially amongst all these overqualified and overconfident people.

'Really? I don't think I've ever met anyone who's done either of those things before.'

Jay gave him a slow grin. 'Well, hell, someone has to make boots or else all those ranch hands and cowboys would be walking around knee-deep in shit.'

Peter blinked once and then resumed smiling. 'I suppose you're right. I've never quite thought of it like that before.'

'We can't all be doctors and captains of industry, Peter.'

'No, I suppose we can't.'

Peter took a sip of his drink, his gaze everywhere but on Jay, as if he was looking for the next important person to come along. Jay had never taken well to being ignored.

'I hear you're retiring.'

'Helen told you that?'

Jay suppressed a smile at Peter's obvious surprise. 'Yeah, we do talk to each other occasionally. People do that when they're in a relationship.'

'I beg your pardon, young man. I was under the impression from David that Helen only brought you to make up the numbers. I didn't realize you were involved with her.'

'I sure am, prof.' Jay winked. 'As you said, she's a real pleasure.'

Peter's gaze switched back to Helen. Jay decided he was done being polite. 'Do you think being seen with me will affect Helen's chances of getting promoted?'

Peter laughed and the false sound grated in Jay's ears. 'Of course not, why should it? We don't live in the Dark Ages, you know. The selection committee is well aware that candidates have a right to a private life.'

'That's good to know.' Jay finished his beer and placed the empty bottle back on the nearest table. 'Because I know first-hand that Helen is a great surgeon as well as a great person, and I'd hate to spoil her chances.'

He strode toward the pool and stared down into its shimmering blue depths. Would Helen really be judged for having an unacceptable boyfriend, and, hell, what made him so bad anyway? He wasn't an idiot, he wasn't getting drunk and insulting the guests. In fact, he'd hardly spoken to anyone yet. Had Helen brought him here to make a point and, if so, exactly what point was she trying to make?

'Jay?'

Helen came up beside him, her soft blonde hair lifting in the breeze, her face animated. He stared at her for a long moment. She fit in well with all this money and these educated people. If he'd stayed with his father and taken the job he'd been offered, would he feel comfortable here too?

'Was Peter being difficult?'

He smiled at her. 'Nope, just looking out for you. I reckon he thinks I'm not your type.'

Her blue eyes flashed. 'It's none of his business who I date. He liked David and look where that ended up.'

'But he's right. David is more like you than I'll ever be.'

Helen crossed her arms over her chest. 'Have they made you feel inadequate, Jay?'

He frowned. 'Of course not, I can do that all by myself.' He sucked in a breath. 'Look at me, honey. I got my GED in my twenties, any money I have is a gift from my brother and my long-term income looks dicey, to say the least.'

'Money doesn't make things right, you know.'

'Easy for you to say.'

Her expression sharpened. 'I wasn't born into this. I worked hard to get where I am just like you did.'

He raised his eyebrows, let her see the skepticism in his gaze. With a frustrated sigh, she swung around toward the barbecue.

'Let's go and eat before I give in to the urge to push you into the pool,' she said.

Jay shifted in his chair and looked longingly over to where Helen was talking to a Swiss guy from the drug company Peter was going to work for. For some reason, this man was very interested in Helen. It made Jay twitchy just to see the intensity of his expression as he focused on Helen's replies.

Unfortunately he was trapped. Carrie-Ann was all over him, asking him questions about his days in the rodeo, making him think about everything he'd lost and would never have again. Was she really this insensitive or was she simply keen to talk about something outside the narrow social world he guessed she now inhabited with David?

'Carrie-Ann? David Junior's nanny is looking for you.'

Jay tried not to look relieved as Carrie-Ann finally stood up and left. His smile faded when David took her place.

'Are you having a good time, Trey?'

'It's Jay and yes, I sure am.'

David leant back in his chair, his gaze fixed on Jay. 'I was worried that you might feel a bit out of your depth.'

Jay slowly raised his eyebrows. 'Now why on earth would you think that?'

'No offense, but I'm sure this isn't your usual Sunday afternoon hangout.'

'None taken, and you're right. I'm usually still asleep.'

He didn't miss the hint of satisfaction in David's eyes.

'If I might offer you a piece of advice, in the spirit of a man who's already been through the mill of Dr Helen's affections. Don't let her order you around. She's very good at it and, to be honest, if she's putting you in situations that obviously make you uncomfortable, how are you ever going to have a real relationship with her?'

Jay sat up. 'Do I look uncomfortable? I sure don't feel that way.'

David carried on as though Jay hadn't spoken. 'If she

gets promoted it will just get worse. As her partner you'll be expected to attend all kinds of parties and social events.'

'And you think that'll be a problem for me?'

David cast him a dismissive glance. 'Well, you don't look like the kind of guy who enjoys standing around being polite to people.'

Jay got to his feet and so did David.

'I've been polite to you, haven't I?'

David took a step back as Jay deliberately crowded him. 'Yes, of course, you have, but . . .'

'If you don't get out of my face, I can stop being polite. Maybe it's time for you to experience a hospital from a patient's viewpoint.'

David tried to sneer. 'I can see why she likes you, cowboy. You're just like Cory. She's always had a taste for lowlifes. As they say, you can take a girl out of the Central Valley but you can't take the Central Valley out of the girl.'

David walked away, leaving Jay by the pool. Helen turned to stare at him and then looked back at Jay, her face full of questions. Jay headed for the house, too angry to be polite to anyone.

He stepped into the kitchen, avoiding the crowd of catering staff, and asked directions to the restrooms. Helen caught him in front of the entrance.

'What did David say to you?'

Jay studied her beautiful face and pulled her close. Her eyes widened as he pushed open the door and locked it behind them. The bathroom was just as overdecorated as the rest of the house. The gold fittings, chandeliers and fur rugs reminded him of a Parisian brothel. He bent his head, kissed her mouth, felt her instant response. This was real. This was what he needed right now.

He slid his hand under her skirt until he reached the apex of her thighs. His fingers brushed her clit and he almost came in his jeans.

'No panties.' He groaned. 'Trust you to get it right today of all days.'

He slipped three fingers inside her and widened her, enjoying how wet she became as he worked her. Still kissing her, he undid the snaps of his shirt so that her silk-clad breasts and hard nipples dragged over his bare flesh. She moaned into his mouth and grew even wetter.

'I want you so bad, Helen.'

'I'm not stopping you.'

He thumbed her clit, felt it swell and pulse beneath the pad of his thumb. He slid his little finger into her ass, settling her on his hand.

'You want to go back out there in front of all those important people looking like you've just been had?'

'We could just leave before they noticed.'

'Honey, they'd notice the moment they saw you, especially if you let me inside you without a condom and my come was all over you, inside you, trickling down your leg.'

She climaxed, digging her fingers into his shoulders, her face buried in the crook of his neck. God, his cock hurt so bad. He kept working her, his fingers so slippery with her juices now they made a sucking sound.

'How about we compromise?' Helen whispered, her eyes wide, her cheeks flushed with desire. 'This is a big bathroom, Jay, how about you lie down on that nice fur rug over there?'

He stepped away from her and moved to the rug, falling to his knees as she followed him down. She pushed on his chest until he lay on his back and then straddled him, her ass close to his face.

Jay groaned as she carefully unzipped his fly, protecting his aroused cock with her hand. He flipped up her skirt, exposed her perfect butt cheeks to his gaze. She leant forward giving him an even more inviting view of her whole wet fuckable sex. In one swift motion, she slid her mouth over his shaft and swallowed him deep.

His hips came off the rug and followed her mouth into a rough demanding dance. He almost forgot to breathe as he grabbed her hips, steadied himself and plunged his tongue into her sex. She shivered and worked him faster, the rasp of her teeth on his most sensitive flesh a turn-on he couldn't deny. With a stifled groan, he came hard, pumping his seed down her throat. Hell, coming in her mouth was almost as good as in her pussy. Hopefully she'd still smell of him when she kissed those other bastards goodbye.

'Keep your mouth on me.' He returned to her pussy, working his tongue deep, his unshaven chin rubbing her sex until she came again, shuddering and bucking around his mouth.

He collapsed onto his back, savoring the taste of her on his tongue. Helen lay against his upraised thigh, her mouth still enclosing his now flaccid cock. Looking up at the fancy chandelier he allowed his body to relax for the first time since he'd arrived at the party.

Helen slowly licked his cock and his shaft jerked. He slid his hand down into her hair and gently pulled.

'Come here.'

He drew her into his arms, enjoying the heat from the

fur rug beneath them, imagining Helen naked and writhing on it. His cock stirred even more. She kissed his
throat, nuzzled his neck. Jay opened his eyes

'Who's Cory?'

Helen sat up so fast his jaw snapped shut. She got to
her feet and started fussing at the mirror. He lay there,
looking up at her, a knot forming in his gut as she
continued to straighten up, erasing all evidence of his
lovemaking.

'Helen.'

She stared at her reflection, noticed the fine lines
around her eyes and mouth. Why had she brought Jay
with her? She'd simply offered David an opportunity to
hurt them both. Her grip tightened on the faucet. Of
course, Jay might not be hurt. He'd managed to get some
sex out of her before mentioning what he heard.

She turned back to him, trying to ignore how gorgeous
he looked sprawled half-undressed and rumpled on the
floor like a *Playgirl* centerfold. His gray eyes were
unreadable.

'Can we talk about it after we leave?'

He moved into a sitting position, one knee bent, his
arm curved over the top. 'Cory's an "it"?'

'That's not what I meant.'

He continued to regard her, his face expressionless. 'All
afternoon I've kept getting this feeling that I've been
judged and condemned before I've even been allowed to
say a word. Did you bring me here because you wanted
my company or because you're still playing some kind of
sick game with your ex?'

Helen swallowed, tasting him in her mouth. 'Jay, I
wanted you to come but I didn't think it through. I
apologize if it's been difficult for you.'

He got to his feet and started to button his shirt, the movements jerky. 'No more difficult than attending one of Beau's little business parties. Despite what your ex and your boss think, I grew up in a shark pool and I survived.'

'Of course, Beau ... Beau Turner, the Texan millionaire and ex-Dallas Cowboys quarterback is your father?'

His smile was cynical. 'Correction, my sperm donor. He doesn't know how to be a father and he doesn't want to.'

She gestured at the overdecorated room. 'Then you belong here more than I do.'

He tucked in his shirt. 'Nope, I preferred to stay with my mother and I paid for that choice by growing up dirt poor. Beau didn't want her anymore and if I wanted her, I couldn't have him.'

Helen gripped the edge of the vanity as Jay's bitterness washed over her. 'What happened to your mom?'

'She died when I was a teenager. She had cancer.' He zipped up his fly, avoiding her gaze. 'Of course, if we'd been able to afford medical insurance, she might have lived. But Beau wasn't willing to pay out for anyone when he had no more use for them.'

'Oh, Jay, I'm so sorry.' Her eyes filled with tears and she stumbled toward him.

He stepped back, his face blank. 'So who's Cory?'

She met his stare. Realized he'd given her an opportunity to repay his honesty with some of her own.

'He was my first husband. I married him when I was sixteen. Now can we leave this horrible party and go home?'

Chapter Seventeen

Helen shut off the engine and studied Jay's profile. He hadn't said a word to her the whole way back. She couldn't decide whether to be grateful for his silence or terrified by it. Peter Hart hadn't been pleased by her abrupt decision to leave, especially when Jay had chimed in and insisted he had to get back to milk his herd of cows. She took a deep steadying breath.

'Do you want to come up?'

'Yeah.'

Helen bit her lip. 'You don't have to. I mean, if you've had enough today ...'

Before she finished speaking, he was already out of the car. She followed him, scooped up her purse from the back seat and located her keys. He waited at the top of the steps. The shadow thrown by the brim of his Stetson concealed his features.

She almost tripped over Tiger, who lay stretched out on his back on a beam of sunlight on the carpet. He acknowledged her with a faint meow and rolled onto his front to glare at Jay. Needing something to do, Helen checked his food and water and then busied herself making coffee. Jay took off his hat and strolled across to the window to stare at the view.

Helen collected two mugs from the cupboard then watched the coffee brew. It was so long since she'd talked to anyone about Cory that it almost seemed like a dream. Gathering her composure, she took the filled mugs over to the low pine table in the family room and set them down.

Jay turned and she watched the rise and fall of his chest as he slowly inhaled.

'Thanks for the coffee,' he said.

'You're welcome.'

He sat down opposite her, one big hand wrapped around his mug, his expression difficult to read. 'Tell me about Cory.'

Helen sighed. 'He came to work on a ranch near my parents' home. I got to talking to him one day in the local store and fell in love, or thought I did.'

'How old were you?'

'Sixteen. What does anyone know about love at that age?'

'That's the same age my mom was when she married Beau.'

She held his gaze. 'I didn't know what I was doing.'

'Neither did she.' Jay studied his coffee mug before looking up again. 'How old was Cory?'

'Twenty-five.'

'Shit.'

'I thought he was the most exciting man I'd ever met.' Helen shifted in her seat. 'Well, he probably was in a Central Valley dust town called Blossom Creek with a population of under two thousand.'

'Sounds like the place I grew up – No Hope, Arizona.'

'Perhaps we have more in common than we realized.'

Jay's gaze flicked away from her. Did he resent the implication that they were alike? She was fed up with him thinking she was some poor little rich girl.

'Anyway, I thought Cory had something special about him and I ... well, I followed him around like some doting sheep. At that point, I wanted to be a veterinarian and he was amazing with horses. I'd never really been into boys. They all seemed immature. Cory was a real man with a job and an interesting past.'

Jay snorted. 'Yeah, right.'

'At first he thought I was funny and then, when he realized how serious I was, he tried to let me down gently. But I was never very good at being told no, so I decided to take matters into my own hands.'

'Don't tell me, you forced him to have sex with you.'

Helen swallowed hard. 'I did.'

Jay slammed his coffee mug down on the table. 'Bullshit, Helen. He was a man, you were just a kid. He could've said no.'

'One Friday night, I stripped naked and waited in his bed for him to come back from the bar.'

Jay almost swallowed his tongue. 'That's a fricking stupid thing to do. Christ, he could have been some kind of pervert or . . .'

'But he wasn't. He was just a guy. And that night he was just drunk enough to do what I needed him to.'

'Fuck you stupid, right?'

She flinched and he glanced up at her, saw the mixture of shame and bravado in her eyes before she blinked it away.

'And did you like it?'

She managed to hold his gaze although her lips were trembling.

'Being fucked, I mean.'

'Yes.'

'It was so fantastic that you ran off and married him? Jeez, he must've been good.'

She brought her knees up toward her chin and

wrapped her arms around them. 'When he said he was leaving to rejoin the rodeo circuit, I was terrified of being left behind. I asked him to take me with him.'

'And he was OK with that?'

'No, he was horrified.'

'But you persuaded him.'

She raised her chin and he recognized himself in the way she set her jaw and the fierce determination of her gaze.

'I told him that if he didn't take me to Vegas and marry me, I'd tell the cops what he'd done to me.'

'Shit, Helen. That's one hell of a threat.'

'I wouldn't have followed through, I'm not that cruel. But I'd realized by then that he wasn't as smart as I was.' She shrugged. 'I hated that town and all the people who told me not to bother even trying to get an education because "people like us" just didn't become nurses or business people.'

'But you walked away from high school. You walked away from all that possibility straight into a fantasy.'

A tear slid down her cheek. 'I thought I'd found something better. I thought sex was the answer to everything.' She attempted a smile. 'I thought I'd finally found a way to make a man do whatever I wanted him to.'

Jay found himself nodding. 'I thought running away to be a cowboy was the answer to everything, too.'

Helen stared at him. 'But then I realized you can't run away from the person you are inside.'

'So did I.'

Silence stretched between them, underscored by Tiger's purring and the sound of more coffee brewing.

Jay tore his gaze away from Helen, his emotions too close to the surface to allow him to speak. Who'd have thought he'd be capable of sitting in Helen's family room as she shared such personal stuff with him?

Desperate to move, he shot to his feet and got them both more coffee. When he returned, Helen had delved into a box of tissues and was furiously wiping her nose. He pretended not to notice.

'How long did it take you to realize you'd made a mistake?'

Her mouth twisted. 'About three months – after I realized that Cory had no ability to hold down a job and no intention of doing so. I began to understand those things were important to me and that I needed something to aim at.'

'So you went home.'

'There was nowhere else to go.' Helen grimaced. 'My parents were reluctant to have me back. I'd shamed them by running off with a no-good cowboy and memories are very long in farming communities like theirs. I crammed as much of my junior and senior years courses into as small a time as possible and graduated a year early.'

Jay tried to imagine her working that hard and could see it all too easily. He could totally understand her desire to get out of that stifling small town, even if her methods were downright alarming. But had he been any less ruthless when he was a teenager? If his mother hadn't died, he would have walked away from her eventually.

'Where did you go after that?'

'I moved to the "big city" of Modesto, got as many part-time jobs as I could handle and was lucky enough to room with Carol's family.' Her face softened. 'They helped me through a few rough years and Carol became my best friend.'

'Cory was on the rodeo circuit, right?'

Helen looked surprised. 'Yes.'

'Is he still doing that?'

'I don't know. He might be.'

'Is that why you help out at the PBR events when Dr Tandy can't be there?'

Helen sat up straight. 'Are you suggesting I'm pining after Cory?'

Jay glared at her. 'Answer the question, dammit.'

'I help out because sometimes I like to be around folks who remind me of home.'

Jay sat back. What the hell was wrong with him? Why was he making such a big deal about some guy who'd fucked Helen all those years ago? The truth rushed at him like a rampaging bull. Because he wished it was him, that's why. He wished he'd been the first cowboy she'd taken to her bed and the last. The pain in his gut intensified and settled like a clenched fist under his ribs.

'Why are you asking me all these questions anyway, Jay?'

'Because I'm wondering what the connection is here. Do you just like to fuck cowboys or what?'

What little color that remained in her face drained away. 'What are you trying to say?'

He shrugged. 'Just asking where I fit in the big scheme of things.'

She stood up, her arms wrapped around her waist and pointed at the door. 'Get out, Jay. Now.'

He stood as well, put his mug on the table and hoped she didn't notice the slight tremor in his fingers. 'We haven't finished our conversation yet. Just because you don't like my question doesn't mean you don't have to answer it.' He took a step toward her. 'You can't run away from everything.'

She closed her eyes as if she couldn't stand the sight of him. 'It's been an exhausting day. I've shared things with you that I haven't shared with anyone since I was married to David and all you can think about is whether I have some strange fetish for cowboys.'

Jay opened his mouth to contradict her and then stopped.

'I like you, Jay. I like you a lot more than I should but I really don't want to deal with your emotional crap right now.'

'My emotional crap? What the fuck is that supposed to mean?'

'It's not always about you. You asked me about Cory and I answered you. That's all there is to it. It was a long time ago and I'm a different person now. I made some bad decisions but I've learnt from my mistakes and I don't repeat them.'

'So you're saying I'm not like him?'

'Jay . . .' She flopped back down into her seat. 'Just go home.'

'No, I'm trying to understand something here. You married a cowboy because you thought sex was the answer, and then you married David because you reckoned you wanted money and power instead. What do you want now, Helen? What is it that I can give you that neither of those guys could?'

She stared at him, her blue eyes wide and almost panicked looking. 'I don't know, Jay. Do you?'

He took two steps away from her before he even realized he was moving and picked up his hat. 'I have to go to class. I'll call you tomorrow.'

She laughed, the sound harsh in the confines of the cozy room. 'Now who's running away?'

Helen waited for the front door to close before she finally allowed herself to collapse. God, what had she done? Telling him all that emotional stuff, thinking he was interested in her, only to realize that he was only thinking about himself. Why was she surprised? He was a man, after all.

She walked slowly down the hall to her bedroom and turned on the shower. It had been a horrible afternoon. Peter and David were bad enough but Jay had proved the frosting on the cake. Joel Franken, the guy from the drug company, had also asked her far too many questions about the origin of the idea for the surgical material that she wasn't willing or able to answer.

She left her dress on the floor and took off her panties. Tiger rubbed against her legs and she bent to pet him. As soon as he realized she was heading for the bathroom, he retreated to her bed and went back to sleep. He didn't like anything to do with water.

The shower was hot and fierce, just what she needed. Had she shocked Jay when she revealed exactly what she'd done to escape her old life? At first she thought he understood and was even sympathetic but then she'd realized he was more worried about himself.

She let the water stream over her face. Perhaps she should try to see things from Jay's side. He'd walked into a situation where he knew less than anybody else. He'd endured David's poisonous suggestions and been patronized by Professor Hart. She could see why he might have felt threatened and overreacted.

It didn't make her feel much better though. She'd shared a private part of herself and he'd let her down.

Jay was so unlike Cory that she never really thought about them in the same way. Jay had all Cory's sexual appeal but unlike Cory, he wasn't a drifter with no ability or interest to plan for his future. Of course, David had all the drive in the world but a total inability to connect sexually with anyone on a permanent basis. She'd already heard rumors that despite his so-called happy marriage to Carrie-Ann he was screwing around on the side again.

Maybe she had disgusted Jay. He probably thought she used people and then moved on. She turned off the shower and grabbed a towel. That might have been true once. She'd certainly used Robert to get what she wanted. Was she just as incapable as David of being honest with the people who tried to love her?

Helen stepped out of the shower and gazed blankly at the steamed-up mirror. An insistent desire to eat ice cream, watch musicals and call Carol for some sympathy came over her. She picked up the phone.

Jay walked three blocks until he realized he had no idea where he was going. Sunday evening wasn't the best time to be taking a stroll through the steep streets of the city. He fixed his gaze on the lights of the Embarcadero and the sweep of the Bay Bridge and kept moving, hands thrust deep into his pockets.

By rights, he should be in bed with Helen by now, not trying to avoid getting mugged. But his knee-jerk reaction to her having fucked another man had kicked him right out of paradise. She'd finally opened up to him and what had he done? Behaved like a jerk. He'd panicked because she'd shared something personal and it had hit him hard. He'd never felt so possessive and territorial before in his life.

The last woman he'd really cared for was his mother and he hadn't been able to help her when she needed him most. Jay kicked an empty can into the gutter. He had to stop reacting like a teenager. He was a grown man who should be able to handle a few home truths. He stopped walking. Except that he hadn't and, in the process, he'd hurt Helen.

To his relief, after about twenty minutes, the lights of Market Street came into view and the welcome sign of a BART station. He checked his bearings again. His knee felt good and he was so close to the apartment he might as well walk the rest of the way. There were six bottles of beer in his refrigerator and he intended to get to know them all – up close and personal.

'You told Jay about Cory?'

Helen nodded and scooped up another cherry from the top of her ice cream. Carol had arrived twenty minutes after her call bearing dessert and a large bottle of wine. Helen had never been so pleased to see her in her life.

'David had already stirred the waters so Jay asked me who he was.'

Carol frowned. 'David is such a prick.'

'It was awful. David and Peter tried to make Jay feel like a pariah.'

'And how did he deal with it?'

Helen found herself smiling. 'He did great. Underneath that lazy charm is a guy who can really stand up for himself. He said he learnt all about being a shark from his father, Beau Turner.'

'*The* Beau Turner?'

'Yup, that's the one, although I don't think they're on speaking terms. It seems as if he treated Jay's mother really badly.'

Carol swigged some wine. 'Don't you read *People*? Beau Turner's notorious for his womanizing, always has been. I think he's on his fifth wife now.'

Poor Jay.

'Anyway, after I told Jay about Cory, he got all self-righteous on me and demanded to know whether I just liked to fuck cowboys. I tried to tell him that that was complete garbage but he wouldn't back down.' She sighed. 'Eventually, I told him to go home and grow up.'

'Maybe he was jealous.' Carol sucked the back of her ice-cream spoon and eyed Helen over the top of it.

'Jealous of Cory? I told him that Cory was a mistake. Why would he be jealous?'

'Because he wants to be the only cowboy in your life?'

'Oh, for God's sake, Carol. Jay's the one who wanted our relationship to be just sexual. He's the one who always backs off when he thinks things are getting too deep.'

'Sounds just like you.'

Helen pointed her spoon at Carol. 'You are supposed to be on my side, remember? Jay Turner is not to be pitied.'

Carol laughed. 'I can't help but feel sorry for him dealing with you. You're not easy, Helen.'

'Neither is he.'

'A match made in heaven then.'

Helen stared at Carol for a long moment. 'He asked me what I wanted from him and I couldn't tell him.'

'Couldn't tell him or didn't want to?'

'I like being with him. Despite the fact that we fight all the time, I feel more like myself when I'm with him than with anyone except you.'

Carol raised her eyebrows. 'Well, shit.'

Helen managed a smile as the repercussions of what she'd just admitted resonated through her. 'Well, shit indeed.'

Chapter Eighteen

Helen skimmed through her email and then returned to the message from the search committee. Her big interview, in front of the whole panel, was set for Friday afternoon. She'd already given two lectures to faculty staff and endured some informal interviews. Apparently the committee was 'looking forward' to seeing her. She sighed as she sent a confirmation. Less than two days to come up with some more convincing lies to dazzle them with. She wasn't sure if she was looking forward to seeing them at all.

She frowned as another email popped up on her screen. What the hell did David want? She clicked on it and her stomach knotted as she read his all-too familiar threats.

She'd never told David about Robert and exactly how they'd come up with the scientific formula for the new polyethylene compound for the surgical procedure. Unfortunately, she had told him about Cory and he seemed keen to use that fact to belittle her in front of the selection committee. He might write about his concern for her bad choices of boyfriends, how that might affect her career and the future prosperity of the hospital. What he *meant* was that he couldn't believe anyone was better than him, either for the job or for her. Helen closed her eyes. David personified the reasons why she now hated getting involved in the politics at work. He was so driven he'd use anything against her.

It took her only a moment to type a reply telling him to mind his own fricking business and leave her personal life out of his plans to woo the selection committee. She knew he wouldn't listen but it made her feel better.

She sat up straight. And why should the committee care about her choices anyway? Cory was in her past, and Jay? Jay wasn't talking to her. She glanced at the phone. Perhaps it was time for her to apologize to him for a change.

Jay wiped his forehead with the back of his hand and studied the pieces of leather laid out on the workbench. The outer brown layer of the leg section was cut in several places to allow the inner red layer beneath to show through. Now all he had to do was line them up, brown on top of red. He moved one strip a fraction to the left and stood back again.

'Stop screwing around, man. Sew it together.'

Jay glanced up at Rob, who had appeared on the other side of the workbench.

'I'm just making sure it's lined up right.'

'You're just procrastinating. You've done everything right so far, made the last, cut the pattern and now the leather.' He gestured at the old sewing machine behind him. 'Now go and put it all together.'

'I haven't finished putting the bottom of the boot together yet. I could always go and do that.'

Rob chuckled. 'You could but you know you don't want to. The machine is free, take advantage of it.'

Jay eyed his fellow classmates. Everyone was busy, heads bent over their work. No one looked like they needed to sew anything. He carefully picked up the four sections of supple leather.

He'd already experimented with some old scraps of hide so he knew how to use the industrial-sized sewing machine. He only hoped his fingers didn't shake too much and get caught up in the sharp teeth. He had no desire to end up sewn into a pair of cowboy boots.

Rob walked away, leaving Jay alone as he laid out the two back parts of the boot, which would join onto the vamp section. The colors looked great together and the red thread he'd chosen would help to blend the colors together. He remembered Rob's instructions and started small, delicately sewing a single line around the first of the star-shaped openings. He had four more lines of stitches to set parallel to the first.

His hands took over, moving the leather with a skill he hadn't known he possessed as the design took place beneath his concentrated gaze. Red stars shone through the dark brown leather, each a different size and at a different angle. He finished the second piece, quicker now as he got into it, confidence making it easier all the time. He cut the strong thread and stepped back as Rob wandered over to take a look.

'That's great, Jay. The design is kind of modern with a real classic touch.'

A couple of the other guys came over as well. He held his breath as they examined his work and was humbled by their praise. Picking up the leather, he returned to his workbench and laid them down beside the remainder of the pieces he still had to sew.

Tomorrow morning he'd cut, cement and sew the side welt, rub the seams down flat, attach the pull straps and finally be able to turn the tops right side out.

He had nothing planned this week. Well, shit, he had nothing planned for the rest of his life so he might as well stay late and try to finish the rest of the boot heel and insole. Bob had given him a flattened 40-penny nail to use as the arch of the sole. He liked the more traditional methods. It reminded him of the men and women who'd come before him.

He touched each piece, reminding himself how it all fit together. The most complicated part remaining was pegging the soles to the boot leather. If he didn't get that right, he might as well throw the boots away.

If he worked hard, he could have them finished by Saturday, when the rodeo was on. He'd decided to take Grayson's advice and do a little advance selling to his fellow cowboys.

'Hey, Jay. Will you lock up for me?'

'No problem. I want to finish this.'

'I figured.'

Rob threw him a bunch of keys, which Jay just managed to catch. He continued to study the leather as the voices of Rob and his classmates faded away.

An hour later, he glanced at the clock. His eyes were straining and a headache beckoned but he'd finished what he set out to do. Tomorrow he'd be able to try to stretch the completed leather boot sides to the vamps and soles.

He wished he had someone to share the news with. Losing his job at the rodeo had taken away all of his friends in one blow. He couldn't bear to talk to the guys yet; the pain was still too near the surface. And hell, why should they care about his small triumph over a pile of leather when they were wrestling with two thousand pound bulls?

The door squeaked and he turned. Helen stood uncertainly in the hall; one hand had a death grip on her briefcase, and the other was in her pocket. He put down the boot.

'Are you coming in?'

She stepped into the room, her blue eyes fixed on his face. She wore a short black skirt, matching jacket and high heels.

'I thought it was my turn to apologize to you.'

Jay shrugged. 'We take turns now?'

She took a step toward him. 'Jay, I put you in a very difficult position. I'm not surprised you felt used. I would've felt the same.'

He stared at her, gauged the sincerity of her tone and her expression. He leant back against the workbench, glad for the solid feel of the wood, and crossed his arms.

'I don't like looking stupid or being lied to.'

'I wasn't lying to you.' She continued to meet his gaze head on. 'I was lying to myself. It wasn't about you at all. I've gotten into the habit of pretending that what happened with Cory was nothing to do with the real me – the person I wanted to be.'

The knot in his gut relaxed. He guessed she was just as uncomfortable exchanging confidences with him as he was.

'OK.'

She blinked at him. 'It's not OK. I haven't finished yet.' She sighed. 'You made me realize that I can't forget that part of myself. That girl who did such terrible things to get what she thought she wanted out of life.'

'We all do stupid things, Helen. I'm not real proud of the way I walked away from everyone when I was sixteen.' He took her hand. 'We agreed to try to be honest with each other. Why don't we just keep trying?'

She covered his hand with her own, her nails digging

into his skin. 'How much honesty do you want, Jay? How about if I told you that even when I was really angry with you I still wanted you?'

He pulled her into his arms, buried his face in her hair. 'I should have stayed and let you show me.'

She brought her hands up and thumped him hard on the chest. 'Dammit, I shared all that emotional stuff with you and you walked away from me! When you got mad, I wanted to sink my teeth into your skin and hit you until I ran out of strength or breath, whichever came first.'

His cock stirred as her fists came to rest on his chest. He bent his head to take her mouth in a savage, possessive kiss. 'Hell, I would've let you. And then when you were too weak to fight me anymore, I would've fucked you until you begged me to stop and then I would've fucked you some more.'

She bit down on his lip and he tasted his own blood. Without further thought, he lifted her up until she sat on the workbench. Her briefcase fell to the floor and her short skirt slid up her thighs. He pushed his body between her legs until he was pressed up against her.

'Kiss me, Helen.'

She slid a hand into his hair and pulled him close. His lips met hers and he outlined them with his tongue before thrusting inside. She tasted perfect to him. A subtle mixture of cool doctor and sexy woman that turned him into a raging fuck-obsessed machine.

She drew back and rested her hands on his shoulders. She was trembling. 'Do we fight so that we can make up?'

'Nope, we just like to fight. This is a bonus.'

He kissed her again, more deeply this time until she

relaxed into his arms. No woman had ever made him feel this way before. She was like a raging fire. He couldn't stop himself from coming back even though he knew he might get burnt. His fingers stroked her knee and kept going up until he reached the soft warm curves of her sex. He rubbed her clit through her panties until she moaned into his mouth and lifted her hips into each stroke. His fingers tangled in the rapidly soaking scrap of silk.

He paused to listen. Calculated how many people were left in the building and the likelihood of anyone walking in on them. He decided he liked the odds. The hall door squeaked when it was opened even a crack, which should be warning enough.

With a satisfied sigh, he slipped two fingers beneath the silk and explored her creamy wet pussy. Her clit was already swollen and ready for him.

'You know how I feel about panties. Take them off.'

He helped her wriggle out of them, then pushed her legs wide so that he could see the slick wetness he'd caused. She gasped as he plunged four fingers inside her and spread them. He kept his thumb over her clit and closed his eyes as her body pulsed and stirred around him.

Keeping his fingers in place, he sank to his knees and stared at her again. He waited for her to complain about being exposed in a public place, but she wasn't complaining. Her breath came in choppy gasps.

He reached up to the workbench, picked up a long scrap of soft leather and showed it to her. Her eyes widened as he wrapped some of it around his thumb and applied it to her clit.

'Did you know that cowboy boots can be made out of almost any kind of leather?'

'No, I didn't.'

'Goatskin, shark, lizard, alligator, ostrich ... good old American bison.' He rubbed her clit a little harder. 'This is deerskin, one of the softest. Does it feel good against your skin, Helen?'

He watched the slow play of his thumb, the way the leather darkened as her juices soaked into it. She tried to move her hips against the solid thrust of his embedded fingers but he kept them still and deep.

'I like deerskin myself. The color, the suppleness and the way it stretches over a last.'

'A last what?'

He chuckled, bent to kiss her mound, just above his rubbing thumb. 'Shoe last. The three-dimensional wooden pattern a bootmaker carves for each customer.' He licked a strip of the leather into his mouth, tasted her unique scent mixed with the animal musk. Licked her again, harder now, from his knuckles and back over his thumb. She shuddered in his arms.

'I bet you didn't know that there are three hundred and seventy-two steps to building a cowboy boot, either.'

'No, no, I didn't.'

He withdrew his fingers, studied how wet they were and sucked them clean. Holding her gaze, he wrapped the strip of leather around them.

'Yup, three hundred and seventy-two. That's a lot of work for a guy like me, but then I've always liked taking my time to get things right.'

'Jay ...'

He slowly slid his wrapped fingers back inside her, felt her internal muscles grip him like a fist as she came so hard she almost fell off the worktop. He kept his fingers still as her internal muscles continued to convulse around the leather.

'Making cowboy boots is a bit like making love.' He withdrew his hand and unwrapped the leather. 'Sometimes you just have to be patient.' He got to his feet, tucked the scrap of leather into his pocket and grinned at her. 'Do you want to get a beer?'

'Beer?'

Her outraged, deprived expression made him want to laugh. He made a shocked noise. 'Dr Kinsale, we're in a community college full of young impressionable minds. You don't really expect me to fuck you here, do you?'

Her blue eyes took on a frosty glare. 'I expect you to drive me to an early grave. And who says I was going to have sex with you anyway?'

'You are. Make no mistake about that.'

He winked at her and rubbed a hand over the huge bulge in his jeans. She slid down off the workbench and confronted him, hands on hips.

'I came here to apologize.'

'You came, all right.'

'Jay . . .'

He picked up her discarded panties and stuffed them in his pocket alongside the leather, wincing as his fingers brushed his erection. 'Do you want that beer or do you want to go home to your lonely bed?'

Jay waited as a complex series of expressions flittered over her face.

Finally, she sighed. 'Oh hell, a beer sounds great.'

He checked that the room was clean, put away his tools and snapped off the lights. Helen waited for him by the door, hands clasped tightly on her briefcase again.

Damn, he wanted her so bad – she was like a drug. She was the first woman who'd ever made him eager to keep fucking her, to keep exploring her, to understand her.

Shit. Not good. Not what he wanted at all. He knew he was in danger but why couldn't he walk away?

Helen noted Jay's abstraction as he took her hand and walked her out of the building into the parking lot.

'Are you sure you want to get a beer?'

He stopped walking and stared at her. 'Why not? I'm already in over my head.'

She got into the car and started the engine. What on earth did that mean? Was he regretting her appearance and his invitation? Perhaps she was a fool to keep coming back to him. But it seemed she was incapable of keeping away. Somehow his raw honesty helped her deal with the insincere world she normally moved through. He reminded her that there were better paths and other choices.

'I can drop you home and then leave.'

'Nope, let's have a beer. I sure need one.'

She smiled into the darkness as she drove off. For once he sounded as confused as she felt. Was that a good thing or a bad one?

His choice of bar was seedy and ill lit. The mud-colored floor felt sticky under the soles of her shoes. Country music blared from a jukebox, reminding her of her youth and her infatuation with Cory. Several guys, including the bartender, hollered at Jay as he walked in. Cowboy hats were much in evidence as was the faint hint of horse sweat and manure. She'd never realized the city had a thriving underground cowboy club. But then San Francisco was renowned for having a little bit of everything.

Helen averted her gaze from a couple kissing at the bar. The woman rode the man's thigh, one of his hands clamped firmly on her ass, the other up the back of her skimpy shirt. No one else seemed to notice.

She wondered if she looked as conspicuous as she felt and if everyone was really staring at her. Jay put his arm around her shoulders and maneuvered her into one of the faded red-leather booths. He kept her close, giving her no opportunity to move away from him.

The warm scent of his body engulfed her and she turned her head to nuzzle his checked shirt. Beneath her cheek, his heart thumped steadily in his chest. Two beers appeared on the table, delivered by a waitress who simultaneously beamed at Jay, thrust her breasts in his face and ignored Helen.

'Thanks, Dee Dee.'

Helen scooted away from Jay and stared at the retreating waitress. 'Her name is Dee Dee?'

'Yeah, what about it?' Jay raised a beer to his lips.

'Is that her real name?'

'I dunno, should I care?'

'She obviously seems to care about you.'

Jay chuckled. 'She's worked here for the last year. That's all I know about her. Are you jealous, honey?'

Helen just stared at him. 'I remember you saying you didn't share. Well, I don't either.'

He regarded her, his gray eyes inscrutable over the upturned beer bottle. 'Good to know. Now why don't you move over here and prove it?'

Helen's sex responded with a rush of cream. She moved closer, sighed as he slid his fingers up her inner thigh and stroked her already swollen clit.

'You just sit here nice and quiet, listen to the music and let me play with you, OK?'

Helen glanced around the bar, realized that no one could see what Jay was doing to her, and relaxed into the caress. God, she was so wet she could hear the slick sound of her juices on his fingers.

He penetrated her with his thumb, curling it up to rub against the underside of her clit. Her nipples hardened in an aching rush and she clenched her hand around her beer.

'Do you want another one, Jay, darlin'?'

Helen didn't dare look at the waitress as Jay continued to finger-fuck her.

'Yeah, that would be great. Thanks, Dee Dee.'

'How about your friend?' Her tone was much less friendly now.

'Helen?'

'I'm fine, thank you.' She just managed to spit the words out without moaning her pleasure along with them.

Jay's mouth brushed her ear. 'You feel good, honey, wide open and ready for my cock.' She bit her lip as he changed his position, pushing her further back into the corner of the booth, his fingers still working her steadily toward a climax.

'Can we go then?'

He chuckled into her hair. 'Not yet. I haven't had my second beer yet. I need that beer.'

She tried to bite his shoulder but he kept her trapped against the seat. His mouth descended for a leisurely kiss.

She kept her mouth closed but he nipped at her lip until she opened for him. Distantly she heard Dee Dee's voice and the thump of another bottle hitting the table.

Dee Dee cleared her throat but Jay kept kissing Helen until Dee Dee walked away muttering. Helen moaned into his mouth as he worked her sex, unable to care what the other woman must think of her. He shifted his hands and she shuddered as the icy cold lip of the beer bottle slid inside her.

'See, I told you I needed that second beer. This one's for you.'

She grabbed Jay's wrist but he kept sliding the bottle deeper. The coldness of the glass sent her hot passage into a series of spasms and her hips surged up to meet Jay's fingers. He murmured his approval into her hair and slowly removed his hand and the bottle.

'Easy, darlin'.'

Deprived yet again of a decent orgasm, she glared at him as he sat back and drank, the muscles of his throat working as he swallowed the second beer. Frustration rose in her and she grabbed her own beer and finished it. She slammed the bottle on the tray and wedged a twenty-dollar bill under it.

'Are you ready to go now?'

He grinned at her, a challenge in his eyes. 'Hey, are you buying tonight?'

She raised her eyebrows. 'If it gets you out of here quicker, yes.'

He stood up. 'OK. Let's move it.'

Helen pushed her way through the crowd around the bar and found the door. Jay followed her out. She kept one of his hands in hers, as if he was a reluctant child being taken to school. Outside it was still surprisingly warm. Wisps of fog illuminated by the red and orange street lights drifted in between the tall buildings and disappeared into the gloom. Even the traffic noise had lowered to a more bearable point, replaced by the sound of people enjoying themselves.

'Shall we go?'

Helen tensed as Jay shook his head.

'Not yet, doc. We have one more place to visit.'

'We?'

He took a step toward her. 'Yeah.' He tried to look scared. 'You wouldn't leave me all alone in the big city would you, lady?'

'At this precise moment? *Yeah*, I would.'

He fell to his knees, pressed his face against her groin and rubbed his cheek against her already sensitized flesh. One of his hands slid up the inside of her skirt and headed for her sex.

'God, Jay, not here.'

'Come to the next bar with me then and give me some privacy.'

She glanced down at the top of his Stetson and resisted an urge to ram it down right over his ears.

'All right, one more place. But that's it. Do you understand me? After that I'm going home.'

He took her hand and led her further down the street. He smiled as the vibrant thud of a rocking bass line shook the sidewalk. Helen stopped walking.

'I'm not going in there.'

Jay turned to look at her. 'Why not?'

'I'm too old.'

He tugged on her hand, kept her moving. 'You're only as old as you feel, or the guy that you feel, so come on.'

As he opened the door, the swell of music almost knocked him back into the street. He loved the sound of a live band. He drew Helen deeper into the small sweating room and found them a space against the wall.

At the far end of the room, a stage was set up. Four guys in cowboy hats were playing a mixture of rock and country, which set his foot tapping. The tiny dance floor was crowded with line dancers and others doing their own thing. A fair number of the patrons wore Stetsons, big belt buckles and shiny cowboy boots.

Unlike the other bar, Jay knew that most of them weren't real cowboys, just people out for a good time. He persuaded Helen to stand in front of him and wrapped his arms around her. After a moment, she relaxed against him. Her tight ass pressed against his already swollen cock.

He rested his chin against the top of her head, amused by how well they fit together, how good she felt in his arms. She sighed and the sound rippled through him. He had the strangest feeling that he would remember this moment for the rest of his life. Helen's body relaxed against his, her scent on his fingers.

The band changed tempo to a slow dance and Jay set his hands on Helen's shoulders. 'Let's dance.'

She opened her mouth, a protest definitely forming on her lips. He settled that by drawing her into his arms and sealing his mouth to hers. As the music played he moved with Helen, caught up in the sway of her hips and the way she held him so close. He kept his head bent, his lips aligned with hers, his cock pulsing against the press of her body, echoing the steady beat of his heart.

After two slow dances, the band took a break, leaving Helen and Jay still on the dance floor. Helen studied Jay's expression as he took her hand and walked back to the bar.

'You didn't say anything mean to me.'

Jay paused to look down at her. 'What?'

'When we were dancing. You didn't say a word.'

A resigned expression flitted over his face. 'You're always telling me to quit teasing you, and when I do you complain I'm too quiet?'

'I'm not complaining.'

She enjoyed dancing with him, the strength of his body pressed against hers, his unique scent surrounding her.

He smoothed a hand through her hair. 'It's late. We both have to work tomorrow. Let's go.'

She followed him back into the street, glad of his strength in pushing aside the many bodies that crowded the club doorway.

'You only wanted the one dance?'

His mouth quirked at the corner. 'It was enough.'

They reached her car and she searched for her keys. 'I'll drop you home, then.'

He got into the car, wincing slightly as he rearranged the prominent bulge in his jeans. She waited while he fussed around with his seat belt and the window controls. Helen continued to stare at his groin, her car keys dangling in her hand. She clicked the door locks and dropped the keys on the center console.

'Uh . . . don't you need those?'

'Not yet.' Helen smiled as she leant across to rake her nails down his fly.

'Damn it, stop that. I'm hard enough to hammer nails.' His groan was almost a growl.

She undid his belt, worked the top snap of his jeans and slid one finger inside. She met the wet tip of his cock and twirled her finger around the thick head. His breath hissed out as she unzipped him, protecting him with her hand. Before he could react, she bent her head and took him in her mouth, enjoying the wet throbbing heat of his shaft as it slid down her throat.

'Christ, Helen, the . . .'

She kept up the tempo. Long sucks at his whole length, little flicks of her tongue over the sensitive slit and head. His hips moved with her mouth, encouraging her to take more which she did unhesitatingly. It didn't take long for him to lose his rhythm and start thrusting harder and harder into her mouth. She took him deeper, held him there while he came so far down her throat she didn't even taste him.

After a final swirl of her tongue, she released him and carefully buttoned him into his jeans. He sat back in the seat, his eyes closed, his hands fisted at his sides. So exhilarating to take him by surprise for a change.

'Put your seat belt on, Jay. We don't want any accidents, do we?'

She turned the ignition and pulled slowly away. A gust of wind blew her hair into her face and she almost pulled over. 'Oh my God, was your window open the whole time?'

Jay opened one eye and stared at her. 'I tried to tell you. But hey, you gave the people on the sidewalk a heck of a show.'

She tried to return her horrified gaze to the road.

'You are such a liar.' She hesitated as she caught the glimpse of a smile on his face. 'There wasn't anyone around, was there?'

He stretched out his legs and chuckled. 'You think I was busy looking out the window after you'd gone down on me? I was watching your mouth on my cock.' He patted her thigh. 'There's nothing to worry about, honey. Nobody could see your face.'

Helen felt her cheeks flush with heat. When had she decided to become an exhibitionist? Obviously Jay's perverted attitude toward sex was rubbing off on her. In a vain attempt to pretend he wasn't there, she kept her gaze on the road, but it was no good.

Her mouth twitched up at one corner as she fought a smile. If the cops had seen her she'd probably be in the nearest police station now being booked as a hooker. That would've been a great conversation starter with the search committee: prominent physician caught with cowboy's cock down her throat.

Jay squeezed her thigh. 'That's it, honey, smile. Let it out.'

Helen drew the car to a stop at the curb as the Ritz-Carlton apartment building loomed out of the gathering fog. She turned to Jay.

'I have my first big interview on Friday so I can't see you until the weekend.'

He took her hand and solemnly shook it.

'Good luck with that, doc. Not that you need it. From what I saw, you're a shoo-in.'

Her smile faltered. 'I'm not sure about that, but thanks for the support.'

He kept hold of her hand, his thumb making small circles over hers. 'Would you like to go out with me on Saturday?'

'Where are we going?'

He took off his seat belt and opened the door. 'To the rodeo, of course. Don't forget your cowboy boots and fanciest chaps.'

Chapter Nineteen

The rodeo?

Helen stared blankly at the notice board on the opposite wall of her office. Why did Jay want to take her to the rodeo? She imagined it would be the last place he'd want to go, especially with her. She closed her eyes as she remembered the bull crashing down on his leg in the Arco Arena in Sacramento, her certain knowledge that he was badly hurt and would need all her skill to help him.

As far as she knew, the National Rodeo tour wasn't due at the Cow Palace for several more weeks. She had no idea where he was taking her. She glanced at her watch, wondering whether the selection committee had finished interviewing the other three remaining candidates. One guy had already dropped out after being offered a research post at Harvard. Unfortunately, it hadn't been David.

She thought she'd done OK. It was always hard to tell. Her relationship with Professor Hart and Nifenberg had come up with every committee member. She dealt crisply with that aspect, insisting that most of the work was Professor Hart's and that she had just helped with the research. She knew Peter wouldn't argue about that. He'd always preferred to take the lion's share of the credit. Before it had infuriated her, but now it seemed fitting. She'd obtained the information in an underhand way and she was allowing Peter to do the same to her.

Helen sighed. Unfortunately, life wasn't that straight-forward. She still had at least one more interview with the whole committee and possibly more lectures and one-on-one time with individual faculty members. Part of her wanted to run away from constantly trying to please everyone. The rest of her enjoyed the challenge of finally coming out from behind Professor Hart's shadow and showing her colleagues and the committee that she could be taken seriously in her own right.

However, the prospect of a day at the rodeo was enticing. Jay had a unique ability to make her forget her workload and her problems. He provided her with a complex challenge that demanded her complete atten-tion both physically and mentally. She even enjoyed fighting with him because he never let her win. Her faint smile died. It would be hard to let him go. If she did get the job, her life would become even more complicated and her time more in demand.

She shivered at the prospect. How many patients would she actually get to see? Would she be too busy weaving through the maze of hospital government to remember she'd trained as a doctor, not as a politician? She shut down her computer. Why exactly was she doing this again? Her desire to show them all suddenly seemed childish.

'Hey, good looking, where's your hat?' Jay smiled as Helen sashayed down the steps from her apartment toward him. She wore jeans, black and white cowboy boots and a blue-checked shirt. She looked as wholesome as Doris Day and twice as beautiful.

'It's in the car. I only got it yesterday.'

He took her hand and kissed it. 'Great, let's go. The fun has already started.'

She pointed at his feet. 'Are those the boots you were making in class?'

'Yeah.' He struggled not to scuff his feet.

She dropped to her knees and pulled up the leg of his jeans to get a better look. 'They are beautiful.'

'Yeah, right.'

'Yes they are.' She looked up at him. 'Don't pretend you aren't proud of them.'

'OK, I'm a little proud. They came out just how I wanted them to.'

She traced one of the red stars with her fingertip. 'I'd say. The design is kind of retro but with a modern twist.'

'I like that. Can I borrow it?' He bent down to help her to her feet.

'Yes, if you tell me where we are going?'

'The Livermore Rodeo.'

'And where is that?'

'It's out in the Tri-Valley. You'll love it there. It'll remind you of home.'

She sniffed as she started the engine. 'I hope not.'

'How long is it since you've been back?' Jay asked.

'About fifteen years.'

He whistled as he studied her profile. 'That's a hell of a long time.'

She shot him a sharp glance as he entered the new directions into the car navigation system. 'You're a fine one to talk. How long is it since *you've* been home?'

'I don't have a home.' He took his hand off her thigh. 'And unlike you, I haven't got anything to go back to.'

She continued to drive and he concentrated on the

scorch-marked hills, determined not to let his nerves overcome him. This was the first time he was presenting himself in his new role as personal bootmaker to the stars. Would his old rodeo pals give him a chance to hawk his wares or would they laugh him out of the barn? He still wasn't sure if it was a good idea.

He figured he'd start small. The Livermore rodeo sure wasn't one of the big ones. It was the kind of rodeo for the up-and-coming, those desperate to increase their overall point standings and guys easing their way back from injury. None of the top bull riders would be there, so he wouldn't have to deal with his closest friends and ex-competitors right away. He'd have to work up to that.

To his surprise, since his last visit, the rodeo park had gradually become surrounded by new housing. Jay wondered how long it would be before the homeowners began to object to the crowds and the smells of the rodeo and vote for it to be moved.

Helen parked and Jay got out to stretch his legs. The heavenly smell of kettle popcorn and funnel cake assaulted his nostrils and he immediately felt right at home. He instinctively searched for the competitors' entrance before realizing he had no right to enter that way anymore. He tried not to think about everything he'd lost, tried to think about the future, but it was harder than he'd imagined.

Helen retrieved her black and white cowboy hat from the trunk and set it on her head. Jay smiled at the picture she made.

'You look good, honey. Even better on a horse, though.'

'I can ride.' Her chin came up. 'Actually I like to ride,

even though I haven't for years.' Before he could answer, she moved close to him, her expression serious. 'Are you sure you want to do this, Jay?'

'What?'

She tugged the open collar of his green shirt. 'The whole rodeo thing. I bet you haven't been near a rodeo or a bull since the accident.'

He took a deep breath. 'Hey, I've got to start somewhere. This is as good a place as any. And I haven't just come here to relive my worst nightmares; I've come to sell myself.'

'I know that, but don't be too hard on yourself if it makes you feel bad.'

He frowned. 'Don't try and psychoanalyze me, doc. I'm not going to break down and sob, if that's what you're worried about.'

She glared right back at him. 'You can cry all you want as far as I'm concerned. I'm just trying to prepare you for any unexpected reaction.'

'Well, thanks, but keep it to yourself. I'm here to sell cowboy boots, not embarrass myself.'

She studied him for a long moment and then nodded. 'Of course, your cowboy boots. What a great idea.' She looked across at the arena. 'Where do you want to start?'

Jay continued to stare at her. Trust Helen to come out fighting on his behalf. She knew better than to expect him to do anything she suggested but it was good to know that she'd be there if he needed her. He bent to kiss her cheek.

'Thanks, honey.'

She frowned. 'What did I do?'

He took her hand, guided her across the rutted open

space to the series of rusty red metal gates where the cattle were held ready for their events. A shout stopped him halfway.

'Hey, Jay!'

He looked behind him and grinned when he saw Mike Fraser, his rodeo traveling companion, waving at him from the back of his horse. Mike was definitely one of the guys Jay hoped to talk with. Mike's hair was as black as his boots, his eyes a pale-green that the ladies swooned over.

'Jay, man, what's up?'

Jay reached up to grasp Mike's proffered hand and shook it hard.

'Nothing much. How's tricks?'

Mike winked. 'Not in front of the lady, Jay.' His gaze slid toward Helen and stayed put. He touched the brim of his hat. 'Howdy, ma'am.'

Jay took Helen's hand. 'Mike's originally from New York. There are lots of cowboys there, he tells me. We used to travel to the shows together.'

Helen smiled and Mike leant so far out of his saddle that the leather creaked with the strain. 'Excuse me, ma'am, but you look kind of familiar. Have we met before?'

'Yes we have. I'm Helen Kinsale. I reset two of your fingers a couple of years ago after you got them caught in your rope.'

Mike laughed. 'Yeah, I remember now. You did a good job, despite me cussing like a fiend. It sure is nice to see you again, doc.' He glanced at Jay. 'Only question I have is, what are you doing hanging around with this old reprobate?'

Helen smiled again. 'I'm taking care of him, of course.'

'Lucky guy.' His paint horse snorted and shifted his feet as if impatient with the conversation. Mike backed him up a few steps. 'Jay, how about we all meet up for a beer in about an hour? I'll get you into the riders' tent, OK?'

'That would be great.'

Jay watched his old friend ride away before turning to Helen. 'I forget how many of the guys you already know.' He hadn't considered it before but Helen was almost as much part of the rodeo family as he was. No one within the tight-knit community would mind her presence or not want to talk to Jay because she was around. In fact, she might be an asset.

'I forget, too. At the hospital I'm so busy that I tend to look at the body part I'm treating rather than the person's face.' She sighed, her shoulders drooping. Jay put his arm around her and drew her away from the stands. It wasn't too busy yet. The big crowds would arrive later in the afternoon when the scheduled events got under way. In this relatively quiet time, he wanted to check out the vendors who lined the thoroughfare behind the stands.

Most of the stalls were for ready-made cowboy hats, T-shirts and ornaments he couldn't see himself buying in a million years. But just behind the cotton candy stall, he spied a leather stall and headed that way. Helen squeezed his hand.

'Checking out the competition, eh?'

'I'm hoping I don't have to hawk my stuff around the rodeo circuit like this. I want to offer something more personal and exclusive to my clients.'

She turned and squinted at him in the sunlight. 'Have you been talking to your brother?'

He shrugged. 'Yeah, he gave me a few hints.'

Helen continued to walk, her cowboy boots scuffing up the dust. 'Good for you. Always helps to ask a professional.'

Inside the booth, they separated. Jay focused on the men's belts, saddlebags and wallets, while Helen did the same for the ladies' side. Jay examined the workmanship of a belt, and admired the neat rows of stitching and the clever way the maker had woven in several black and silver beads.

'It's one hundred and twenty dollars.'

He looked away from the belt to find the bored-looking teenage stallholder staring at him. Despite the heat, the kid was dressed in black from head to toe. Even his fingernails were painted black to go with his three nose studs.

'It's real nice. Do you make them?'

'My dad does. He's kind of crazy about getting the details right.'

'Is he here?'

'Nope.'

'Is he going to be here at all today?'

'Nope.'

Jay felt as frustrated as an interrogator failing to get the necessary details out of a reluctant witness. He tried again.

'Are you based around here?'

'Yeah.'

'Does your dad have a business card?'

For the first time the boy looked vaguely interested. 'Why would you want that?'

'So that I can contact him.'

'But I told you how much the belt was.'

Jay held up his hand. 'I know. I just want to talk to your...' He sighed and put the belt down. 'Do you have that business card?'

The guy returned with a slightly grubby square of cardboard. 'Here you go. He's not very techno so phoning might be best.'

Jay smiled and retreated to the other side of the stall where Helen was trying not to laugh. He took her hand and walked back into the sunshine.

'How do you ever get injured kids to tell you what's wrong with them? It was like extracting milk from a wild cow.'

'I suppose you get used to interpreting the grunts. Sometimes I ask a parent to translate.'

Jay shuddered. 'I'm not sure I'd ever want kids. They seem so alien these days.'

Helen looked up at him. 'Really? I've always kind of pictured you with a family.'

He held her gaze, tried to imagine her carrying his child and realized he'd be OK with it. He quickly erased the thought.

'Nope, not for me.'

Helen looked around. 'How about something to drink? It's definitely warming up.'

Grateful for her change of subject, Jay nodded. 'Yeah, it gets really hot around here. I'll get a beer. What would you like?'

Helen sipped her lemonade and studied the ever-increasing crowd. Big families complete with babies, grandparents and assorted kids roamed the stands or hung out on the steep grassy banks next to the main arena. In adjoining areas, competitors practiced with their horses or simply rode around getting used to the noise and the new sensations surrounding them. The smell of popcorn made her mouth water and drew her thoughts back to the county fair where she'd first persuaded Cory to kiss her.

Jay's positive attitude about the rodeo and how he could make use of his contacts to advance his new business had surprised her. Beneath that lazy exterior she glimpsed the hardness and intelligence that had enabled him to leave school at sixteen and still succeed. She could only respect that. He'd made something of himself once and he was going to do it again. As a fellow survivor against the odds, she could only applaud him.

Jay waved at her from the bottom of the stairway and she made her way down to him, carefully avoiding all the kids who were using the steps as a playground.

'Are you ready to go and meet Mike?'

Helen touched his arm. 'Do you want me to come? I can go and find something else to do if you like.'

'I'd like you to come along.' He held her gaze, his gray eyes steady on hers. 'You can kick me in the shins if I say anything stupid, OK?'

'That will be a pleasure.'

He guided her down to the back of the chutes where yet another cowboy, who seemed to know Jay well, let them through. Mike was already seated at a table in the riders' tent with four other guys. He got to his feet when he saw Jay and Helen.

'Hey, I found some of the old gang. Come and tell them what you've been up to.'

Jay grinned as he pulled out a chair for Helen and then found one for himself.

'It's nice to see that nothing's changed. You're all still losers.'

Inwardly Helen sighed. Why did guys express their friendship with insults and macho back slapping? How about someone asking how Jay's leg was healing up instead of making jokes about his pretty face? She smiled when someone handed her a beer and let most of the conversation drift over her.

Someone poked her in the back. 'Hey, doc, do you remember me?'

She swiveled round in her seat. 'Show me your left hand.' She watched him take off his glove and expose the clean lines of his hand and wrist. 'That healed up pretty well, didn't it, Justin?'

Her hand was taken in a huge paw and shaken hard. 'You saved those bones, doc. I never got to say thank you. I couldn't believe it when Mike said you were here.'

'Just doing my job.'

Justin grinned. 'Hey, Jay, good idea getting the doc to follow you round. Are you hoping she'll stop you getting injured?'

Jay slid an arm around Helen's shoulders. She could feel the tension in his fingers.

'Hell, it's too late for that. I'm done.'

'Holy crap, Jay.'

Silence fell as all the men sitting at the table contemplated their worst nightmare. Helen glanced at Jay and realized he couldn't speak.

'Didn't Jay tell you that he's moved on to bigger and better things?' Helen said.

She caught Mike's eye in a blatant appeal for help and he sat up straight.

'Like what, Jay? You're not training to be a nurse, are you?'

Jay cleared his throat. 'Nope, I'm setting up as a maker of fancy handmade cowboy boots and leather goods.'

Mike nodded. 'Yeah, you were always messing around with leather. It sounds like just your thing.'

Justin pointed at the ground. 'Did you make those?'

Helen moved her chair out of the way as Jay stuck out his legs to reveal his brown and red boots. She held her breath as the guys crowded around him.

'I like 'em.' Mike said. 'They remind me of the old boots my granddad used to wear. Do they feel as good as they look?'

'Of course they do. Handmade to your size and fit using the traditional slow methods of a real craftsman.'

Justin whistled. 'Pretty pricy then.'

'Not for you guys. If you'll take a chance on me, I'll keep the costs to the minimum.'

'My momma told me never to look a gift horse in the mouth.' Mike stuck out his hand. 'You can start making a pair for me whenever you're ready.'

Helen started to relax as Jay directed the conversation into a discussion about what made a boot comfortable and what were everyone's favorite designs. The rodeo community was relatively small and slow to trust outsiders. Jay's chances of winning their business were better than most because he truly understood what they needed.

She studied his face as he became more animated and confident. When he started handing out business cards, she knew he'd taken his first step away from the past and toward a new future. A strange desire to cry flooded her. She'd worried that she'd be the one having to leave him, but perhaps it would be the other way round.

Helen gave herself a quick mental shake. That was good, wasn't it? If both of them moved on, they'd remember their time together with pleasure rather than guilt and acrimony. Jay laughed and his smile warmed her right to her toes. It would be so hard to let him go . . .

'Jay, I still had some of your rodeo gear loaded in my truck. I left it at the back of the tack room under the main stand.' Mike stood up and pointed in the general direction of the stand. Jay got up as well, bringing Helen with him.

'Thanks for hanging on to my stuff, Mike, I appreciate it.' Jay paused to look down at Helen. 'Do you think we can get some of it in your car?'

'It depends what it is. Maybe we'd better go and take a look.'

He took her hand, led her through the competitors and out into the maze of gates, chutes, and livestock behind the stand. The bulls looked remarkably quiet, all huddled together in one enclosure, probably dreaming up new tortures for their unfortunate riders. In contrast, the calves jumped, kicked and hollered like spring lambs.

Helen stopped to look at them. 'I used to do team calf-roping with my brother.'

'You have a brother?'

'As far as I know.' She kept her gaze on the calves. 'I think someone would've called me if he'd died.'

'You sure about that?' Jay asked.

She glared at him. 'That's uncalled for. Just because I don't choose to associate with my family doesn't mean I'm some kind of uncaring monster.'

His mouth set in a firm line. 'You should go see them.'

'Stop telling me what to do!'

He stepped closer until she had to look up to see his face. 'Shit, Helen, you have a family. Don't leave it until you get that phone call saying someone's sick or dying. Go back and see them.'

'I'll go back when you go and live with your father.'

He caught her upper arm. 'I tried that. It didn't work out. By the time I realized what an asshole he was, my mom was dying and there was nothing I could do but sit by her bedside and hold her hand.' Abruptly, he set Helen away from him. 'I have to go get my stuff.'

Turning on his heel, he walked away from her. She watched as he veered to the right, ducked his head and disappeared through a low doorway. She took a steadying breath and followed him. As darkness closed around her, she was surrounded by the scent of leather and wet horse. She slowly inhaled. Vibrations from the stand above her head made the cavelike space tremble and flex like a continuous mini-earthquake.

Jay was at the far end of the cramped space, his back turned toward her. She reached out a tentative hand and touched his arm. 'Jay . . .'

He turned so suddenly he almost knocked her over.

'Hell, I'm a fine one to talk. I left my mom for a fucking year because Beau promised he'd help me get into the rodeo business and I was so damned selfish, I wanted to believe him. While I got the best of everything, he cut off my mom's money and ignored her pleas for help.'

Helen swallowed hard against the pain in his eyes. 'But you went back. You realized he didn't have the power to give you what you really wanted, didn't you?'

He continued to stare at her, his breathing harsh, his attention fixed on her face.

'So you shouldn't blame yourself. You were there with her at the end and that's all that matters,' Helen said.

He sighed. 'Helen ... why do you make everything I do, everything I'm most ashamed of, seem so damn reasonable?'

'Ssh.' She put her finger over his lips and then replaced it with her mouth, putting into the kiss everything she wanted to tell him. He responded with a deep groan, opening his mouth to her questing tongue and kissing her back with a strength and desperation that quickly turned the kiss molten.

She pressed against him, nuzzling at his chest, breathing him in, instinctively trying to make things right, even though she knew she couldn't.

'I should've stayed with her, Helen.'

She framed his face with her hands as he blinked back the glint of tears. 'I should have stayed home too, but I didn't. I can't change that and neither can you. But maybe we can learn and move on.' He tried to speak but she kissed his mouth. 'Do you think your mom would want you to feel bad about this? You were there for her when she needed you most.' Emotion flooded her. 'Oh hell, I'll go see my parents, Jay. I promise.'

He drew her into his arms and hugged her tight. He was right. She owed it to herself and to her family to go back and set things straight. Even if they chose not to accept her, at least she could say she'd tried.

Jay kissed her, his mouth eager and demanding and she replied in kind, desperate to get as close to him as she could. His fingers slid around her waist, unbuckling her belt and zipper, delving between her legs where she was already wet and swollen for him. He thrust two fingers inside her, his thumb grinding against her clit as he struggled to move within the restrictions of her jeans.

Helen managed to drag her mouth away from his. 'We don't need to rush back. Let's get a hotel room and do this properly.'

Jay bit her ear lobe, making her writhe. His voice sounded hoarse. 'That is one heck of a good idea, doc.'

Chapter Twenty

Jay kept his gaze on the undulating golden hills as Helen drove them to a hotel near the freeway. Since he'd nearly cried like a girl on the doc's shoulder, he'd been unable to meet her eyes. What was it about her that made him tell her stuff he thought he'd buried and forgotten long ago? She made him angry enough to forget to hide all his worst shit but somehow he also knew she'd deal with it and move on.

'This motel should be fine. It's only been here a year.'

He glanced at the modest brown façade. 'Yeah, looks great.'

'I'll go see if they have a room.'

Helen stopped the car and headed for the main office. Sun glinted off the tinted windscreen as the temperature continued to rise. Jay stayed in the car, the scent of leather and horse all around him. The back seat and trunk were packed with his stuff. He'd traveled with Mike on and off for years and it was amazing how much junk he'd collected along the way.

He turned to touch his second-favorite saddle. His fingers lingered on the smooth, worn leather. Would he ever use this gear again? If push came to shove, and he wasn't able to ride at all, he supposed he could always give it to Grayson for his ranch. Damn, he wanted to be back in the saddle so bad.

Helen reappeared, a card key in her hand. 'We're in room twenty-six. We can park outside.' She slid into the driver's seat. Jay stared straight ahead, his hands gripped together on his lap. 'In your professional opinion, do you think I'll be able to ride again?'

'I don't see why not.'

He shot a quick glance at her. She looked pretty confident.

'As I said before, I don't think you'll be able to compete at world-class level but there's no reason why you shouldn't be able to ride,' Helen said.

He let out his breath. 'I don't think I could bear to do without that. Horses have been part of my life since the beginning.'

She patted his hand. 'I know, Jay. And I'm not trying to give you false hope here. I'm telling you the truth. Most of my ex-rodeo athletes learn to ride again.'

'Thanks for that, doc.'

She started the car. 'You're welcome.'

Less than a minute brought them to their designated parking space. Jay let Helen open the door while he brought in a few items from the back of the car. She turned as he came in. 'What do you need that for?'

'You'll see. Go get naked for me.' With a nod, he watched her go into the bathroom and shut the door. The hotel room was a blur of beige and cream and still smelt of new paint. After locking the outside door and making sure the blinds were down, Jay turned his attention to the saddle. Mike had kept it in great condition. He wiped it over with his handkerchief, smelling leather-care products and warm sunlight. Helen would love it.

With a grunt, he hefted it onto the bed and pushed it into place. Absently he stroked the bulge in his jeans as he waited for Helen to emerge from the bathroom. She didn't take long. She moistened her lips as her attention flicked between him and the saddle on the bed.

He sauntered toward her, loving the way her nipples were already hard and begging for his mouth.

'You like leather, right?' Jay asked.

She nodded, her attention now fixed on his face.

'So you'll like being fucked on my saddle.' He raised an eyebrow as her eyelashes flickered down to conceal her gaze. 'No answer? It's hard for you to admit what you want, isn't it?' He pinched her erect nipple between his finger and thumb. 'But we both know you'll be begging for it soon.'

He took her hand and drew her toward the bed, arranged her so that she sat sideways on the saddle, one knee hooked over the horn, the other over the cantle. Her upper body rested against the nest of pillows and the headboard.

He stepped back to study her and nearly came in his jeans at her wanton provocative expression and acceptance of his demands. Without thought, he bent and licked her pussy until her cream ran into his mouth and she was writhing on the saddle. He eased back.

'I'll go get washed up. Don't move.'

When he returned, she lay where he'd left her, blonde hair falling over her face, lips already swollen from his kisses earlier in the afternoon. Her gaze was strong and steady, as if she'd never doubted he'd come back to her. Why was that, when she already knew that he was capable of running out on anyone who'd ever cared for him?

Jay worked at his belt buckle, aware that his shaft was so engorged that it was trying to escape his jeans. He almost moaned as he dug into his pocket for the leather ties he needed to secure Helen's hands.

He crawled back onto the bed, feeling as ungainly as a seal out of water. The scent of Helen's arousal swirled around him and he fought a groan.

'Jay.'

He glanced down as he tied her wrists together and brought them over her head. 'Yeah, honey?'

'I want you to fuck me like this.'

He smiled at her. 'About time you asked nicely.'

He kissed her mouth, his tongue slow and gentle. He knew she liked it fast and hot but seeing as how she trusted him enough to tie her up, she would soon figure out he was all about slow today. She tried to lift her hips against his but he moved away. Kneeling between her thighs, he pulled her nipple into his mouth and settled into a thorough suckling. Without touching her with any other part of his body, he changed to the other breast and took his time there too.

By the time he lifted his head, she was panting, her blue eyes hazed with lust.

'What's up, doc?'

She glared at him and then at his groin. 'Obviously not you.'

He chuckled and moved away from her. 'Oh, I'm up, don't you worry about that.' Gritting his teeth, he eased the zipper of his jeans down over his thoroughly over-excited shaft. He picked up his discarded belt and coiled it up into a tight circle. Knowing she was watching him made every movement an erotic torture. He showed her the belt, letting it uncoil in his hand.

'Sometimes, when I'm alone and horny as hell, I like the feel of leather on my skin, too.' He glanced down at his cock. 'Sometimes I wrap this belt around my shaft as tight as I can and make myself come.' His breath hissed out as the belt buckle grazed the sensitive crown of his cock. He coated his fingers into the dripping pre-come and crawled back onto the bed. Helen tensed as he slid his wet fingers inside her ass.

'How about here? How about I give you my fingers here and my belt in your pussy? Do you think you could take it?'

She moaned and her sex gushed more cream. He fingered her clit, which was as hard as his cock. 'Yeah, take my belt. I want to watch it slide up inside you.'

He folded his belt into four and pressed it against the opening of her pussy lips. Her cream eased his way. He managed to get most of the belt in. The gold buckle glinted against her pale skin.

'You look beautiful,' Jay said.

He couldn't stop fingering her clit, letting his thumb dip inside her ass just below his belt buckle. He slid his four fingers inside her ass, stroked the bulky leather through the thin sensitive wall that separated him from the clench of her passage. As soon as he moved his fingers, she came, bucking her hips and riding his hand. Her cream pooled on the leather of his saddle as he leant in to kiss her. The smell of the leather became indistinguishable from that of her arousal.

Helen bit down on her lip as Jay used his tongue and teeth on her clit. She wanted to come again so badly. Every time she got close, he eased back and made her wait. She wanted to lift her hips and grind her swollen sex into his face, make him as desperate as she was.

'Please, Jay.' The words were out before she could stop them. 'Make love to me.'

He rocked back onto his knees and looked up at her, his mouth and chin gleaming with her juices. She moaned as he removed his belt from her swollen sex.

'Don't you worry about that.'

He got off the bed and slowly unsnapped his shirt, giving her tantalizing glimpses of his chest and the fair hair that tapered down to his navel and below. Next, he bent to remove his boots and jeans. She swallowed hard as he revealed his perfect tight ass and then his thick erection.

'Don't wear a condom.'

He went still. 'Why the hell not?'

'Because I want to feel you. You and the leather.'

He straightened and studied her, his gaze moved over her flushed skin and came to rest on her face. 'Aren't you doctors always preaching safe sex?'

'Jay, I've seen your medical records. I know you're clean. I'm on the pill.' She swallowed hard. 'Please, just this once.'

His breath hissed out in a curse. Reaching over her head, he untied the leather cord that connected her to the bedpost but didn't untie her wrists. Instead, he wrapped the excess leather around his hand until she was pulled toward him.

Just before she lost her balance he caught her around the waist and turned her until she straddled the saddle. Her bound hands came to rest on the saddle horn and she gripped it hard. He moved behind her, his cock a hot pulsing presence against her spine.

'Let's pretend we're out for a ride. You're naked, because that's how I like you and I'm sitting right behind you ready to get naked too.'

She shuddered as his thighs rubbed the back of hers and he urged her to kneel up.

'Let's say we take a ride down Main Street first, with you all naked so that every man can see just how fuckable you are.' He thumbed her nipple. 'You do remember how to ride, right?'

'Yes.'

In one swift motion, he pulled her down onto his shaft. After being stuffed full of his belt, she took him easily. She came fast, her hips pressing down onto his cock, eager to prolong the incredible sensation of being so full. He held still and deep until she finished pulsing and finally remembered to gulp down some air.

'Nice, honey. Do it again.' One of his hands came down to cover her mound and he rolled his hips in a fast circular motion. 'Let's pretend the horse is trotting, so post.'

She had no choice but to move with him; her body wouldn't have allowed it any other way. She locked her hips to his and worked with him, whimpering as another huge climax crashed over her. Again he held still while she convulsed around him, his hands gentle as he stroked and encouraged her. His mouth moved in tantalizing circles against her throat and the nape of her neck.

As the scent of warm leather and sex rose around them, she forgot where she was and embraced the demands of the man who was controlling her every move. He stroked her clit, brought her tied hands down to feel it too, rubbed the end of the leather binding her wrists against her flesh until she came again.

She arched her back and pushed against him. 'Jay, come with me, I want to feel you.'

'Not yet, honey, I'm still enjoying the ride.'

She moaned as his cock seemed to grow even bigger inside her.

'How about we lope?' He changed the rhythm from the up and down motion of the post to a longer horizontal oval. She leant forward as he slammed into her. Each upstroke hit her G-spot and made her scream. His breathing shortened and his strokes became less smooth and shallower. Sweat made their bodies slide against each other with sensuous ease. Helen could only brace herself on her knees and hold onto the saddle horn as he pounded into her.

'Helen, I...'

He sank his teeth into her shoulder as his hot come filled and overflowed her. He rocked back and forth as if he wanted to crawl inside her and never come out. His pulses seemed to go on forever and she gloried in every one.

Groaning, he rolled onto his back, bringing Helen down on top of him. He untied her hands and dropped his belt onto the floor. She remained pressed against him, her head tucked under his chin. He kissed her hair.

'Let me move this saddle,' Jay said.

With one mighty shove, he pushed it to the ground and drew them into the space he'd created. Helen wiggled against him, aware of the wetness between her thighs but strangely reluctant to move away from him. She liked the feel of his come on her skin and his body entwined with hers. Her eyes began to close. She'd sort it out in a minute.

She woke to the sound of thunder and then realized Jay was snoring in her ear. She kissed the underside of his prickly jaw and he turned his head away from her, revealing the leather ties from her wrists on the pillow beside him. Helen sat up and eyed her sleeping cowboy. Maybe it was time to turn the tables.

Jay blinked as Helen's hair drifted over his face. He tried to blow it out of his eyes, tried to use his hand. Shit, what had happened to his hand? He couldn't move it closer to his face.

His eyes snapped open as Helen's fingers closed around his ankle. She'd moved her weight off him but he still couldn't use his hands or his legs.

'What the hell are you doing?'

She had the nerve to turn around and smile at him. 'Tying you up.'

He pulled hard on the leather belt that constricted his wrists and realized he was hog-tied to the bed, arms above his head and legs spread wide. His cock responded with enthusiasm. 'Turn me loose, Helen.'

She shook her head, her hair catching his oversensitive cock. 'I've always wanted to try this. It seemed like the perfect opportunity.' She touched the leather around his ankle, the leather he'd used to tie her wrists earlier. 'I hope my knots hold. I wish I'd brought the leather cuffs with me.'

He continued to glare at her and struggle against his bonds. The leather bit into his wrists. 'I'm supposed to be the one in charge of the sex, not you.' He groaned as she bent her head and licked the tip of his already straining shaft.

'That's OK. Tell me what you want me to do to you.'

He tensed as she slid a pillow under his butt, raising his hips and groin so that he had a clear view of what was going on. She knelt between his outstretched thighs, a picture of cool innocence.

'I want you to let me go.'

She sucked the first inch of his cock into her mouth, swirled her tongue over the slit and penetrated it with tiny stabbing licks.

When she lifted her head, he struggled not to whimper. She raised her eyebrows. 'Not talking, Jay? That's not like you.'

'Hell, you don't talk much either when I've got you over my knee.'

'Exactly. That's because I don't want you to stop, and really, Jay –' she cupped his balls in her hand '– you don't want me to stop either, do you?'

He groaned as she lowered her head, took his balls into her mouth and swirled them around her tongue like the finest cognac. His cock throbbed and pre-come trickled down the sides. He tried to move his hips forward but had no leverage, had to rely on her mouth to find the right angle for him and, boy, did she know how to find his sweet spot.

When she sat back, he couldn't speak, couldn't even look at her because she knew how much he enjoyed her mouth on him. No chance to run away from her now – not that he wanted to. No way he'd let her down and spoil her game.

'I want it all in your mouth next time.'

'Are you talking to me?'

He pretended to look around. 'Yeah, I don't see anyone else here.'

She crawled forward on all fours until her breasts brushed his chest. 'If you want me to be nice, you'd better say please.'

He held her gaze, felt his wet cock slide against her stomach. 'And what if I don't want you to be nice?'

'Then I suppose I'll just have to please myself.'

She cupped her breasts and brought them close to his lips, just out of reach of his tongue. He groaned as she touched her nipples until they were two hard points. God, he wanted them in his mouth so bad. She straddled his hips and sank down onto his stomach, her sex rubbing against his rough hair in a sensual slippery glide.

His hands fisted as she continued to touch herself, her eyes hazed with lust, her scent overwhelming him. He held his breath as she slid one hand down over her belly and knelt up, fingers buried in her mound. He could see the swell of her clit now as she worked herself.

'Helen, "please" touch me.'

She opened her eyes and stared at him as if she'd forgotten he lay tied to the bed beneath her. 'Not yet.'

He watched, enthralled, as she fingered her breast and sex faster and faster, until he could hear the sucking sound of her juices and see the flush of her skin as she climaxed. She leant into him, kissed him hard as she collapsed and writhed against his belly. She bit down on his lower lip as another wave hit her. He even enjoyed the slight stab of pain and the taste of his blood.

'Helen, I want my cock inside you. Let me in.'

He bit back an urge to roar as she climbed off him. Out of the corner of his eye he could just see her perfect ass sticking up as she searched the floor. When she got back on the bed, she had her own narrow leather belt in her hand. His mouth went dry as he stared at the soft leather. She crouched between his thighs.

'What are you going to do with that?' he managed to croak. She smiled. He guessed he wasn't fooling her with his bravado.

'This.'

He dug his heels into the mattress as she slowly wrapped the supple leather around his cock. When she reached the base of his shaft she encircled it with her hand, protecting his balls from the rasp of the metal buckle.

'Mmm, perfect. Leather and you. My two favorite scents.'

His whole body started to shake as she lowered her head and licked the leather, the point of her tongue clearly visible to his heated gaze. She licked all the way down, stopping to investigate every gap in the binding, every clear drop of pre-come that overflowed his bonds. He wanted to close his eyes against the startling intimacy but found he couldn't. He had to watch her own him, make him her plaything and make him her slave forever.

He wanted to come more than he wanted to breathe, to explode through the tight leather right into her mouth or all over her, covering her in his seed. But he held on, craving the ultimate satisfaction of climaxing inside her.

Helen glanced up at Jay, felt the fierceness of his stare and his struggle to keep from coming. His breathing was labored, his tight abs flexing as her hair trailed over them. After her little experiment with the leather, his cock seemed to have grown even bigger. She shifted her grip on his cock, saw how tight his balls were against his shaft and let the buckle of the belt drop onto the sheet below.

Carefully she straddled Jay's narrow hips and positioned his cock at the entrance to her sex. Sweat gleamed on his chest. She inhaled slowly, loving the sensation of his leather-covered shaft as it disappeared inside her. She was wet enough to take the extra width and gloried in the slight roughness of the leather as it spread her swollen engorged flesh.

'Oh God, Jay, you feel so big.'

Jay's breath hissed out as she lowered herself until she couldn't go any further. A climax roared through her, making her quiver and pulse. His cock jerked within her and his body arched like a bow.

'Helen, I'm gonna come. Shit!'

She reached around to cup his balls, squeezing them against his shaft as he groaned his pleasure and climaxed inside her. Despite the leather binding, his hot come filled her and drove her to another orgasm. She fell forward onto his chest, heard the frantic beating of his heart under her cheek start to slow down.

Her own breathing slowed as she stroked the curve where his shoulder met his neck. He might be the one tied up, but she might as well be. He gave her so much more than the freedom to be herself in bed. He'd given her back herself.

With a groan, she carefully pulled away from him and unwrapped his now flaccid cock. She untied his hands and feet, pausing to kiss his wrists where the leather had bitten into his skin.

With a growl, Jay caught Helen around the waist and rolled until he was on top of her. He spread her legs with his knees and pinned her wrists over her head. He stared down at her, noting the signs of arousal on her face: her flushed cheeks and swollen mouth. She'd tied him to the bed and he still wasn't able to walk away from her.

He kissed her mouth, taking his time, smoothing the hair away from her face. He didn't want to let her go, period.

'Jay?'

'We're not done, honey.'

He winced as his cock thickened and lengthened. He wanted his come in her. He wanted her so full of him that she could never get his scent off, so that every other guy who came within fifty feet of her knew she was taken. With a long satisfied sigh, he slid one hand under her ass and gripped the base of his shaft with the other. He groaned as his cock responded to his touch. It was time to fuck her senseless until he convinced her that she never wanted another man between her legs but him.

Chapter Twenty-one

Helen closed the door of her apartment behind her and surveyed the quiet space. Jay had decided to stay at his apartment and she was glad. Her emotions were too close to the surface to stand much scrutiny. And he demanded honesty from her. She sensed he always would. Tiger strolled over to say hi and wound his way in and out of her legs. Her knees were so weak she almost fell over him. Jay's last session of lovemaking had almost robbed her of the ability to walk, let alone think.

With a sigh, she set the coffee to brew. Jay's possessive lovemaking gave her the notion that he wasn't going away anytime soon. Did she even want him to? She smiled as she recalled the intensity of his gaze as he'd climaxed inside her, the heat of his come at her very center.

He might have been the catalyst for all the emotions recently stirred up, but arguing with him had forced her to face several important issues about how she'd conducted her past relationships. He gave her no quarter, came back at her for every perceived slight and hadn't flinched when she'd done exactly the same in return. Every time she walked away from him, the pull to return became stronger. She suspected it was the same for him, too.

Her phone rang and she leant across the counter to pick up the receiver.

'Hi, Helen. You're home, right?'

'Of course I am. How else would I be able to pick this up?'

Carol gave a snort of laughter. 'Get with the program, old lady. You can practically pick up a call on the moon these days. Where've you been?'

Helen tucked the phone under her chin and went to investigate the refrigerator. She frowned at the lack of food. 'At the rodeo.'

'I didn't realize you were working today.'

Helen poked a piece of cheese. 'I wasn't. I went with Jay. He needed some company.'

'Don't tell me he's riding again.'

'Nope, just meeting old friends and making contacts for his boot-making business.'

'Ah, I see. You felt you had to go along to stop him leaping on a horse and ruining all that fine surgical work you did on his knee.'

'Yeah, right.' Helen gave up on the cheese and stuck two pieces of bread into the toaster. 'It was fun.'

'Fun? Are you sure this is Dr Helen Kinsale I'm talking to?'

'You're talking to the new improved version. I want to have fun. I want to remember how I was before I met either of the guys I married. I was an OK person then, wasn't I?'

There was silence. 'You were more than OK, Helen. I can't wait to see that girl I knew again.'

'Thank you, Carol.'

'That's OK, sweetie. Give Tiger and that cowboy of yours a hug from me and come by the shop and tell me all about it as soon as you can.'

Helen hung up and stared at the phone. It wasn't just

fun she wanted back in her life, it was integrity. Who would've thought that a washed-up rodeo cowboy would teach her that? She glanced down the hall to the open door of her home office. It was time to repair the damage and start again.

Jay picked up the phone and punched in the number he'd scribbled down from his messages. His body ached from all the sex with Helen but he didn't care. He'd learnt something valuable and that was worth every twinge. He smiled as he heard Grayson's deep voice.

'Hey, Gray, what's up?'

'Do you really want to know or are you just being facetious?'

Jay grinned at his brother's fractious tone. 'I really want to know.'

'I'm living in a banged-up trailer waiting for my house to be built and my land is full of fricking construction workers, burst water pipes and mud holes.'

'Sounds like fun.'

Grayson gave a reluctant laugh. 'Hell, it will be. I just have to keep telling myself that. Give me a few months and you can come and see for yourself.'

'I'd like to. Thanks for leaving me your new number.' Jay shifted his stance. 'Listen, Beau's been calling me asking where the hell you are. Do you want me to give him your number?'

'Not yet. The last thing I want is him coming up here and getting in my face. The way things are at the moment, I'd probably kill him and bury the body in one of these convenient holes.'

'Understood. I'll keep stonewalling him then.'

'Don't get into too much shit on my behalf. You take

enough of your own. How's the boot-making going and how's Dr Helen?'

Sensing his brother had said all he had to say about their father, Jay gladly changed the subject.

'The boot-making is going great. There's something else I'd like to talk to you about when you get settled.'

'Shoot. I'm sick of shoveling dirt.'

Jay slid down the side of the kitchen cupboard until his butt hit the floor and stretched out his legs.

'I've been thinking about all the cowboys who can't afford a handmade pair of boots but still want something different from the stuff that's available to the general public.'

'You mean something that's designed specifically with cowboys in mind?'

'Yeah. I'm sure there are other companies out there that have products like that but I'd like to think I can produce something better.'

'You'd need to do some research into what's available already, but with your inside experience, I don't see why you couldn't make a go of it.'

Jay let out his breath. He'd wondered if Grayson would tell him he was nuts.

'I have an old colleague called Barry Levarr who would be a great guy for you to talk with. I'll tell him to call you.'

Jay straightened so abruptly he banged his head on the wood behind him. 'Hold on, bro, I'm only speculating here. I don't have the money or the experience to do this yet.'

His brother's sigh sounded loud even down the phone. 'Don't worry about the money, OK? Just work on the idea and let me know.'

Jay closed his eyes. 'I don't want your money, Gray. I want to do this myself.'

'You're my brother. If I can't help you out, who can I help? Where else are you going to get the money? Do you think Beau will pony up?'

Jay tried to relax his grip on the phone. 'If I do what he says, he might.'

'Jesus, Jay – whatever you're thinking, don't do it. Trust me, nothing is worth working for that bastard for, nothing.'

'I'll talk to you later, bro.'

Jay hung up even though Grayson was still shouting. He stared at his new cowboy boots, touched the smooth, rounded toe. Pointed toes were definitely for Hollywood cowboys only. If he went to work for his father for a few years, he'd be able to save enough money to start up his company and give Helen the kind of lifestyle she deserved. Was he willing to suck up to Beau if it meant achieving his dreams?

Hell, yeah.

He dialed an all too familiar number and held his breath.

Helen listened as the unfamiliar international dialing tone continued to ring. She checked the clock. It wasn't too late, was it? She almost dropped the phone when someone picked up.

'Hello?'

'Hi, is this Dr Robert Grant?'

According to the internet, Robert was now head of a very successful research facility based at the Cambridge Science Park near the university campus. She was glad he'd done so well for himself.

'Speaking.'

His distinctive English accent took her straight back to the drunken summer vacation they'd shared while students in southern California.

'This is Helen Kinsale. We haven't spoken for several years but I hope you remember me.'

Robert's chuckle made her smile. She relaxed her grip on the phone a little.

'Of course I do. Who could forget someone with your brains and beauty? I seem to remember, conceited oaf that I was, trying to convince you to marry me so that we could have the smartest kids in the universe.'

'I'm not sure you'd want to marry me now.' Helen took a deep breath. 'I have a confession to make.'

Jay hung up. After ten minutes of abuse, Beau had agreed to meet up with him next week to discuss his future within the company. He groaned and lowered his face into his hands. He had a raging headache and a bad feeling in his gut. He reminded himself why it was necessary to go ahead with his plan. It didn't help. Shit, he wanted a beer.

He tried to think of Helen, of how pleased she would be to see him taking charge of his life. Tried to picture her agreeing to stay with him as he slowly bled to death working for his father. *Dammit, Jay, stop thinking like that. It doesn't have to be that way, does it?*

If he remembered correctly, she was at the clinic until seven tomorrow evening. He'd take the belt he'd made for her and try to convince her they should stay together for as long as they both wanted, which he hoped meant forever.

He managed a grin as he got off the floor and headed for the refrigerator. You could never tell with Helen. She might just tell him to get lost and then where would he be? Right back on her doorstep asking her again. Even if he had to strip her naked and tie her to his bed until she gave in. His smile widened. Hell, she'd probably like that.

Helen sat back and contemplated her hands. Her fingers still shook from the stress of making the call. After all those years of deceiving herself and those around her, she was finally able to come clean. Robert Grant was a true gentleman and if what he said was true, she didn't have a thing to worry about. She smiled. Now all she had to do was think of a way to break the news to Professor Hart.

Chapter Twenty-two

It was another busy Monday at the hospital clinic. Helen groaned as she studied the long list of patients she was expected to see that day. She might as well forget about lunch. She often wondered why people waited until the start of the working week to bring their injured bodies into the ER. Did they only notice something was wrong when they tried to get to work or was it because they assumed the weekend would be too busy?

Helen wasn't sure anymore but there were always extra patients who needed to be squeezed in on the already full lists. It was also strange how many of them she seemed to acquire when Nancy was doing the re-scheduling. She gulped down a cup of coffee, put on her white coat and pinned on her name badge.

As soon as she'd arrived at work she scheduled an after-hours meeting with Professor Hart to discuss the Nifenberg research. He'd agreed to meet her in her office at seven-thirty. Despite the workload, Helen found her-self smiling at everyone she encountered in the halls. It would be interesting to see how the search committee evaluated all the candidates and whether she'd impressed them. She still hoped to be offered the job. Whether she took it or not was still up in the air.

'Helen, how good to see you.'

Her smile disappeared as she encountered David emerging from the residents' lounge. 'What are you doing here?'

David's eyebrows rose. 'Wow, you really should work on your hostility issues. I can recommend a good therapist if you need one.'

'I'm fine, David. I just wondered why you were here at this time in the morning. It's a perfectly reasonable question. I work here and you don't.'

He stuck his hands in the pockets of his white coat and flashed her that amazingly insincere smile. 'Just getting to know the place so that when they announce me as the new boss, I'll be familiar with everyone.'

Helen pretended to look around. 'Have they made a decision already? That's weird, I haven't heard anything and I'm scheduled to give my last lecture to the faculty tomorrow.'

'You're so amusing. I'm just about to meet with some of your colleagues. They asked me to come in for an informal chat before the patients started to arrive.'

Helen crossed her arms over her chest. 'Let me guess. They're concerned that a bimbo like me might get control of their lovely department and ruin it.'

'Well, they didn't actually say "bimbo".' David made exaggerated quote marks with his fingers. 'But that's the general impression I get.'

Helen took a step toward him and he blanched.

'Have a lovely gossip, dear, and give my love to Carrie-Ann.'

She turned away from him and headed back to her office, a distinctly sour taste in her mouth. If she did get the job, she'd have to spend the first months of her tenure weeding out all the people who would make life difficult. Not something she looked forward to at all, despite her reputation.

'They sure are interested in hearing about you and your cowboy.'

Helen stopped walking and turned around. She ignored the several interested faces behind the reception desk and concentrated on David. 'I'm not the first doctor to date an ex-patient and I'm sure I won't be the last.'

David's smile was smug. 'Ex? I hear from the nursing staff that he's still listed as a current patient of yours.' He shook his head. 'Now that is definitely not ethical.'

Helen spared a scathing glance for Nancy who glared triumphantly back at her.

'Believe what you like. My conscience is clear.'

His laughter made the knot of anger in her stomach grow until it felt as if it would force its way out of her throat.

'Surely your colleagues should know that you don't always obey the rules? Leaving school at sixteen and running off to marry a cowboy doesn't make you seem like a very reliable person or the kind of leader a great department like this needs.'

A collective gasp ran through the staff gathered in the hall. Helen was only grateful that they hadn't opened the doors to the patients yet. She raised her chin.

'This from a man who's fucked more medical personnel than an afternoon soap star?'

David shrugged. 'That's right, Helen, attack me because you can't defend yourself.'

She held his gaze. 'I don't need to defend myself. I'm not ashamed of what I've done. Are you?' Without waiting for his answer, she turned on her heel and walked away. She shut her office door quietly behind herself and locked it. There was still ten minutes before the patients flooded in and she'd need every one of them to calm the shaking rage David had roused in her. It was a special talent of his to stir up her life and expose her to public ridicule.

She tried not to think about what her colleagues must be saying about her now. Would they believe David and despise her for being such a fool? Hospitals were small places. It wouldn't be long before the rumors of her 'interesting life' came to the ears of one of the search committee.

Helen drew a long steadying breath. She was done with hiding. If the committee preferred to base their choice on gossip and innuendo, then perhaps she wouldn't want the job anyway. It was a revolutionary thought. She'd fought so hard to get to her present position; perhaps it was time to realize that she'd slowly been losing herself in the process.

Maybe David had done her a favor after all. She bit her lip. Soon she'd have no more secrets left to hide. A knock on the door made her jump. She turned to unlock the door. Tara Davies stood there, her face concerned.

'Are you OK, Helen?'

Helen managed a smile. 'Wow, rumors really do fly fast.'

Tara jerked her head back down the hall. 'Actually I was at the reception desk and I heard everything that jerk said. Who is that asshole, anyway?'

'My ex-husband.'

Tara's horrified expression made Helen want to laugh. 'Oh man, you're kidding.'

'It's OK. I divorced him and I don't regret it one bit.'

'I'm not surprised. What was he trying to do?'

'Get Professor Hart's job.'

'Interesting way to go about it.' Tara nudged Helen in the ribs. 'Um, is it true? The bit he said about you running off with a cowboy when you were sixteen?'

'It's true.'

Helen found herself engulfed in a huge hug. When she emerged, Tara was still grinning.

'Wow, that's amazing. How on earth did you get to be so smart and successful after such a bad start?'

'I just learnt to make better choices.'

'You make it sound so simple and I bet it was anything but.' Tara patted her shoulder. 'Don't you worry. I reckon your ex has done himself more harm than good. Everyone will be talking about you, not him.'

Helen groaned. 'That's not what I wanted, either.' She returned to her desk to gather up her files and beeper. 'Walk me down the hall, will you? I feel a sudden desire to hide.'

'What a day,' Helen muttered to herself as she collapsed into the chair behind her desk. She rested her head in her hands and stared fixedly down at the hospital issue mouse pad. Tara's attempts to protect her hadn't helped much. She'd spent the whole day being asked whether it was true she'd gotten married at sixteen and whether she really did have a thing for cowboys.

In the ten minutes she salvaged for lunch, she typed a note confirming the gossip and stuck it on both of the staff notice boards. The questions kept coming but she was surprised that not all of them were hostile. Some people were impressed she'd managed to get as far as she had. Others avoided her, obviously thinking the worst.

She let out a long slow breath, realizing she didn't feel

as bad as she had thought she might. She was beginning to believe that Jay was right and that all this telling the truth was good for you.

There was a knock on the door. She glanced at the clock. It was only twenty minutes past seven; surely Peter Hart wouldn't arrive early?

The brim of Jay's cowboy hat appeared, followed by his face. Helen sat up straight.

'Is this a good time?'

She gestured for him to come in. 'Professor Hart will be here soon but come in anyway.'

He took off his hat and held it in front of him like an awkward teenage girl clutching a purse. Helen drank in the long elegant lines of him, his rumpled blond hair and tanned skin.

'What can I do for you, Jay?'

'I brought you this.'

He placed a brown paper bag on her desk. She tipped the contents out onto her desk and gasped. He'd made her a belt of intertwined colored leather which was as soft and supple as her skin.

'It's beautiful. Thank you. I'll wear it with pride.'

He grimaced and then cleared his throat.

Helen frowned. 'Is something wrong?' she asked.

'Nope, I'm just thinking how best to say this.'

A knot of dread blossomed in her stomach and she put the belt back in the bag. 'Just spit it out. I find that's usually best.'

'Not with you,' he muttered.

Her irritation rose. 'Are you sick? Are you going away?'

'I'm not sick. I might have to leave San Francisco for a while, but it's not what you think.'

Even as her heart plummeted, Helen gave him her coolest smile. 'I don't have the right to "think" anything, Jay. You're a free man.'

He sighed, ran a hand through his thick blond hair, making it stand up on end. 'I knew you'd do this.'

'Do what?'

'Make it difficult.'

She bared her teeth at him. 'I'm not doing anything. I'm just sitting here very patiently waiting for you to leave.'

He took a step toward her, his gray eyes blazing fire. 'You see? There you go again, making assumptions, telling me to fuck off because you're scared you might want me to stay around too much.'

'Who asked you to psychoanalyze me? And why the hell would you think I'd mean that?'

'Because that's exactly what I'd do!' He slammed his hands down flat on her desk and loomed over her. 'Look, I need to make some money so that I can give you the kind of life you deserve. When I've done that I'll come back and –'

'What are you talking about? You don't have to do anything for me. I'm perfectly capable of looking after myself!'

Jay bowed his head, drew in an audible breath, and then looked into her eyes. 'Helen, will you please listen to me –'

'Am I interrupting?' Peter Hart stood in the doorway, his normally bland face avid with interest.

Helen shot to her feet and forced a smile. 'No, come in, Peter. I was expecting you.' She glanced at Jay. 'Do you want to continue this conversation later?'

'Sure.'

He strolled across to a vacant chair by the window and sat down.

Helen glared at him. 'Wouldn't you prefer to wait outside?'

He raised his eyebrows. 'Nope.'

Peter Hart cleared his throat. 'Mr Turner, we will be discussing private hospital business. It might be better if you leave.'

'That's OK, Prof.' Jay waved a hand. 'I'm so dumb, I won't understand any of it anyway.'

Helen clenched her jaw so hard it hurt. Today was definitely turning into a disaster so why not make it complete by letting Jay see the real her at work? She smiled sympathetically at Peter Hart.

'Jay's right, Peter. He's way too stoopid to understand what we're talking about. Let him stay in the corner.' She had the brief satisfaction of seeing Jay's smile wiped off his face.

'I'll wait outside,' he grunted, leaving the room.

'Very well, then.' Peter took the chair in front of her desk. 'What did you want to see me about, dear?'

Helen took a deep breath. 'It's about the research papers we produced. I wasn't entirely honest with you at the start.'

Peter frowned. 'In what way?'

'I didn't come up with the chemical formula for the new polyethylene compound all by myself.'

'Well, I know that. If you remember, I perfected your basic suggestion.'

'No, you didn't. I let you take credit for that, but I also let you believe the basic idea was mine.' Peter looked as if he wanted to speak but Helen kept going. 'In fact, I wasn't the originator of the formula at all. Ten years ago, the summer after you became my mentor, I met a guy called Robert Grant. He was an exchange student from England studying at M.I.T.'

'Go on.' Peter sat forward.

'One night, we got drunk at a bar and I started complaining to him about the problem of using the current polyethylene implants for professional athletes and children. We ended up having a really deep technical discussion about the different ways we could crosslink the elements to improve resistance.'

She took a folded bar napkin out of an envelope and held it up. 'Robert wrote down a series of chemical formulas on this napkin. That's the basis of what I brought to you.'

'Why didn't you mention this before?'

'Because I was desperate to succeed. Because I knew that once Robert returned to England, he'd probably forget all about our evening together and I'd be able to benefit from his insight.'

'And why are you telling me this now?'

Helen went still. 'Why do you think? I can't take all the credit for something I didn't do.'

'But you said this man was in England and that he probably had no recollection of what he'd told you.'

Helen put the napkin back in her desk drawer. 'Are you suggesting I should just keep quiet?'

Peter shrugged. 'It depends what you want to happen, my dear. If you go public with this information now, the only person you'll damage is yourself, particularly at this delicate stage of the selection process.'

Helen tried and failed to capture his stare. 'Professor Hart, your name is on those academic papers. You chose which parts of my research went into the content. In fact, you did your best to minimize my contribution.'

Peter got to his feet. 'Helen, relax, it's a win-win situation. I'll pretend I didn't hear your confession and you just carry on confirming that the majority of the work was mine. I'll get my job at Nifenberg and I'll make sure you're in line to bring a nice big fat grant to the hospital when you get that promotion.' Helen stared at her mentor and he finally met her gaze, his expression unmoved. 'Hospital politics is no place for a weakling. You can't change the past, nor should you want to, especially when you have benefited from it. Let's just pretend this conversation never happened and carry on as before.'

Helen stood up too. 'But Peter, you don't understand...'

'I do understand. You've allowed yourself to get rattled during the selection process. When you're running this department you'll realize what a mistake you almost made and you'll laugh at your own foolishness.'

He nodded and turned to the door. Helen watched him walk down the hall, her mouth open in disbelief.

Jay knocked once on the open door and strolled back into the room toward Helen. 'Professor Hart didn't look too happy. What did you say to him?' he asked.

Helen had her head in her hands. 'Why do you want to know? You're leaving, aren't you?'

Jay sat on the chair Peter had vacated. 'Spit it out. What did you do?'

'It's complicated.'

Jay crossed his arms and sat back. 'I've got plenty of time. Surprise me.'

'Oh hell, why not? It will only confirm your worst

suspicions of me. Ten years ago I lied to get my name on some academic papers.'

Jay shrugged. 'So what?'

'Jay, I lied.'

'So what?'

She gave an exaggerated sigh. 'To get to where I am, at such a relatively young age, I had to do something out of the ordinary. I co-authored a series of academic papers with Peter Hart about a new formula for crosslinking polyethylene elements to enhance resistance to wear.'

'Oh *right*, of course, yeah.'

'I realized that athletes and people who were more active, needed orthopedic polyethylene implants that were more resistant to wear and tear than average folk.'

'Well, that makes sense.'

'But the thing is, the new formula wasn't all mine.' She finally looked up at him.

'Whose was it then?'

'An English guy I met that summer called Robert Grant who was studying at M.I.T.'

'What did you do? Torture the information out of him?'

She gave a defeated sigh. 'No, we got drunk and he came up with it and scribbled it down on a bar napkin.'

'Wow, impressive. I suppose I should be glad that you didn't sleep with him.'

'Jay, that's not fair.'

'What's fair?'

Her blue eyes bored into him. 'I found the napkin in my pocket a few days later and realized Robert might have been on to something.'

'But you kept that bit of information to yourself, right?'

'Well, I didn't tell Robert. He'd gone back to England. But I did tell Peter Hart and the rest is history.' She swiped a hand across her eyes. 'I just wanted him to notice me. I didn't really understand that he had the connections to make my pathetic little attempt to succeed into a whole big drug company sponsored mess. After continuing my own research, I wasn't even sure if it would work anyway. But Peter wasn't really interested in my opinion by then. All he cared about was the academic acclaim.'

'OK, I'm no medical expert but if your paper was published, doesn't that mean that your Robert guy, or some other brainiac, could've seen it and said that your deductions were all wrong?'

Helen held his gaze. 'You're absolutely right but Robert wasn't involved in the medical community and lives in a different country and Peter ... well, Peter used the information I gave him very creatively.'

Jay stared at her. 'So what did you just do?'

Helen groaned. 'Why haven't you left in disgust? You must realize by now that I'm not a very nice person.'

Jay's lips twitched. 'You found Robert, didn't you? You told him what you did.'

She peered at him through her fingers. 'Yes, I did and it's your fault making me feel I have to be honest with everyone. He's a very nice man.'

'How nice?'

'Nicer than you. He was always a perfect gentleman.'

'So why didn't you hook up with him, then?'

She removed her hands from her eyes to glare at him. 'Because he was too nice. I used him, Jay. That's what I do with men. I use them and then I move on.'

He studied the toecap of his boot. 'You don't use me.'

'That's because you won't let me.'

'That's right.'

He fought a smile as she tried to regain her usual icy composure. She looked at him, her hands twisted together on the desk.

'You have to remember I was very ambitious then and I needed something important to get his notice. I didn't really think it through. It never occurred to me that there would be interest outside the small world of academia and that Peter and I would end up being courted by several drug companies.'

She gripped her hands together until her fingers whitened. 'Peter took nearly all the credit and I was OK with that. Even then I felt guilty about taking Robert's idea and presenting it as all my own work. But hell, I liked the attention and the prestige too much to dream of giving it up. It was all I had.'

Jay nodded. He understood her desperation all too well. When Beau offered him the opportunity to succeed at the rodeo, he'd walked out on his mother without thinking it through either. He crossed one leg over the other. 'What did Robert say when you contacted him?'

Helen's lips twitched. 'He told me that Nifenberg would soon find out that the chemical formula I used in the original proposal wouldn't hold up in high-level testing.' She shrugged. 'He said he'd tried something similar in his lab and abandoned the effort. He even apologized for not contacting me earlier when he decided to test out our theory. There was some complicated reason why things didn't work out, but his explanation went way over my head.'

She glanced down at the napkin on the desk and smoothed it with her fingers. 'Robert did say he'd be happy to work with me and Peter to see if we could come up with any new solutions. I intended to pass Robert's phone number and all the additional information over to Peter, but he didn't really give me a chance to explain. He prefers to leave it all buried in the past. He seems to think we could continue to protect each other's asses.'

'So Nifenberg isn't going to be able to develop the product after all?'

Helen nodded. 'That about sums it up. It's not an uncommon occurrence. A very high percentage of ideas fall by the wayside during intensive research.'

'But Professor Hart doesn't know that yet.' He met her gaze. 'Are you going to try to tell him the truth again?'

'I'm not sure. Part of me thinks he deserves whatever happens to him, but the rest . . .' She shrugged. 'I wouldn't be in the position I'm in today without him.'

Jay raised his eyebrows. 'Will this affect your chances of getting the head of department job?'

'I don't know.'

She slumped in her chair. He'd never seen her look so defeated.

'Maybe I should withdraw my application. I feel like such a fraud. It's going to get complicated from here on in. It takes months for the selection committee to make a decision. If Nifenberg pulls the plug on the research during the wait, Peter might decide not to leave after all and if that does happen, I doubt he's going to want me working with him anymore.'

She sighed. 'It might be better to just give up and resign now.'

To her surprise Jay avoided her gaze and studied his fingernails. 'You're right. You don't have to take the job if you don't want to.'

'Why is that?'

'Because I'll take care of you.'

She got to her feet, her stomach churning. 'What the hell is that supposed to mean?'

He stood up too. 'I'd like to take care of you. That's what I was trying to tell you earlier. I have it all worked out. I'll go and slave for Beau for a couple of years to earn a load of money. Then I'll focus on building the boot-making company and another more commercial idea I have going with Grayson.'

'Really.'

Helen barely restrained herself from vaulting over the desk and smacking his handsome, smug face. He straightened as she stormed toward him.

'In the meantime,' he said, 'you can give up work if you want to, and just look after me.'

He flinched as she poked him in the chest. 'Is that how you'd like me, Jay? Barefoot and pregnant? Catering to your every whim?'

He met her gaze. 'Well, hell, yeah.'

She tried to breathe deep, tried to remember that inside she was still an intelligent, civilized human being. Her voice rose to a screech.

'And are you seriously contemplating going to work for that bloodsucker of a father of yours? Are you nuts? He'd destroy you in five seconds flat.'

He frowned. 'I want to give you a good life, Helen. I need money to do that and Beau has more than enough to go around.'

'I am perfectly capable of giving myself anything I want.' She emphasized each word with another jab to his chest. 'And I am perfectly capable of getting this job. I deserve this job, I've worked hard for this job and even if I have to tell the world about Robert and acknowledge his part in my achievements, I still deserve to succeed.'

'You think?'

'I know!'

He smiled down at her. 'That's my girl.'

She stared at him, her breathing ragged. 'Did you just say all that to make me mad?'

'Some of it.' He shrugged. 'The bit about you stopping work was just to get you riled up and ready to fight for what you really want.'

There he went again, forcing her be honest to the person who mattered most – herself. What did she really want? She wasn't sure if she would take the job, even if it was offered to her. Part of her yearned to be free of the hospital completely. Perhaps it was time to return to her roots and work full time as a rodeo doctor. She sure had a lot to think about. Jay flinched as she laid her hand on his chest.

'Tell me you're not going to work for Beau.'

He stepped away from her and put his hands in his pockets. 'I want to be successful, Helen. I want to be able to give you what you deserve.'

Her hands fisted at her sides. 'Now who's being an idiot?'

His gaze flew to her face. 'Shit, Helen, I'm trying to do what's best for you here.'

'And you get to decide what's best for me, do you?'

He closed his eyes. 'We both know what it's like to live with no money. It ain't fun. It isn't something I'd wish on anyone.'

Tears threatened her self-control and she ruthlessly converted them into anger. She moved closer until they stood toe to toe.

'Listen to me, you complete idiot. This is the twenty-first century. I don't give a damn about how much money you earn. I admire you for pursuing a dream and having the talent and guts to achieve your goals. I bet Grayson has offered to fund you and I would, too.' She met his gaze. 'I will *not* admire you if you go crawling back to your father. Is that clear?'

'Helen, I can't keep taking, not from Grayson, not from you. I'm not a kid anymore.' His voice cracked and she touched his cheek.

'How about you don't think of it as taking? How about you think about it as us giving because we love you?'

Damn, had she said that out loud? Had she just admitted to loving him? She shivered when he closed his fingers over hers.

'I suck at being loved, Helen. I have no idea how to handle it.'

'Again, may I suggest you take your own advice and just accept it, deal with it and move on?'

He let out a breath and brought her fingers to his mouth for a kiss. 'How come you make it sound so simple?'

'Because it is.'

He drew her into his arms and kissed her again, his mouth rough as it moved over hers, her body tight against his. He whispered, 'I don't know if I can say the words, yet, but I promise I'll work on it.'

She pulled back to smile at him. 'You'd better. Even high-powered doctors need to be told they are loved occasionally.'

He smoothed her hair away from her face. 'I promise I won't go and slave for Beau. We'll work it out somehow, although I don't imagine it will be an easy ride.'

Helen nodded. They were both far too hard-headed and stubborn to make concessions. But being with Jay would never be boring. She looked up as he cupped her chin in his big hand.

'I don't want to walk away from you anymore, Helen. I want to stay right here.'

'I don't even need to hog-tie you to the bed anymore?' Helen pretended to pout. 'That was fun.'

His gray eyes took on a familiar lustful glint. 'You can tie me up anyway you like, just as long as you allow me the same privileges.'

She shuddered as his lips met hers. After another long kiss, he set her away from him.

'Honey, just remember that as soon as I get my company up and running and I can support you, we're going back to plan A,' he said.

'And what might that be?'

He winked at her. 'You, barefoot and pregnant.'

Helen took great satisfaction in kicking him in the shins.